Curveball

A Love Story

Anne Trowbridge

Curveball

A LOVE STORY

Anne Trowbridge

AUTHOR OF *OUT OF THE PARK*

© 2022 Six Dog Productions, LLC

This is a work of fiction. All of the characters, organizations, and events portrayed in this novel are either products of the author's imagination or are used fictitiously.

All rights reserved.

ISBN: 979-8-9865072-0-0

For my parents who, deep in their souls, absolutely believed I would be "the next Erma Bombeck." I love you both.

Acknowledgments

I WROTE THIS BOOK after a trip to Ireland in 2010. I was pregnant with my son at the time, and life soon had me tucking this manuscript away for more than a decade. A dear, wonderful friend, Wil Mara, helped me pull it out, dust it off, and finally give breath to my words. Thank you, Wil, for all of the encouragement, help, patience, and goofy side comments. You're the best!

Thank you to all my early readers, editors, and helpers, including Camille Trentacoste. Special thanks to my talented sister Amy Smith for all your help (and an early thanks for all the other website and video stuff I'm no doubt going to ask for your help with!). Thank you, also, to my sister Marisa Trowbridge, who read the final prologue—after it had been scrutinized in dozens of reads and edits—and immediately spotted a sentence with a missing word. (Face palm.) I couldn't have completed this journey without any of you! (Special shout out to Marisa, who bravely sauntered across the rope bridge that Emma and Zach cross in this book while I stood on the observation deck, pretending the pregnancy and the need for cool pictures were all that was holding me back from joining her.)

I also want to acknowledge my dearest friends for all their ongoing love and support, including Sally Bennett, Shannon Kastner, Cathleen Reed, Marlo Teal, Linda Rowland-Buckley, Laura Burgess, and Camille (again!). You guys are the best!

Thank you, also, to my loving parents, Gary and

Sarah, who always encouraged my dreams, and who always viewed me as a writer. I think that started around the time I was in the second grade and trying to craft stories with endings that would surprise my teachers. I desperately wish my dad was here to see my first book—and all those years of dreaming—become a reality.

My brother Matthew wasn't an early manuscript reader for me, didn't make the Ireland trip, and is too young to remember the elementary years of my writing career, but I can't leave him out! Love you!

Thank you to my kids, Madelyn and Alexander, just for being great kids, but also for supporting and believing in me. And finally, of course, thank you to my husband Wilson, who believes in me, loves me, and supports me always. I love you forever!

The Curveball Incident Series

Curveball (Book One)

Out of the Park (Book Two—coming soon)

Standalone Titles

The Honeymoon (coming in 2023)

The Bridesmaid (coming in 2023)

Prologue

"BALL ONE!" the umpire called.

That one was too low. Zach walked off the pitcher's mound to catch the return ball from Jose Diaz, his catcher. He bounced the ball once, then rolled it in his hand, watching as Jose gave him the signs. Two fingers followed by four. Jose wanted another fastball. Yeah, that was a good call. The rookie he was facing, Tommy Layton, wouldn't know what hit him. He wouldn't be expecting another fastball. Zach had a few pitches in his arsenal, but it was his curveball that he was known for. That's what Layton would be expecting.

This was the part Zach loved about being a pitcher: the battle. The *strategy*. He loved working with his catcher to figure out the best combination to get those strikeouts and eventually the wins, which were the ultimate reward.

He'd give Jose the fastball he was asking for, but he was going to move it in toward the batter. *Can't have these guys getting too comfortable on that plate.* He wound up the pitch and sent it hurtling toward home plate.

"Strike!"

Yes! The fastball worked. It had flown right over the inside corner, making the batter jump back instead of swing. This kid Layton had been knocking the leather off the ball ever since he got called up from Triple A by the Orioles earlier in the year. It was time to teach him a few things about being in the Majors.

Jose gave him the sign. He wanted a cutter this time. Zach nodded and prepared his wind up. He stared in long and hard at the batter before going forward and then hitting his release point.

"Ball two!"

The cutter had stayed too high. Layton had a good eye and hadn't chased it. Zach reminded himself not to underestimate the kid just because he was a rookie. That was part of the challenge too: Knowing your opponent, knowing his weaknesses.

Jose gave him the sign again. Another cutter. A second chance to actually get it to cut low this time. He prepped the ball in his hand, stared at Layton again, and finally entered his wind up.

"Ball three!"

The cutter hadn't cut again. Zach walked around the mound in frustration and kicked the dirt with his cleats before settling down. He shook off Jose's signs. *No, forget the cutter. Go back to the fastball or bring out the curve*, he thought.

He'd get this kid. This strikeout would be his.

Along with talent, Zach was filled with confidence. No situation was too stressful, and no opposing player was too intimidating. In fact, those were the parts of his job that really made him tick. Last inning of game seven of the World Series all coming down to whether he could execute a series of pitches that would lead to the final out and bring home a championship? Bring it on. He lived for the thrill of those big moments.

Jose called for the fastball again. Zach nodded. Once again he focused on Tommy Layton's face, prepped the pitch in his glove, and went into his wind up.

"Strike two!"

Yes! Zach smiled. This kid was his. He would get this.

It was exactly that mentality that had made Zach a pitching phenom at a very young age. He'd been drafted right out of high school by the Yankees and had rapidly risen through their farm system. When he finally was called up to the Majors, the team had tried to hold him back, issuing pitch limits and pulling him out of games when they thought their young star's arm had taken enough of a beating. But Zach had worked tirelessly to prove to the Yankees that he could handle it. He'd logged countless hours in the weight rooms. He had always been the first player at the stadium every day, running, shagging balls in the outfield, working with the trainers—whatever it took. The trainers, managers and team brass had taken notice of his work ethic, and gradually the restrictions had fallen away. Now there was nothing holding him back.

Jose laid down the sign for the curveball. *Yes.* Perfect time for his best pitch. He was going to go in close again and sweep this kid right off the plate with his curve. Layton was getting too comfortable up there on home plate. Time to remind him who was in charge.

Zach stared at the kid, the ball clutched in his hand. It was time to get that third strike. He wound up the throw and put everything he had behind it, executing a perfect release. His momentum carried him forward a few steps before he came to a halt. He slowly raised his eyes under the brim of his cap just in time to see the ball take the sharp curve toward the batter that it was designed to take. But it was too high. It was going faster than a curveball should. He'd thrown a wild pitch. And Layton wasn't expecting it. He wasn't jumping out of the way. Before Zach could fully process what was happening, the ball had made contact. *Loud* contact. But it wasn't with the bat.

Zach watched in horror as the kid fell to the ground. The pitch had hit him right in the temple.

"No," Zach said quietly, bending over in horror. "No, no, no."

The crowd fell silent as the team trainers raced out to Layton, who hadn't moved since he hit the dirt.

Zach took a couple steps forward before he was stopped by Jose and his manager, Hank Wilson, who'd come out on the mound to talk to him.

"Just wait son," Hank said. "Let them take care of him."

"I didn't mean to hit him," Zach said, never taking his eyes off the kid, who was still lying in the dirt.

"It was me," Jose said. "My fault. I was the one who called for the curve."

"I was trying to go close with it, move him back. But I wasn't trying to hit him."

"Listen to me Z, no one would ever think you'd try to hit a guy with three balls and two strikes on the line," Hank said. "Calm down, son."

The trainers worked on Layton until a cart came out on the field. They loaded him on the back of the cart and drove his still-unmoving body off the field.

"I want out," Zach said, looking at Hank for the first time. "Have someone warm up."

"Okay, but you've got to take one more batter."

"No, no," Zach said, shaking his head. "I...I need to know how Layton is doing."

"First you gotta get back on that horse, son," Hank said. "There won't be news for a while anyway."

Zach stared down at the ball in his hand, but he couldn't really focus on it. He kept hearing the thunking sound of the ball hitting Tommy Layton's head.

"I didn't mean to hit him," he said again as Jose trotted off the mound. Hank clapped him on the back and then he walked away, too.

A pinch runner took Layton's place at first base. A new player took some practice swings in the batter's box. The crowd was still quiet.

The mound seemed lonelier than it had ever felt to Zach before. There was a ringing sound in his ears. He couldn't focus on Jose or make sense of the signs he was giving him. He just stood there, frozen on the mound, the sounds and smells of the ballpark all around him.

"No, no, no," he muttered again, this time to himself. "I didn't mean to hit him."

Soon enough there came the booing. Zach was glad to hear it, in a way. It felt right. He deserved their contempt. He hadn't meant to hit him. He didn't mean for Layon to get hurt. But he was the one who'd thrown that pitch. He was the one who had been trying to sweep the batter off the plate. It was him. His fault. And now Tommy could be seriously injured. Those batting helmets offered some protection, but a projectile to the temple at 80 miles per hour could easily kill a man.

Oh God, Zach thought. *He could die.*

Jose came running over to the mound again.

"Z, come on. Just take on one more batter. Come on, you got this."

Zach stared at Jose, trying to make sense of what he was saying. He battled to catch his breath. He was starting to panic.

"Z? Buddy? Calm down. You *got* this."

Jose returned to the plate and gave Zach the sign

again. Fastball.

Zach tried to force himself to go through the usual routine. To find comfort in the steps he'd taken over and over a million times before. He stared at the batter. He prepped the ball in his glove. But he just couldn't go into the wind up. He still wasn't breathing right. The noise of that ball striking Tommy Layton was still repeating itself in his mind. And the boos were getting louder.

Finally Jose ran back to the mound.

Zach just shook his head at him and handed Jose the ball.

"I can't," he said as he turned to walk off the mound. The crowd's boos got even louder as he went to the dugout. He didn't look up at any of his teammates when he got there, and he didn't look back at the field. He reached the clubhouse steps and kept walking.

Chapter 1

TWENTY-TWO MONTHS LATER

"You're an American!" Emma said, astonished.

"And you must be...a world-renowned linguist?" the bartender asked, setting her drink down.

"Very funny," she said with a smile. "I just didn't expect it. I came to a pub on my very first day in Dublin to have a genuine Irish experience, and I end up being served by an American. From...I'll guess...North Carolina?"

"Texas."

"I was right!" Emma said, triumphantly.

"Texas is not the capital of North Carolina, you know," he said, a slow and lazy grin working its way onto his face.

"I was close!" she said again, returning his tentative expression with a full-wattage beam.

"You were like five states off," the bartender said, his face finally breaking into a full smile now.

"They're both in the south though! We're practically re-enacting *My Fair Lady* here. I heard your accent, and I instantly knew. My skills as a linguist are going to be legendary."

"I don't even know what you're saying," he said, shaking his head, but still smiling.

"Okay, Texas, let's start over. Hello. My name is Emma Crawford," she said, extending her hand. "It's my first day in Dublin. I am totally not a linguist. Thank you for my drink, and thank you for my first genuine Irish experience, which involved chatting up a guy from Texas."

"Hello Emma," he said, reaching his hand out to meet hers. His firm handshake was anything but tentative. The hand looked huge and work-roughened. *Like someone on a ranch*, she thought idly as his fingers wrapped around her own, sending a jolt of electricity right up her arm and into her chest. Emma gasped at the sensation and raised her eyes to meet his again.

"I…uh…." she began, her thoughts scattering. Any attempt to verbalize the feeling abandoned her as she gazed at him. He was tall and muscular; he had to be well over six feet. His sandy brown hair was short, but a little longer on top. It was combed to the side, a few lazy strands hanging over his forehead. Sexy. And his eyes were startlingly blue. *Genuine Irish Texas bartenders are so very deliciously yummy*, she thought.

"Uh, I need my hand back if I'm going to serve anyone else today," he finally said, breaking into her dreamy reverie.

"Oh, uh, yes, of course," she said pulling back awkwardly. "But you never told me your name, Texas."

"Nope," he said as he turned to wipe down the counter.

"Oh come on!" Emma fired back before taking a sip of her beer. "We just had a moment there. And…you're the first person I've met in Dublin. You have to at least tell me your name!"

"You can stick with 'Texas' if you'd like," he told her.

"No, tell me your actual name, Texas. Please? You're thoroughly ruining my first genuine Irish experience. Please tell me your name is something like Colin or O'Shaughnessy or McGregor or…I don't know. Bono?"

The bartender cracked another smile and sized her up. Finally he took a deep breath.

"Z," he said, fidgeting with a towel.

"You're going to make me guess it one letter at a time? Should we just play hangman on a napkin?"

"No, that's it. Z. People…they call me Z," he said, still messing with the towel, and now looking a little like he was sorry he'd told her.

"Z? Really? Okay, then. Well, people call me Em a lot, so I guess we have a whole alphabet thing in common here."

Emma was lost in a happy trance, thinking again how his smile was mesmerizing. Then, *Okay, I can't just stare at him all day.*

"I feel like I'm in an episode of *Sesame Street*," she said finally. "This conversation was sponsored by the letters Z and M and the number 2. Or maybe we're in *Men in Black*. J and K are probably around here somewhere." Then she gave herself an imaginary kick. *Stop babbling!*

"Nice to meet you, Em," he replied before breaking their eye contact and turning to help a couple who had just sat down at the end of the bar.

Geez. She'd scared him away with her nervous chatter, and she was annoyed with herself. Nevertheless, she couldn't help continuing to watch him work as she sipped her beer. There was something about him. Something she couldn't put her finger on. It was almost like she knew him somehow. But she'd stake her life on the fact that she'd never met him before.

Okay, that made no sense. She did feel like she'd seen him before, but she was certain she had never met him. That was just nuts.

She pulled out her travel guide and began to flip through the pages. She couldn't spend her entire time gawking at a bartender, no matter how fabulously gorgeous he was.

Gorgeous, she thought as she thumbed to the pages about Dublin. *Gorgeous and...familiar.* Her mind wasn't letting it go. There was a definite puzzle here. Had they gone to college together? Maybe he was a former neighbor? Or someone who she used to see at the bus stop or the grocery store or something like that?

No. She still was convinced that she'd never actually met him before. She'd remember the way her body had reacted to him. The chemistry had been palpable in just a simple handshake and introduction. She would definitely remember that.

Unless he was someone famous...? He certainly was good looking enough to be a model or an actor. Maybe that was it. She turned the idea around in her mind as she sipped her beer and tried to keep watching him inconspicuously. But if he was a male model or an actor who had landed a big enough role to be recognized, what in the world was he doing pouring drinks at a tiny pub in Dublin? No, that didn't make any sense. Unless he was immersing himself for a role as an Irish bartender or something? *Whatever...enough is enough.* She had to stop obsessing about this guy.

"How long will you be in Dublin?" asked the guy in question all of a sudden.

"Wow, you move fast," she replied, startled. "You were clear across the bar like two seconds ago."

"You were lost in your book," Z said. "What are

you reading?"

"Oh, this? Just my travel guide. Trying to make sure I see all the sights while I'm here."

"And how long is that? A week?"

"No, all summer, believe it or not. My friend Tracy is here on a research grant. I had this fabulous idea that I'd take advantage and come stay with her. But I didn't exactly think through the part where she's going to be super busy and hard at work, and I'm going to be alone all summer in a strange place." Emma shrugged. "I mean, don't get me wrong, this is a once-in-a-lifetime opportunity and I'm glad I'm making use of it. But it's also going to be…."

"Lonely?" Z finally asked when Emma trailed off.

"Yeah, I guess so. Part of exploring new places and experiencing new things is getting to share them with someone else, you know what I mean?"

"I know exactly what you mean," he said with a nod. "I'm here by myself, too."

"Ooh, really? Okay, now I sense a story," she said, closing her book. "Tell me the Z story."

"I…there's nothing to tell," he said as a look of…was that panic?....chased across his face.

"Oh, I'm sorry, I don't mean to be nosy," Emma said, feeling uncertain now. "I just really have a strong sensation that I know you from somewhere. Not that we've met before, but it's more like…I *recognize* you."

Z shook his head like he was trying to look nonchalant, but Emma could almost see the wheels furiously turning in his head as he searched for a reply. That was interesting. He was definitely hiding something from her. He looked a little desperate now.

"Impossible. We've never met. I…we've never met before," he said before turning and walking away.

Now she was beyond intrigued. She had to figure out how and why she knew him. *There's a full-on Nancy Drew kind of mystery here*, she thought. She was sure of it.

She sipped her drink and read her book a little while longer, hoping Z would come back. But now he seemed to be avoiding even eye contact. Finally she gave up, tossed some money on the counter, put her book in her bag, and walked down to the end of the bar where he was stacking glasses.

"I'm sorry," she said. "I didn't mean to upset you before."

"You didn't," he said. "How could you? I told you—we've never met before."

"Right, yeah, okay," Emma said, feeling awkward as the icy wall Z had erected around himself radiated an actual chill in the air. "So…nice meeting you."

Z stopped his furious glass-stacking activity long enough to look up at her. Their eyes met then, and Emma held her breath, wondering what he was about to say. He looked like he was carefully choosing his next words, but in the end it was nothing more than, "Enjoy Dublin, Em."

"I…okay, thanks. I will. And I really am sorry I made you uncomfortable," she added as she turned and hurried out.

As she reached the sidewalk, she stopped and leaned back against the building, waiting for her heart to stop racing. What kind of reaction was she having? she wondered. And why was she reacting to a simple conversation at all? Okay, so it was a simple conversation with the sexiest Texan bartender in all of Dublin and maybe all of the world. *But I seriously need to get a grip*, she thought as she gradually regained her equilibrium and started walking toward Tracy's apartment.

When she got there, she dropped her bag and headed straight for her laptop. But what in the world was she going to Google? The letter *Z*? *Blue eyes + Texas*? *People I might recognize*? In the end she pushed the laptop away with a frustrated sigh. Clearly she wasn't going to solve this mystery today. She walked over to her bag again and pulled out the guidebook.

She needed to find a way to take her mind off the incredibly sexy—and mysterious—Z.

Chapter 2

ZACH COULDN'T STOP panicking even though he knew he was being ridiculous. *But knowing you're being ridiculous and making yourself calm down and not hyperventilate are two different things*, he thought as he checked the clock on the wall behind the bar again.

Finally, blissfully, his shift was over. He yanked off the stupid green apron he had to wear and tossed it in a hamper in the back room. Then he pushed out the door and into the low light of late afternoon, not bothering to say anything to any of his coworkers. They wouldn't be surprised, of course. He was known as a loner there—which was exactly the way he wanted it.

He shoved his hands into his pockets and headed down the sidewalk toward his apartment.

Finally he could give some real consideration to what had happened today. He'd almost been *recognized*. And by the most adorable woman he'd ever laid eyes on. *Emma the linguist*, he thought with a tiny smile.

He'd been attracted to her the minute she'd sat on the stool across from him. Everything about her had knocked him off center. First that she was beautiful, of course. But it wasn't just her looks that had grabbed his attention. There was something about her presence and sense of self.... She had opened the door, walked into the pub, and sidled onto the stool with an easy confidence that he found irresistible. And yes, she really was gorgeous. She had long wavy blonde hair—and did it have a little red in it? Were her eyes brown or hazel? It was hard to tell in the dim light of the pub. But fine details aside, she'd been so cute sitting there sipping at her beer and reading her travel guide. There hadn't been anything cute, however, about the sizzle of electricity that had coursed through his arm when she shook his hand. Pure chemistry had been arching in the air between them, and he knew she felt it, too. There was awareness and mutual attraction written all over her face.

He'd been emotionally shut down for so long. A zombie slogging through his day-to-day routine, unmoved by almost anything that happened around him. So when the adorably sexy Emma had sparked some life into his soul, some actual feeling, he'd been so taken aback that he'd just decided to enjoy something for once. Enjoy *her*. The company, the conversation, the smiles…and now he exhaled in frustration. The old version of himself would have asked her out right then and there. Old Zach had been confident and carefree; he was a flirt who always just had *it*, that indefinable magnetism when it came to women. They'd always flocked to him, and he'd always welcomed their company. He would have been flattered if they recognized him and wasn't at all above playing the 'I'm a sports star' card.

But that's not how life was anymore. Not for *this* Zach—the one who felt like a fugitive from everything and everyone he'd ever known. This Zach had been hiding out in Ireland for almost two years now. Ever since the big incident. Ever since Tommy Layton had taken that pitch to the head. That's when everything changed. When something inside of Zach just died. His parents, his manager, his teammates, his agent….

absolutely everyone had tried to talk sense into him, console him, get him to see reason. Layton hadn't died, after all.

But Zach still couldn't forgive himself. He couldn't get past it. All his old swagger had withered away. A pitcher in the Major Leagues needed confidence and bravado. He had to be able to stand on that solitary mound, with the weight of an entire organization on his shoulders, and make pitch after pitch to get those outs and secure those wins. After the Curveball Incident—as he privately referred to it—he just couldn't get any of it back. He couldn't even figure out how to *start* getting it back. His old confidence had shattered, and like all the king's horses and all the king's men in the nursery rhyme, he just couldn't put the pieces back together again.

So he walked away from it all. Broke his contract. Made his agent do some fancy footwork to avoid a breach lawsuit. He'd left millions of dollars on the table and signed papers from the Yankees swearing he wouldn't pitch for another Major League team for ten years. Then he just walked away from his whole life. As far as the entire sports world knew, Zach Hiller had become a ghost and vanished. His parents, brother, and sister all knew where he was, of course. But to the rest of the world he was yesterday's headline. A sports phenomenon who, in the end, didn't actually have what it took to make it big.

Choosing Dublin as his landing spot had almost been a random decision. He wanted to flee to another country, somewhere he could get lost in a sea of strangers who couldn't care less about a burned-out athlete. But he also wanted to make sure he wouldn't have to learn a new language. So he'd picked Ireland on a whim and put in a little bit of work to get the necessary papers for a long-term stay. He gave up his apartment in Manhattan, put his stuff in a storage unit in New Jersey, sold his car, and headed to Newark Airport.

Disappearing had actually been sort of disappointingly easy. There was a part of him—he eventually came to accept that it was his bruised ego—that was startled by how few people had actually noticed or cared. After the initial furor of headlines and sports-radio talk shows devoted to picking apart what had happened after he walked away, things had died down quickly. He hadn't left behind a girlfriend pining for him or a posse of close friends who missed him. His inner circle had been people who were paid to be there. When the checks stopped coming, so did they. So he'd come to Dublin alone and lost and broken, and almost two years later he still didn't really have a plan. All he knew was that he liked being there and being anonymous. Not having any eyes on him, nor any expectations. Until today, that was—when a stunning blonde and her travel guide had breezed into the pub and into his life, and tossed him right out of the solitary little cocoon he'd been living in.

No, he told himself. *I'm still overreacting....*

First of all, what were the odds that Emma was going to be able to identify him? Not very good. He hadn't been in the papers in all that time. Yes, she seemed to vaguely recognize him. But that didn't mean she was a baseball fan. Or even a sports fan. It was true that he'd been a fairly big star in the baseball world. And just being on the Yankees gave a guy a bit more press than, say, someone on the Pittsburgh Pirates would get. But he'd never been a *superstar*. He wasn't a household name like some players. So even if Emma was a casual sports fan, the chances still weren't high that she'd be able to place him.

By the time he got to his apartment, he felt calmer about all this. *Also*, he thought as he grabbed his mail and walked through his doorway, *she's just a tourist*. He'd probably never even see her again.

When that thought brought a wave of disappointment crashing over him instead of the relief he'd expected, he tried not to analyze it further. Maintaining his anonymity was the important thing, right? Staying hidden, that was what he needed to survive. What he definitely *didn't* need was the beautiful woman who in one short conversation had made him feel more flickers of humanity inside than anything or anyone else since his life had fallen apart.

But those feelings weren't important, he reminded himself. *Just the opposite, really.*

If he could continue to not feel anything, then he could keep wandering unchallenged through the murky, solitary life he'd made for himself. And that was precisely how he wanted it.

Chapter 3

"SO WHAT DID you do today?" Tracy asked as she walked into the apartment that evening. "Anything fun?"

"I didn't get as much done as I thought I would," Emma replied. "Mostly I just drank a beer in a real Irish pub and talked to the super-sexy bartender, who was actually from Texas. That southern drawl was so not what I was expecting in Dublin."

"All I heard was the word *sexy*," Tracy said. "Since I'm the one who's single, why don't you tell me more about this guy?"

"I'm *technically* still single," Emma clarified. "Engaged isn't married."

"No, but engaged *isn't* technically single, either. So dish. Who's the guy? I need to live vicariously through you this summer since I'm otherwise just going to be hidden in libraries and records rooms, working."

"I don't know really. He was being totally mysterious. He wouldn't tell me anything about himself, not even his name."

"He wouldn't give you his name? That seems weird," Tracy said with a frown as she started pulling ingredients out of the small refrigerator to start supper.

"Yeah, it kind of was. All he'd say is that he was from Texas and that people call him 'Z.' Must be a nickname. Short for Zaid or Zach or Zebediah or something," Emma mused.

"I totally hope it's Zebediah," Tracy said, filling a pan with water for pasta.

"Can I help with that?" Emma asked.

"Nah, this kitchen is too small. Let's just switch off handling dinner. Your turn tomorrow. Is spaghetti okay tonight?"

"Sure. And hey, my Irish experience is getting richer by the minute," Emma said with a laugh. "First a bartender from Texas and now supper from Italy."

"Yep, you're just marinating in the authenticity, aren't you? So come on, tell me more about the mysterious Zebediah."

Emma shrugged. "I don't know. It wasn't a big deal, I guess. We just talked and flirted a bit. It was harmless."

"Nah, not harmless. I can totally tell there's more to this story than you're saying. You're attracted to him, aren't you?"

"I...yeah, okay, there was just this instant connection that totally caught me off guard. We just had *it*. You know, chemistry? But I promise you I won't act on it. As you reminded me, I'm engaged. It wouldn't be right to pursue it."

Tracy made a funny muttering sound. Then, "Emma, can I ask you something personal? Something potentially uncomfortable?"

"Trace, geez, of course. You're one of my closest friends. And you're opening your home to me for an entire summer. The least I can do is answer a question or two. Ask me anything."

"Okay then, here it goes—why did you and Jim get engaged right before you came here? Why now?"

"Why? Why do most people get engaged? Because we want to get married. Because he asked. Because I said yes." Emma had a perplexed look on her face.

"Uh huh," Tracy answered, turning back to the sauce she was warming up.

"What? That 'uh huh' carried a tone of sarcasm. What exactly are you saying?" Emma asked, trying not to sound annoyed.

"Why couldn't you have just come here unattached? Free? Open to any sort of adventure that you could find? Why did you have to tie yourself down to Jim first?"

"I…because…Tracy? What's up with these questions? Jim proposed and I accepted. End of story. I seriously don't understand what you're getting at."

"Emma, you're a doll. You're an absolutely fabulous person. But you seem to have this need to live your life by some kind of checklist. You're always doing what you *ought* to do instead of what you *want* to do."

"How do you know that what I ought to do and what I want to do aren't the same thing?" Emma asked.

"You're telling me, from the bottom of your heart, that you didn't get engaged to Jim because his proposal was perfectly timed to coincide with you finishing your degree? Education? Check. Husband? Check."

"That's not true! Jim's a great guy, and I love him."

"Mmm-hmm."

"I do! You know I do. You've seen us together."

"Yeah, Em, I have. I'm telling you, as one of your closest friends and someone who loves you like a sister, that I think you haven't really, really thought about this. I just don't think Jim's the guy for you, and I just want to hear you say that he's absolutely The One."

"Well no one knows *absolutely*," Emma said, starting to get a little annoyed.

"I think *you* would know absolutely, Emma, I really

do."

"How'd we leap from 'How was your day?' to 'You're marrying the wrong guy' in less than ten minutes?"

"I warned you it was a personal question. I'm sorry, Em. But it's just been on my mind, and I couldn't live with myself if I didn't tell you what I thought before it's too late. So I'd been tossing around how to bring it up, but then you come in here dreamily talking about this sexy bartender who you're obviously smitten with…"

"It was one meaningless conversation!" Emma interjected.

"It doesn't have to be meaningless or just one conversation. Tell Jim you want to be on a break this summer and then please, for once, just go have fun without worrying about whether it fits into your master plan."

Emma shook her head. "I'm not breaking up with Jim. And seriously, I don't have a master plan. That's totally a myth that everyone keeps perpetuating. Like Bigfoot."

"Emma, if Jim's the right person for you, then he'll wait for you. Please think about it. Just find a way to enjoy this summer with total abandon. It's your time, Em. You just finished your degree. You haven't entered the drudgery of slogging into work every day. You're not tied down to a mortgage or kids or a husband. Accept a little bit of freedom. Fully enjoy this unencumbered time in your life. Embrace it with both arms."

"I'll think about what you're saying, Trace, I will. And I appreciate that you love me and want what's best for me. But having a fling with a stranger just isn't my style."

"Interesting," Tracy said as she stirred the spaghetti.

"What?"

"I never said a thing about a fling, you jumped to that conclusion all by yourself. Which probably means you're thinking about Mr. Texas way more than you're letting on."

"Oh come on! It's what you were *implying*! If you're just defining freedom as, I don't know, just an opportunity to rent a car and amble around the countryside taking pictures of sheep, then whether or not I'm engaged wouldn't matter."

Tracy just shook her head silently, looking frustrated now.

"I can't win in this conversation, can I?" Emma said with a laugh as she reached over to give Tracy a hug.

"Nope!" Tracy said, returning it. "I'm sorry Em. I'll drop it now. Just think about what I said though, Okay? Promise?"

"I promise," Emma said, giving Tracy one last squeeze before pulling free to set the table.

It was touching that Tracy was so worried about her, but she'd never actually go through any type of sordid affair. Why shake the foundation of her existing relationship on a whim? Nope, this summer was just about seeing the sights and having fun. Period. No worries. No master plans.

And no bartenders.

Chapter 4

OKAY, THIS IS RIDICULOUS, Zach thought, angrily untying his green apron and tossing it in the hamper before slamming his way out the back door of the pub yet again.

He'd convinced himself that he was never going to see Emma again, and that it was really for the best anyway, since he desperately didn't want her to figure out who he was. So how, then, could he explain the crushing disappointment he'd felt every time the door to the pub had opened and she hadn't come waltzing in with her infectious smile and her trusty guidebook?

I can't....

The last thing he needed in his life was another complication. If he met Emma again and they started talking, how long would it be before she either realized who he was or figured out a way to make him tell her? And *then* what? He'd have to sit there in agony as pity clouded her face? Be unable to answer her inevitable question about why he just couldn't go back and recapture his old life? Try to tell her why part of him had died and could never be brought back? Explain it? Hell, even he didn't understand it.

No, he didn't need it. He didn't need any of it. The complications, the questions, the pity, the forced explanations. Nope, he didn't need any of it. Or anyone. And he most certainly didn't need Emma Crawford. Fine, so it was settled.

Except it wasn't...because he couldn't get her out of his mind. It had been one tiny, inconsequential conversation. A little flirty bit of banter that ultimately hadn't meant a thing. Except, of course, that it had. In those seemingly tiny and inconsequential moments, Emma had made Zach feel more than he had at any other time since the Curveball Incident. How was that possible? He didn't *want* to feel anything, right? So never seeing her again was the absolute best thing that could ever possibly happen...right?

He continued to wage a mental war with himself as he made his way down the sidewalk toward his apartment, head down, shoulders hunched in frustration.

Why? Why now? Why her? Why....

"Oomph!"

He barreled right into someone—a woman—without even realizing it. He reached out to steady her as her bag fell to the ground.

"I'm so sorry," she said. "I wasn't watching where I was going." She leaned down to pick up her bag and...was that a travel book?

Zach's heart felt like a marching band came alive in his chest as the woman raised her eyes to meet his, and he found himself looking down at Emma. *Her eyes are brown*, he thought to himself, finally able to see their color now that they were outside the bar. While he'd been cataloguing all the reasons why it really was best that he never see her again, he'd managed to run right into her. Classic.

"Emma. Hi. Again," he stuttered. Geez what was wrong with him? This was bad. Had he completely forgotten how to talk to a beautiful woman? He couldn't even form a sentence—but he also couldn't deny how unbelievably happy he was to see her.

"Z! My Texas bartender! I'm so happy to see you again," she said, a happy smile chasing across her face as she flipped her hair over one shoulder and hooked the bag back onto her arm.

"I...you too," Zach managed. He was starting to feel like a complete idiot now.

"Are you done with your shift?" she asked, seemingly fine with his sad attempts at conversation.

"Yes. Just finished up." There, that was better. *That had been a complete sentence, right?*

"Great! Come have coffee with me," she said. "Are you free? Am I interfering with any plans?"

"No, no plans. Just heading home," Zach said. Then he remembered that he wasn't going to see her again, right? So this wasn't good. She might figure out why she knew him. He had to avoid her, not go have coffee with her. And yet in the end he couldn't stop himself from adding, "I'd love to go get coffee."

He gave himself a mental kick. A million reasons. There were a million reasons why he should be avoiding this woman, up to and including the fact that he really wasn't even a coffee drinker. And yet he suddenly found himself walking alongside her, unaccountably thrilled by this turn of events.

Oh man, I'm in so much trouble here.

"What have you been up to today?" he asked, giving up trying to talk himself out of the coffee. He could itemize reasons why he should never see her again later. For now he was just going to enjoy walking next to her.

He glanced back down at the top of her blonde head again. She was probably 5'8" or 5'9" he guessed. Quite a bit shorter than he was. *Perfect for dancing*, he thought before he could stop himself. Honestly! Where had that thought come from? He wasn't going to be dancing any time soon; not with her, not with anyone.

"I got a ticket for the hop-on/hop-off tourist bus today," she told him. "I ended up riding the whole loop, but I only stopped at a few spots along the way. Mostly I was enjoying listening to the bus drivers talk. I'm never going to get tired of listening to Irish accents."

"Where'd you stop?"

"I got off at Trinity College first. Have you ever seen the library?"

"No."

"You haven't? Oh you really should! It's amazing. There are books stacked as far as you can see—I think they said there are like 200,000 or something. And they're these amazing, ancient books, too. It's just stunning. I think it's going to end up being my favorite thing on this trip. It was *that* amazing. I can't believe you haven't seen it. How long did you say you've been in Dublin?"

"I didn't. I, um...it's been almost two years," Zach said, feeling a little hesitant. How many details should he give her? Would supplying a timetable help her figure out who he was? Should he be concocting an elaborate cover story to throw her off the trail instead?

"Oh, wow, two years. What brought you here?" she asked, looking up at him as they continued their unhurried pace down the sidewalk.

Okay, yes, he decided, he totally should have made up a cover story. He could feel himself starting to sweat. *Oh this is great*, he thought. *She's going to think I'm a complete freak who can't even answer the simplest of questions.*

"I, uh...," he started, feeling himself really start to

panic now. "I just wanted to travel. See someplace new."

That seemed like a reasonable answer. He worked at trying to calm himself as he waited for her reply.

"It's great that you were able to go on such an adventure, and for so long," she replied. "Wow. Didn't you say you're here alone?"

"Yeah."

"Two years all alone in a foreign country seems, well...kind of lonely," she said. "How have you filled up the time? I'll bet you've investigated every corner of the country by now, huh?"

"Well, no, actually. I...I really haven't gotten outside of the city."

"What?" Emma said, stopping with a look of complete incredulity on her face. "You've been in Ireland for two whole years and you never set foot outside of Dublin?"

"Nope," Zach said, starting to sweat again.

"You haven't seen the Cliffs of Moher or kissed the Blarney Stone or...seen a single puffin or sheep?"

Zach shook his head mutely. He was such an idiot. If she wasn't suspicious about him before, she certainly would be now. He was really doing a stellar job of staying under her radar. By the time he finished this conversation, she'd have reason to hire a private investigator.

Emma stood there a moment longer, studying his face and obviously searching for answers. Finally she shook her head and started walking again.

"What?" he asked.

"Z, you are a fascinating man. I just can't put my finger on it, but, well, I feel like there's a mystery here to be solved."

"No!" he said way too sharply. "No...there's no mystery. Seriously, there's nothing interesting to my story at all. I'm just a guy. A guy who's taking some time off to, uh, find himself, I guess."

"Okay, right," she said, looking doubtful.

He realized he needed to divert this conversation away from himself, and fast. "So come on, tell me the Emma story," he said. "Where are you from?"

"Oh, well, there's not a whole lot to that, either, I guess," she replied. "How about stopping here?"

Zach looked up and saw she was pointing to a nice little café that he'd never noticed before.

He nodded. "Sure."

They walked in and found only a handful of other customers seated at the dozen or so round tables that dotted the room. After they sat down, a waitress came by quickly. Emma ordered coffee. Zach hesitated, then ordered a cup anyway, mostly so he'd have something to do with his hands. He'd always been fidgety, and he didn't want to give her more reasons to think she was conversing with some lunatic, which was pretty much how he figured he must be coming off about now. Why was a simple conversation with a beautiful woman such a struggle?

"So," she said, turning back to him after the waitress left. "You asked about me. I'm from Massachusetts, which of course means I probably have a funny accent to you. And, because it's practically the law there, that of course means I'm a huge Red Sox fan."

Zach's eyes shot toward her at the mention of a pro baseball team, but she was idly playing with her spoon and didn't seem to notice. *Okay, it had just been an off-hand comment*, he thought. She hadn't been trying to get a reaction from him.

"I just finished my master's in early education from U Mass in Amherst," she continued. "I'm taking the summer off before diving into the fast-paced life of a substitute teacher, which is pretty much all I can expect to be for a while. It's hard to get your foot in the door with a full-time position straight out of school."

"So you'll sub until you can find an opening?"

"Yeah, that's pretty much the plan. I probably would have been smarter to use this summer to blanket the state's school districts with my résumé. But like I told you, my friend Tracy's here and, well, I just couldn't pass up on the opportunity to take this trip," she shrugged as the waitress put their drinks down.

"Makes sense to me," he said, reaching for the cream and sugar. If he was going to drink this cup of coffee, it was going to feed his sweet tooth and be as sugary as possible. He stirred the liquid until it was a light mocha color, then picked it up for the first wretched sip.

"And, well, I guess the other big part of my story right now is that I just got engaged right before I came here," she added.

"You're engaged?!" Zach asked, clunking the coffee back down on the saucer harder than he meant to. A swirl dribbled down the side of his cup. *Smooth*, he thought, as he attempted to wipe up the mess with a napkin.

"Yeah, I am. It's so new that it feels weird to even say out loud. Jim and I met at college and dated for years. And, I don't know...I finished my master's, but he's working on his PhD, so he'll be there for a while. I think the fact that I was leaving and starting this whole new phase of my life just made him…pop the question,

I guess. So he did and I said yes and then I left for Ireland. We haven't really set a date or anything. This is all really, really new."

"So new you don't even have a ring yet?" Zach asked, nodding toward her bare left hand.

"Oh, that? Yeah, I just didn't want to lose the ring while traveling, so I left it at home."

"You left it at home?" Zach asked before even realizing the question was coming out of his mouth. This was seriously none of his business.

"Yeah…what? Is that weird?" she asked, sipping her own coffee now.

"I don't know a thing about engagement rings or etiquette. But I just thought women got so attached to them. I wouldn't figure you'd want to let it out of your sight."

"Yeah, you're right I guess. I just…I don't know. It seemed so extravagant and fancy to be casually wearing on a trip, you know?"

"Yeah, sure, that makes sense," he said, looking down at his cup again. Why was the news that Emma was engaged hitting him so hard? Hadn't he just spent the last 24 hours creating an elaborate list of reasons why it was best that he never see her again? What was wrong with him? This should be fantastic news. Emma wasn't free, which meant she wasn't free to be spending time with him and nosing around in his past and trying to figure out who he was. This was the best possible bit of news she could give, right?

But it one-hundred-percent does not feel *like good news*, he thought. *Not at all.*

"What's wrong?" Emma asked. "You look down."

"No, nothing's wrong," he said. "You just, uh, well you got me thinking about how crazy it is that I haven't seen more of Ireland. You're right. I should be soaking in the sights and sounds a whole lot more than I've been doing."

"Okay, so what are you doing tomorrow?" Emma asked, looking excited now.

"Nothing I guess. I don't work tomorrow."

"I was going to hop on the bus again and stop at more of the sights. Come with me! If you haven't ever been to the library at Trinity College, then my guess is that you've never done any of the other big touristy things, either. Am I right?"

"You are right, yes," he admitted, feeling like an idiot now. Seriously, what the hell had he been doing with himself for two years?

"Ooh, fun! Then come with me tomorrow! We could tour the Guinness Brewery! And we could go to Phoenix Park! Are you a zoo person? Or we could tour the old jail! It's called the...." she paused to pull out her guidebook.

Zach smiled as he watched her flip excitedly through the pages. Who got this worked up to go see an old jail or tour a brewery?

"...the Kilmainham Gaol! We can see the site where hundreds and hundreds of political prisoners suffered. Okay, maybe that's not such a great first place to take you."

"You mentioned Phoenix Park," he said. "Maybe we could just take a walk? It's actually supposed to be pretty nice tomorrow. Perfect for a park outing."

Wait a minute, why am I agreeing to this? he wondered. He was just giving her more of an opportunity to figure out his secrets, or at least to further cement in her mind that he *was* keeping secrets.

All of that made perfectly logical sense, and yet in

the end he just smiled and made no effort to back out of their plans as she happily read Phoenix-Park facts to him.

He wasn't going to fight it, he decided as he listened. Nothing could ever really happen between them anyway because she was engaged to someone else. So what was there to fear? And the thought of spending a little time with someone he actually liked being around was just too enticing to pass up. He'd been alone too long. Here he was, after two years of almost complete social paralysis, feeling the first stirrings of life in his soul again.

It wasn't something he could just ignore.

Chapter 5

"OKAY, I THINK I just did a dumb thing," Emma said that night as she made dinner at Tracy's apartment.

"A dumb thing with the food we're about to eat?" Tracy said, not looking up from her laptop.

"No, not that. I ran into Z, that bartender I told you about yesterday."

"You mean that *sexy* bartender from Texas who you totally want to have a torrid love affair with? That bartender?" Tracy gave Emma a wink.

"Shut up! I do not! I seriously don't know a thing about him. We spent an hour or so together and I think I know less about him than I did before. He is so secretive!"

"So what was the dumb thing? Talking to him for an hour?"

"No, actually, the dumb part was that I made plans to go to Phoenix Park with him tomorrow."

"Em, that's great!" Tracy said, shutting her laptop, standing up and walking over to her. "I told you that this summer should be all about having wonderful experiences! This is exactly the kind of thing I was talking about. Seriously, what's the dumb part?"

"I don't know this guy, like at all. Like I said, I don't even know his name. What if he's an axe murderer? What if he's a perv who wants to make a necklace out of my teeth?"

"Does he give you mysterious or creepy vibes?"

Tracy countered.

"Just mysterious, I guess. He's very guarded. It's like he's got so many walls up around himself he can't even move. And I feel like those walls are guarding him from...something sad, I guess, but that's just me trying to read the tea leaves. So, okay, I'm babbling here. But no, I don't really think he's dangerous. Still...again, I don't even know his *name*."

"Well, it's probably smart to keep that in mind. Don't go wandering to some remote part of the park. Stay with the tourists. Can't be too careful, especially since you know outright that this guy has something to hide."

"Yeah, I'll be careful. But the other dumb part is, seriously, what am I doing spending time with another guy anyway? I'm committed to Jim. So this just feels a little...wrong, I guess." Then Emma said, "I hope you don't mind an omelet for supper. It's all I could think to make."

"An omelet's great," Tracy told her. "But don't change the subject. Did you tell Z about Jim?"

"Yeah, actually I did," Emma said as she chopped an onion.

"Okay, then what's the problem?"

"Well, I don't know. I guess the problem is that I didn't tell Jim about Z. And I really don't want to. Is that wrong?" The onion-chopping started to make her eyes burn, so she wiped them on her arm.

"I'm probably not the right person to ask," Tracy said. "I'm the one who just yesterday was telling you to dump Jim for the summer."

"Yeah, true. I don't know. I keep saying I'm committed to Jim, and yet today when I ran into Z I just...I don't even know the last time I felt that happy.

It was so great to see him again. But I keep asking myself why? He's a total stranger to me. And yet before I knew it, we were chatting over coffees and making plans to meet again, and...I don't know. Jim's feelings didn't seem important at all in that moment. Okay, so I'm a horrible person. I heard how that sounded as it came out of my mouth."

"Stop torturing yourself. You weren't ready to get engaged. I could see that from clear across the Atlantic. And now that you're here I'm even more certain. Seriously Em, what's the hurry? You've got your entire life to be tied down to Professor Jim. Go figure out what secrets Z is hiding, and for God's sake, have some carefree fun for once. Stop thinking so much."

"You are a terrible influence, Trace!" Emma said with a laugh. "You're supposed to be talking me out of doing dumb things, not helping me justify them."

"Says who?" Tracy asked, pulling plates out to set the table.

* * * *

Later that night, Emma lay in bed thinking over her conversations from the day. Was she making too big a deal out of this? Should she just go and have a nice time with Z and not worry about it? Or was Tracy's idea about breaking up with Jim something she should think about more seriously? *Okay, what? Where had that errant thought come from?* Was she really considering breaking up with Jim? Over a guy who wouldn't even tell her his name? *Ridiculous....*

Tracy clearly believed she'd made a mistake in saying yes to Jim, period. She seemed to think that Emma should break up with Jim *and* spend time with Z, not break up with Jim *in order to* spend time with Z. Like their relationship was flawed, and that it really didn't have anything to do with this summer or Z at all. What was Tracy seeing? she wondered, rolling the question around in her mind. What was missing in their relationship that a friend could see from the outside but Emma herself couldn't? Or was the mere fact that she was dying to find ways to justify spending time with Z her answer?

She rolled on her side, and bunched her pillow under head as she tried to make sense of it all. Jim Taylor, future English professor. They'd met at U Mass. Her friends and his friends had ended up sitting near each other at dinner one evening, and they'd struck up a conversation that continued after they all left. Jim had asked her out right on the spot, and she'd said yes.

That simple story pretty much summed up their entire relationship—easy and uncomplicated. They'd met and seamlessly fallen into each other's lives. There never had been any huge ups or downs, no big drama. She had fun with Jim, period, so she'd continued to date him through the rest of her time at U Mass. She trusted him and she liked him. A strong marriage could easily be built on that foundation. So when he had asked her to marry him, it never occurred to her to say no. Why should she walk away from such a great guy?

But she supposed if she was really being truthful, the lack of drama could also be interpreted as a lack of fireworks. They never really had a sizzling chemistry. Maybe that's what Tracy was picking up on. And maybe that's why being with Z felt so exciting. He might be a secret-keeping stranger, but they definitely created a spark together. *Then again, just because you have chemistry doesn't mean there's anything else there*, she reminded herself. With Jim, she honestly had everything. Caring, compassion, honesty, and the promise of a secure future.

She smiled with affection into the darkness of the room. Jim...she really did love him. She'd always been attracted to his seriousness and sense of purpose. Jim was one of those people who'd always known who he was and what he was going to do with his life. When everyone else was stealing off on impetuous ski weekends or trips to Boston, Jim would hang back to study. He was a man with a life plan, and he would never veer from it. She'd always liked and admired his determination. She herself liked making plans and appreciated that skill in others. She liked that he wouldn't be thrown off course by the little things.

So he certainly wouldn't be shaken up by his fiancée having a perfectly harmless walk in a park with another guy, right...?

Emma rolled onto her back again and stared up at the ceiling. There was nothing going on with Z, so there was nothing wrong. She had *done* absolutely nothing wrong. There was no reason in the world for her to be analyzing and agonizing about this. She was going for a harmless walk in the park with this guy, not having wild sex with him.

At that moment Emma could actually feel her face turn red as a ferocious heat washed through her from the offhand thought of having sex with Z.

Okay, yeah, this is bad.

She needed to hear Jim's voice at that moment. She needed to remember what was truly important in her life.

She grabbed her phone off the nightstand. Jim should be home, probably studying. That's pretty much all he did these days, although he was the graduate assistant for a freshmen-level English lit class this summer, so he might actually be at his office. She couldn't remember his exact schedule.

He picked up almost immediately. "Hey Em!" he said. "How's Dublin?"

"Great!" she replied cheerfully. This was good, she thought. Hearing his familiar voice felt so comforting and right. "I saw the library at Trinity College. I was blown away."

"The Long Room, they call it," he told her. "And did you see illuminated gospels? But then you must have—you wouldn't have gone to the library and missed seeing them." He was in professor mode, as always. She rolled her eyes with an affectionate smile. Good old Jim.

"The Book of Kells? Yes, I saw the whole tour, of course. They were beautiful, but it was the library that really blew me away."

"What else have you done?" he asked.

"Well, not much. Although I did go to a pub. I was talking to the bartender, and it turns out he's from Texas," she said. Okay, here was her chance to tell him everything.

"That's nice, Em. Hey, a student just came in, so I have to go. Have a great time, Okay?" He finished with a quick *Love you!* and then disconnected the call without waiting for a reply.

That hadn't exactly gone the way she'd wanted it to, she told herself. But at least she'd mentioned the conversation with Z. *Well, sort of.*

She put the phone down and rolled onto her side again. This was ridiculous. She was getting all worked up because Tracy had planted some seeds of doubt in her mind. If she hadn't said those things, Emma never would have even felt the slightest bit guilty about her innocuous plans with Z. Honestly. It was just a walk in

the park.
 What could possibly be wrong with that?

Chapter 6

HE WAS SO NERVOUS. Too nervous. Way more worked up than the situation called for, and yet the stress ball clenched tightly in his fist was getting a complete beat-down. Seriously, it was a walk in the park with a woman. *Newborns in strollers go to the park all the time, right?* And they're so happy and relaxed they all seem to sleep through the whole experience. So why couldn't he calm down?

He rolled the stress ball around in his left hand again, a nervous habit he'd acquired since he arrived here. He'd always been a tightly wound supernova to begin with, the kind of person who could never sit still. Even tucked into a movie theater or a team meeting, he was always jiggling his leg up and down or playing absentmindedly with a pencil or some other object. But never completely still. He remembered his mom putting her hand on his knee to calm him while they sat in church. He'd try so hard to stay that way, but the moment she removed her hand, he'd be moving again. She used to say he came with an internal motor that couldn't be turned off. That energy was part of the reason his parents had let him channel so much time, money, and other family resources into baseball by the time he was old enough to lift a bat. The sport had helped him burn off that extra power while giving a focus and purpose to it.

But when baseball had been torn from his life, he

no longer had a way to channel it all. So he'd started carrying a stress ball. And that was largely why he'd taken the job as a bartender. He didn't really need the money—with the modest way he was living, he could draw from the nest egg earned through his pitching forever. But he needed to stay busy and have some sort of focus and purpose, even if that was just pouring beer for chatty tourists.

He squeezed the ball again and realized he wasn't being totally truthful with himself. This wasn't fidgeting, this was practically a full-blown panic attack. *But what was there to panic about, really?* It should be simple. He'd make casual conversation with Emma—a woman he really enjoyed spending time with—and he'd walk. Easiest thing in the world. Walking and talking. No problem.

Except that it was totally a problem.

He tried to focus on breathing slowly and calming down as he made his way to the bus stop where they'd agreed to meet. If he was just a guy with no secrets, then obviously this outing wouldn't be a big deal at all. But he was actively trying to hide his identity, so everything he said would have to be carefully chosen and analyzed beforehand.

Okay, so part of him—a quiet voice deep down inside—kept asking what the big deal would be if Emma did find out. Really, what was she going to do with the information? Hold a press conference? Write a tell-all book? Laugh at him? Pity him?

Yeah, you nailed it at the end there.... It was the pity he was trying to avoid, and the inevitable questions that would follow. For example, she might ask why he ran away from his life like a big baby when things got tough. Or she might say, "Why don't you just recapture your old life and stop feeling sorry for yourself?" Oh, and of course there was the biggest question of all—"Two years away from professional sports is a lifetime. Could you pitch again even if you wanted to?"

Did he want to answer any of those questions? No. And not only did he not want to answer them, he didn't even want to *think* about them. And the fewer people he had pressuring him, the better. He already was hearing about it from his family; he didn't need Emma questioning him, too.

So he needed to protect his secret. How should he go about doing that? What was the best way to approach the situation? He had been thinking about his options almost nonstop since he had left Emma after their talk at the café. He figured he had a handful of choices.

One was to stick with being vague. Not really answer any questions about himself. Work to continuously shift the conversation back to her and her life. Act perplexed if she came out and asked him why he was being evasive. However, this wasn't a truly effective approach. It was just too hard. Eventually she'd either get annoyed and leave or she'd get scared, thinking his secret had something to do with him being a criminal or a serial killer or whatever. He knew Emma was engaged and could never really be a permanent part of his life anyway, but he didn't want her to leave their brief time together thinking he was some kind of crime lord. Basically, he didn't want her to hate him or be afraid of him. So being vague and mysterious was out.

The second choice would be to straight-out lie to her. He could concoct some sort of cover story and fake identity. Give enough details so that she wouldn't be suspicious or afraid, but not so many that she'd be able to fact-check the story. It would have to be something she wouldn't be able to disprove in ten minutes on Google. Like maybe tell her he was in the Witness Protection Program. That was a vaguely reasonable story, right? It had a mysterious air of credibility to it, plus she couldn't really ask any further questions or expect him to say more. Zach liked this idea to an extent. It'd be easy and would explain almost everything, like why he couldn't give his real name or why he was alone and removed from his old life. Actually it was kind of perfect...except for one tiny problem....

He didn't want to lie to her.

That almost didn't even make any sense. Why should he care about what he told a woman with whom he'd only had two conversations? A woman who was happily engaged to another man? Seriously, what would be the harm in telling her a little white lie? It wouldn't hurt her, and it would protect him. All good, right?

No.... Because he knew he couldn't do it. Yes, it had only been two conversations. And yes, Emma could never be in his life long term even if she *wasn't* engaged. Zach had no future and nothing to offer Emma, so there was no scenario where their friendship would ever last longer than whatever time she planned to stay in Ireland. Her stay was inevitably going to come to an end, and when she got back on a plane and headed home, their story would be over.

But even given all of that, and as irrational as it sounded, Emma was still somehow important to him. Whatever small amount of time she let him share this summer would, he instinctively knew, become cherished memories in the aftermath. He just knew it. So, in the end, it would kill him to lie to her.

Yep, building up a fake cover story was also out.

All that really was left, then, was to be as honest as he could. Just tell her straight out that he did have a secret that he wasn't comfortable sharing with her. Let her know that it wasn't anything criminal or something she should fear. Just a tiny secret. He could tell her he enjoyed spending time with her and simply ask her to respect his privacy if they were going to continue to be friends. That would work, right? No lies. No elaborate cover stories with tiny details he'd have to manage to avoid carefully as he tromped his way through a conversational minefield.

As he approached the bus stop, he saw Emma waiting for him. She was scanning the sidewalk, looking at the faces of the people hurrying by. As he watched her, he caught the moment her eyes landed on him, and the recognition flashing its way across her face.

Zach's breath caught as he saw a smile radiate from her face. He could tell she was every bit as happy to see him as he was to see her. She looked stunning today, in a sexy pair of cut-off jeans with her long hair casually pulled back in a high ponytail. *I will be in so much trouble if I'm not careful*, he thought as he continued toward her, feeling slightly dreamy and hypnotized. Her sunny disposition had the power of a tractor beam.

A wave of relief sloshed through him as he closed the distance between them and returned her smile. At least he had a plan for how he was going to get through this day with this gorgeous creature.

Chapter 7

"HEY, Z," she said finally. It was either that or just stand there beaming at each other like dopes for the rest of the day. He looked as goofy-happy to see her as she felt seeing him.

"Hey Em. You look beautiful today," he said before a tiny flicker of regret stole its way across his face.

Was he really feeling as guilty for pursuing this friendship as she was? she wondered. But why should he be guilty? He wasn't the one who was engaged here. *Or who knows, maybe he is....* Maybe he was even married. He could be married to five different women, for all she knew. She had to keep reminding herself that she knew almost nothing about this man.

But despite all the facts—or, if she was being precise, then despite the *lack* of facts—she couldn't escape one big truth: the mere act of spotting him in the crowd had made her unaccountably happy. And she didn't want to deny herself that little slice of happiness. She was going to enjoy this day and let the guilt and worry take turns battering her later.

"I'm so happy to see you," she said, actively trying to ignore her warring emotions now.

"Me too," Z said. "I've really been looking forward to today. But, well, there's something I want to tell you first."

Emma spotted the little green bus making its way

to their stop. "Hold that thought. Let's get on first."

"Right."

Once they were aboard, they made their way to the back while most of the other tourists climbed the stairs to reach the top deck. Emma took a seat by a window and watched as Z folded himself awkwardly into his own, his tall frame comically at odds with the small space around him.

"You are totally squished there," she said.

"I'm used to it. I'm too tall for pretty much everything," he said, looking hilariously uncomfortable.

All the movement caused her to glance down at his left hand. He was holding something. *A ball*, she realized. "What were you going to tell me?" she asked, looking to his face now.

"I...um, yeah. I just wanted to acknowledge what you probably already know, I guess. You're right that I do have a secret and a reason for not wanting to give you my real name," he said, a pained look on his face.

"Oh, yes. Actually, I deduced you're keeping a lot from me," she told him, uncertain how to handle this suddenly heavy conversational turn. She decided on an impulse to just put all her cards on the table and be upfront about her concerns. "Honestly, Z, it made me wonder if I should go to the park with you today. I don't know anything about you at all, except that you appear to be in hiding. Are you in danger? Am I in danger by being with you?"

"No, no, there's no danger. I'd never...." Z stopped to take a deep breath. "I'd never do anything to harm you, Em. I'm not in danger, and I'm not dangerous. I'm not wanted for any crimes or anything like that."

"Oh. Good," Emma said. "I'm not going to lie: It crossed my mind that maybe you were some kind of axe murderer."

"Yeah, I figured you'd think that if I continued to be mysterious with you." Zach exhaled with a look of frustration. "I didn't know how to handle this. I've been hiding from my past for two years now. And you are the very first person I've come across in all that time who I had even the smallest urge to tell. But...I just can't. I can't."

"It's okay, Z. I won't push you," Emma said, giving him a reassuring smile.

"Thank you, Em. I appreciate that."

"Can you tell me whether you're married?" she asked before giving herself a mental kick. Why should it matter? She was the one who was spoken for...and yet she couldn't deny she was happy when he met her question with a shake of the head.

"No. No wife. No kids. No fiancée," he said.

Silence fell over them as Emma tore her gaze away. He seemed so sad and alone, she thought, like he was pained by whatever his secret was. She glanced at his hand again as an awkward silence surrounded them. The object he was holding was a stress ball, she decided, and she watched him roll it around in his fingers. But the funny thing was that he wasn't squeezing it. Wasn't that what you were supposed to do with a stress ball?

She kept watching. No, he definitely wasn't squeezing it. Instead, he seemed to be repeating some sort of little nervous ritual with it. Everything this man did or said was a riddle she wanted to solve, she realized, down to his mindless fidgeting. He carefully lined his fingers on the ball and then rolled it around in his palm again. Each time it was the same—he'd roll the ball, set his fingers up on it in what seemed to be some sort of deliberate pattern, hold it that way a moment, then roll the ball again. Most surprising was the fact that it looked like something she *knew*. Something familiar. *Why...?*

She was fascinated. Everything about Z was such a puzzle. And now he'd confirmed what she suspected—there *was* a mystery here to be solved. But he was telling her he didn't want her to try to figure it out, so she really should drop it. Well, she certainly wouldn't hire a private investigator, if that's what he was afraid of. But she'd be lying if she didn't admit she was beyond intrigued. She absolutely couldn't help wanting to figure him out.

"Tell me something about yourself that you *can*," she said. "I want to get to know you better, or at least as much as I can. Despite all your secrets, I can't help but like you, Z. I'd like for us to be friends if possible."

"If you don't mind that there are things I just can't tell you, then okay," Z replied, "I absolutely would love for us to know each other better."

"Right now we're essentially strangers," Emma reminded him. "So let's break the ice in a big way. Tell me something you've never told anyone. Not about your big secret of course. But just something no one else knows."

"Well, you don't make things easy, do you?" Z said with a laugh.

Emma smiled. Had she ever heard him laugh before? She didn't think so. Whatever his secret was, it seemed to be holding him back from simple human responses like joy and laughter. She wanted to hear it again. She wanted him to be happy and carefree, not burdened by whatever was haunting him.

"It doesn't have to be anything big," she said.

"Okay, well, I think I have one. But it might sound a little whiny."

"Oh, just tell me. If you can't whine to someone you met a couple days ago, then who can you whine to?" She nudged him with her elbow. "Spill it."

"Well, here it goes—I've sort of always had...certain things...come easy to me," he said haltingly. "People, they...cleared certain pathways for me my whole life. And now, looking back, I can see that maybe it would have been better if everything hadn't been so easy. If I'd had to struggle more."

"Wow, I totally know what you mean," she said.

"Really?"

"No, not at all. You were just talking like a fortune cookie there. I literally have no idea what you just said," Emma told him, laughing now.

Z gave her a crooked smile. "You're teasing me," he said.

"Yeah, I am. Seriously, though, I do think I know what you were saying, *kind of*. But since you can't fill in the blanks for me, well...."

Z looked genuinely remorseful. "I'm sorry."

"It's okay," she said, wanting nothing more in that moment than to comfort him. She reached over to put her hand on his leg before really thinking about what she was doing. Z glanced down at the hand and then back up to meet her gaze again. She couldn't tell what he was thinking, so she awkwardly pulled her hand back. She had merely wanted to comfort him, but the sizzle of electricity between them at her innocuous touch had knocked her back into reality. It just wasn't a good idea to go around putting her hand on other men, even if she didn't mean it as a come-on.

"It's our stop," Z said, breaking yet another

awkward silence between them. Then, to her utter shock, he stood up and offered *his* hand. "Let's go, Em," he told her.

She reached out slowly, very slowly, until their fingers met. She tried to stifle her gasp as he gently closed his big hand around hers and she let him tug her up. She unfolded herself from the seat until they were standing face-to-face, a raw tension crackling around them. Then, wordlessly, Z broke their gaze and turned to make his way off the bus, still holding her hand in his own.

She followed him off the bus in a dreamy trance, speechless from the emotions that were spinning around her. Her touch to his leg had been the spark that had sent her senses into overdrive. Z seemed to be feeling it too as they stood at the bus stop, staring at each other.

Jim, Jim, Jim, Jim.... Her conscience was doing its best to break her out of the reverie, but she continued to stare into Z's face. His blue eyes were her only reality in that moment.

"Jim," she finally managed to blurt out.

"What?" Z asked.

"Jim…is…my fiancé," she spluttered.

"Right," Z said, dropping her hand awkwardly and taking a step back. Then he ran his fingers through his hair in what appeared to be considerable frustration. Emma was filled with regret over the loss of contact as she took a step back, too. She noticed he was still fidgeting with the stress ball in the other hand. *Spin the ball…pose the fingers…hold it…spin again....*

One of them needed to say something.

"So I guess it's only fair that I tell you something I've never told anyone else, since you told me yours," she finally said.

"Yeah, okay, but let's keep moving," Z requested.

"Of course."

They turned and headed toward a pedestrian walkway brimming with couples, families with young children, joggers, and so on.

"Looks like we weren't the only ones who thought today would be a good one for a stroll in the park," Emma commented.

"Nice try diverting the conversation," Z said, smiling at her sideways. "Remember, it's your turn to tell me something you've never told anyone else."

"Right. Well, mine might sound whiny too, so brace yourself."

"Bring it on."

"Okay, you asked for it. Well, I sort of have this reputation as a major planner. No, not just that I like to make plans, but that I live my life by them. Like they're a checklist, you know what I mean? Like I'd never do anything spontaneous, anything that wasn't a part of the plan. Tracy even accused me of getting engaged to Jim because it fit in with my master checklist. She said something like, 'You got your degree, check. So you had to find a husband, check.' You know what I mean?"

"Yeah, I get what you're saying. But is it not true?" Z asked.

"No. That's the thing that no one understands, not even my family, and honestly it drives me crazy. But it's become such a thing, that if I protest they just tease me about it."

"You're sure they're wrong? If every single person you know thinks the same thing, maybe there's something to it."

"I know it seems that way, but no, I honestly think people just sort of enjoy the joke. So it takes on something more than it is, and it becomes everyone's easy shorthand for knowing you. Like if you once said you sort of like turtles, and before you know it every single person you know is giving you turtle figurines, turtle pendants, turtle Pez dispensers. You end up stuck in this whole turtle thing, but mostly because people like having a shorthand for knowing you. They don't *actually* know anything, but hey, you're the turtle lady," Emma looked directly at Z. "I officially just talked myself into a box. I don't even know what I'm saying right now. Lists, blah blah, Pez dispensers, blah blah, turtles, blah blah."

"Oh stop it. Tell me what the *truth* is," he said.

"The truth is that I enjoy the practice of planning in and of itself. I like scheming up an itinerary almost as much as I like taking the actual trip. I like planning the route more than the journey. I like coming up with various options and then seeing how they might work out. But I can be totally spontaneous, too. Just look at this vacation. The opportunity came up and I jumped at it without any hesitation. The 'I live my life by a playbook' thinking would have told me to stay home and hunt for a full-time job and pay off student loans, not incur *more* debt. But I wanted an adventure, so here I am. Yes, I like to make plans. But sometimes life throws you a curveball, and you just have to go with it. Know what I mean?"

She looked up at Z, and she was startled to see all the color had drained from his face. In fact, he looked like he was going to pass out.

"Z? Oh my gosh! Are you okay? Are you feeling sick?"

"I...no...." he stammered. "It's just…nothing. It's nothing."

"Are you sure? Wait, was it something I said? I've been yapping about myself for five solid minutes. I'm sorry." She pointed toward one of the park benches. "Here, let's go sit down."

"Nothing's wrong, Em. Seriously, relax. And it was nothing you said," Z replied, then followed her to the bench and sat down despite his protests.

"I'm pretty sure you got upset about something just now," Emma told him. "Z, does it have anything to do with your secret?"

"Emma, seriously. Nothing's wrong," he assured her, his left hand still moving around the stress ball. "Here, let's change topics to something lighthearted. Tell me one completely goofy thing about yourself."

"Goofy?" Emma asked, full of exaggerated indignation. "I am completely offended that you would even suggest there's anything goofy about me in the first place."

"Oh come on," Z persisted. "Everyone does. So spill it."

Emma exhaled, thinking what she could share with him in this subject area. But she also continued watching him work with the ball. Her mind was still trying to figure out what was familiar about the way he was doing it. And now there was an extra layer to the mystery—something she'd done or said had just upset him.

"Okay, well, here's something," she said finally. "I am completely, one-hundred percent addicted to sports talk radio. I listen to it constantly." She was about to deliver another smile along with this confession when she realized he looked pale again. *It was something I just said,* she thought. *I'm sure of it now.*

"You're a huge sports fan?" Z asked.

"No, that's the goofy thing," she said. She was getting close to a nerve here, she decided, and she wanted to see how it played out. "I don't watch games. Well, I do go to Red Sox games at Fenway sometimes. I wasn't lying when I said I'm a fan. But other than that, no, I'm not really all that into sports."

"But you listen to sports talk radio?"

"Yes, when I can," Emma said, realizing this topic was making him more and more uncomfortable. "Ask me anything. I can tell you about how the Knicks really need a point guard. I can discuss, at length, the salary cap situation for any of the NFL teams. Ask me which baseball clubs need to start manufacturing runs and stop relying on the long ball, despite what the sabermetrics say."

Z was laughing now. "Incredible, but you really don't watch many games?"

"Nope, I just listen to people talk about them," she replied. "Which makes me certifiable. You asked for goofy, and I delivered big. I totally realize how weird that is."

Z shook his head in disbelief. "Yes, you are a complete nut, Emma Crawford."

"Now tell me your goofy thing," she said. "It's only fair after I revealed what a psycho I am."

"Okay, um...I guess my goofiest thing is that I never stop moving. I was that weird hyper kid in school who never settled down."

"I have no trouble believing that. I noticed you're fidgeting with a stress ball."

"Yeah, exactly. I can't keep still. I'm constantly juggling this thing around in my hand, or tapping my fingers to a beat, or jiggling my knee. It drives everyone around me insane. There, I've called attention to it. You won't be able to not notice it now, and it will start to slowly make you lose your grip on your sanity." Z stood up. "You're welcome, by the way."

"Oh my gosh, the calories you must burn!" Emma said, laughing as she stood up, too.

"Well, I do channel some of that energy into workouts. That's like my one big expense and luxury here besides the apartment. I joined a fancy gym. I wanted stay in game shape." Z turned to her quickly. "Oh, uh, that's just a saying. I...wanted to talk in sports lingo for you. You know, speak your language?"

"Yes, game shape. That *is* my language! I know exactly what you're saying now."

They were both still smiling, yet Emma could tell he was feeling uncomfortable again. She decided not to analyze all the evidence while she was here at the park with him. *But I'll snap those pieces together when I get back to the apartment,* she thought.

Z's mystery, she firmly believed, was about to be solved.

Chapter 8

HE WAS TERRIBLE at keeping secrets. Seriously, how had he managed to keep his identity private for this long? A toddler would have been able to pick up the clues he had dropped so far today, and Emma certainly was no idiot. He had been as transparent as glass during every conversation they'd had. Short of handing Emma his contract from the Yankees and asking her to proofread it, he had done absolutely everything he could to give his secret away today. It was almost like he *wanted* her to know. But that was ridiculous, right? Of course he didn't want her to know.

And yet...he'd handed her clue after clue. First, he almost passed out when she said the word *curveball*. Honestly! One word from her, and he had panicked so hard that she freaked out. And that panic had been set off by what was otherwise the most innocent conversation ever. She had been talking about herself, just chatting. Obviously she wasn't trying to get a reaction out of him. But he'd sure given her one. And then when she told him she listened to a ton of sports radio? Yeah, that had driven him to a near heart attack. He'd wanted to disappear on the spot. Just vaporize.

But again, she had been chatting about herself. No big deal. Clearly, if she was going to recognize him based on her knowledge of the sports world, she would have done so already. But then how *could* she? She didn't really watch the games or the highlights or the interviews. She listened to radio chatter. How could she possibly recognize him from the radio? They didn't talk about him anymore. Hadn't for years.

Okay, so the Red Sox and the Yankees were legendary sports rivals who played each other about a million times every season. If she went to Red Sox games, chances were pretty good that she'd seen the Yankees play a time or two. But a starting pitcher only works every fourth or fifth game. And even if she'd caught as many Sox–Yanks games as she possibly could, chances were good that she'd never actually seen him pitch.

In the end, it didn't matter anyway. She hadn't put the clues together. She would have told him if she'd figured it out, right? He had asked her not to dig into his past, and she'd accepted his wishes at face value. It was fine. There was no problem...and yet, despite knowing she really wasn't onto him, he'd persisted in overreacting to the point that just about anyone could have figured it out by now. So he needed to get it together. *Fast.*

I certainly didn't miss my calling as an international spy, he thought bitterly. He'd fold like a cheap tent in under thirty seconds of even the lightest interrogation. He could just hear the questioning now—"We think you're the spy known as Captain Obvious and we—" *Yeah, okay, you got me.*

But stressing over his secret hadn't been the only problem up to this point, he thought as he glanced at Emma from the corner of his eye. They were on the bus headed back to their apartments now. He was glad this outing was almost over. Being near her but unable to touch her was agony. There was no escaping that truth—he was beyond attracted to her. If it wasn't for her fiancé, he would have been unable to control himself. So, in truth, the existence of her fiancé was actually a good thing, he realized. Knowing she had Jim in her life helped keep him on course. The mountains of problems that were piled all throughout his life wouldn't be easy to get past. He'd never have anything to offer her. To offer *anyone*.

The attraction was really strong though. So strong that it made him stupid. It made him forget the countless reasons why he needed to guard his privacy. So the whole thing with the fiancé...yeah, good old Jim was the splash of cold water he needed to keep his head straight.

"Tell me about Jim," he said impulsively. Yes, this was good. Get her talking about him. Remind her of how committed she is to this guy. *And remind myself why she could never be mine.*

Emma looked startled, like he'd yanked her out of a daydream.

"What? Oh, Jim? Yeah, okay. Well, he's a great guy. He's working on getting his PhD. His focus is American literature of the 20th Century."

"Huh. Fascinating."

"Really?"

"No, not at all," Zach said with an awkward laugh. "That's definitely not my field."

"It's not mine, either," Emma replied. "My thing is early education, although I guess I already told you that. What's yours? Is that something you can tell me?"

"Well, actually, I never went to college," Zach admitted, already wondering once again if he was saying too much.

"Oh, okay. Did you learn a trade?"

"You could say that, I guess," Zach said, then realized it was time to change the subject again. "So why didn't Jim come with you this summer?"

"He's teaching a freshman-level class this summer. Plus, I don't think he'd ever do anything this spontaneous or frivolous. He's also a hardcore planner, probably even more so than me. The one who never deviates from his life goals. But, like I said, everyone thinks I'm the one who's like that." Emma shrugged.

"So what do you two do for fun, then? Collect turtles?"

Emma laughed and nudged him with her elbow. "No! You're going to make me sorry I made the turtle analogy, aren't you?"

"No, not at all. I thought it was cute," Zach said, then immediately regretted it. He was supposed to be getting her to talk about her fiancé, not giving her a list of the ways he found her adorable. *I really am pathetic.*

"Wait, isn't this our stop?" she asked abruptly.

"Oh, yeah. Okay, let's go."

Zach stood up and let her walk in front of him, silently thanking the bus driver for the excellent timing. He needed to end this now, for both of their sakes. No, he didn't want to. Not at all. He knew he'd miss her. That much was obvious to him now, although how was it even possible? How had she become so important to him so fast? She'd come hurtling out of nowhere, smashing her way into his tidy little world like an asteroid crashing to Earth. And yet it couldn't lead to anything but pain. If the thought of cutting her out of his life hurt this much now, how much worse would it be if he kept seeing her all summer? If he let her get closer to him? If he actually let himself fall for her? He felt like someone was squeezing his chest in an icy fist as he climbed off the bus and onto the sidewalk to face her again.

"I had such a great time today," Emma started. "Talking to you is so easy. I just…I really can be myself with you. I feel like you understand me without my saying anything. Which, of course, doesn't explain why I then proceeded to chat your ear off."

"No…no, you didn't talk too much," Zach said. "Not at all. I liked talking to you. I…I feel like I can be myself with you, too." He wasn't sure how he was going to tell her he didn't think they could be friends anymore.

"Oh good!" she went on. "I know it's hard for you, since you're always censoring what you can and can't tell me."

"Yeah, listen, about that. It *is* hard. Too hard. I just…." He trailed off as he tried to sort out his thoughts. He didn't want to do this. That's what was making it so difficult. But he had to. Being with her was like being injected with truth serum. She made him say too much, think too much. And want too much.

"What, Z? What is it?" she asked, looking concerned now.

"This is too…I'm sorry, I just can't do it. I don't think we should see each other anymore. I don't even think we can be friends." The words almost choked him on their way out, but at least he'd said them. It was over. He'd just walk away now and never look back.

"Oh come on, lighten up, Z!" Emma replied. "You told me your secret wasn't anything dangerous or criminal. So what's the big deal? I think you've been alone too long, you dope. You've forgotten how to interact with people. Come on, why don't you come over for dinner sometime this week? You could meet

Tracy. We could talk about completely safe subjects, I promise. No questions about your past. I'll let Tracy know where your boundaries are, okay?"

Her beautiful brown eyes were just about pleading with him, making him silently recite the list of reasons why he should tell her no. He had to protect the safe world he'd made for himself here. He couldn't let her in. Being with her was too painful. She could never be his. Their friendship could lead to nothing but misery. So he had to say no. He *had* to say no. He had to say....

"Okay, sure," he heard himself tell her. "I'll come over for dinner." *Oh, for God's sake, this woman is my kryptonite.*

"Great! What's your work schedule? When are you free?"

"Uh, I could do tomorrow, I guess," he said.

"Perfect! I'll text you the address. What's your cell number?" She started digging in her bag for her phone.

At that moment he realized he couldn't give her the number. It was from *New York*. He'd be giving her yet another clue.

And yet, in the end, he said it anyway, watching as she plugged it into her phone and then save the contact as "Z."

"Great, thanks. Here, I'll call you so you have my number too," she said cheerfully.

Well, that's just terrific, he thought. Now they had each other's contact information. His firm resolve was approximately as strong and impenetrable as a sandcastle.

"Okay, then. Thanks Z. I'll see you tomorrow at 7?"

"I'll be there," he said, offering her a little smile as she turned to walk away. He gave himself a mental smack as he watched her go. He was in some major trouble here.

When it came to Emma, he didn't seem to have a chance.

Chapter 9

SHE WAS SO CLOSE to figuring it out. It was right there, tucked in the shadowy corners of her mind. She knew it was. She just had to put all the clues together, and then she'd finally be able to solve the riddle, Emma thought as she walked home from the bus stop.

She felt guilty about trying to solve Z's secret, but it was seriously driving her crazy. And maybe she was wrong to do so, but she had this strange feeling it would *help* Z in some way. He couldn't bring himself to be the one to tell her, but what if she just suddenly knew? Maybe it would help him work his way out of his lonely, sad existence. And watching his suffering was breaking her heart. She just couldn't let it go.

If she could help him, then who knows? Maybe it would help her be able to leave him here at the end of the summer. It might be a way to find peace and closure to this little problem. Because the truth of the matter was that she was attracted to Z. Wildly, crazily attracted to him. And the thought of leaving him behind when her time in Ireland came to a close was painful to even consider. It was irrational to feel this way after knowing him for such a short time. And yet she was.

Yet there were a million reasons why she could never act on those feelings. Starting with the fact that she didn't even know his name, and ending with the fact that a little more than a week ago she'd accepted Jim's ring and promised to spend her life with him. How could she possibly have changed her mind so quickly? No...that made no sense. No one was that fickle and flighty.

So she'd just focus on helping Z. Being his friend. Supporting him as he worked through whatever it was that was keeping him hidden away from his family and friends and his former life. Then he could move on. And she could move on, too.

Okay, so solving this puzzle was something she absolutely had to do. And she was doing it to help him, not to hurt him. Right? So she shouldn't feel guilty, not at all. Not one bit.

But...she totally did. Super, super guilty. He had specifically told her not to stick her nose in the middle of his secret. And yet she couldn't help herself. She *had* to know. And she knew she was close to figuring it out, too.

All right. So she was doing this. She just needed to catalogue all the evidence and the answer would present itself. What were the basic facts of what she knew? Well, whatever happened had occurred about two years ago. So she had a timeframe. That part was easy.

He was from Texas, but she didn't think he'd given her a Texas number. She pulled her phone out and looked at the number again. That area code was familiar. She stopped on the sidewalk to type it into Google along with the words *area code*. Bingo—*New York*. So whatever had happened had likely occurred in New York. Around two years ago. Okay, she was getting somewhere now. She started walking again.

As she walked into the dark apartment, she called out, "Trace? Are you home?" Nope, didn't look like she was. Emma locked the door behind her, dropped her purse, and flipped on a few lights. Picking up her laptop, she flopped down on the couch. *All right, time to get busy.* What else did she know...? He was a bartender now, but she got the feeling that's not what he'd been doing back home.

What could his secret possibly be? She rolled the millions of options around in her mind.

A disagreement? A family feud? A fight? A broken heart? Could this have something to do with a woman? He'd told her he wasn't married or engaged. But that didn't mean some woman hadn't been involved. *But so what? People break up all the time.* If every person who suffered a bad breakup ran to Dublin, the entire island would tip on end and slide right into the ocean.

Okay, speculating wasn't getting her anywhere. She needed to get back to the facts as she knew them.

He didn't go to college. So what had he been doing? He said himself he was full of energy. He must've been doing something productive. He'd even agreed that he'd had a trade of some sort. Z wasn't the type who would have been mooching off other people or playing video games in his mom's basement.

The stress ball....

Her mind kept going back to it. Somehow it was a clue, she knew it. She'd watched him play with that thing all day long. It was driving her crazy because she knew it meant something. He'd spin it. Place his fingers. Hold the pose. Spin the ball again. But he wasn't placing his fingers in the same pose each time. Sometimes his fingers were lined up on the top, and sometimes he'd split them down the sides.

Split fingers.

Split finger...fastball.

That was it! Those were *pitches* he was setting up!

She pulled up the search engine screen and typed *pitching finger positions.*

The first link was a guide to pitch grips. She clicked on it. That brought up an index page with a list of the various pitches. How to grip a two-seam fastball. How to grip a knuckleball. How to grip a curveball.

Curveball.... The word flashed through her memory like a bolt of lightning. Hadn't she said something about a curveball today? She'd said life sometimes throws you a curveball, and that was right before all the color had drained out of Z's face.

She clicked on the link for curveball. It showed a picture of a hand gripping a baseball. Yes, that looked like one of the finger positions Z had made today. She went back to the index and clicked on the fastball. Bingo. Yes, Z hadn't been just messing around with a stress ball or just fidgeting in general. He'd been setting up pitches all day long. She was absolutely sure of it.

Excited now, she went back to the search engine home page and typed $Z + $ *pitcher.*

The first hit was for a water-filtration system. She laughed out loud. There was actually something called the Z Pitcher. But below that was an article about Zack Greinke. Wasn't he a pitcher for the Dodgers? No, wait, the Astros? She clicked on the link. Could Z be Zack Greinke?

No, the picture was definitely not of Z. Besides, she was pretty sure she'd heard about Zack Greinke playing in the last two years. He was still in the Major Leagues. She was almost positive of it.

She needed to stop and put this together correctly. A pitcher. Who was no longer pitching. From New York.

She knew. Right in that moment she knew exactly who Z was.

Her hands were trembling now as she went back to the search engine and typed *Zach Hiller, New York Yankees*.

And there he was. She saw the picture come up before she even had a chance to read the headlines. It was most definitely him. *I'd know those blue eyes anywhere.*

Emma stared at his picture, surprised at the realization that tears were pooling in her eyes. What was she crying about? She should be ecstatic. She had just solved the mystery!

She wiped the tears away as she clicked on the first link—

Hiller Breaks Contract, Leaves Yankees Stranded Without Pitching Ace

What had happened? She remembered hearing all about the broken contract and the speculation about why he'd done it. But what led up to it? That part wasn't coming back to her. She clicked on some more links.

Layton Loses Rookie Year to Head Injury.

Hiller Throws Killer Curveball, Strikes Layton.

Hiller Unable to Finish Pitching Start After Layton Goes Down.

Emma stopped at the last headline and read the article—

Orioles' rookie phenom Tommy Layton was hit in the head by a pitch from Yankees starting pitcher Zach Hiller in

Wednesday's 2-1 Orioles win.

With a 3-2 count, Hiller fired the lethal pitch, a curveball gone wild, which turned sharply toward the inside corner of the plate, catching Layton on the temple. The game was delayed for 12 minutes as the training staff worked unsuccessfully on Layton, who never regained consciousness on the field.

Hiller was visibly shaken, and could be seen saying, "I didn't mean to hit him" to his manager, Hank Wilson, and his catcher, Jose Diaz. Wilson gave Hiller the ball back, but he walked off the mound and into the dugout, refusing to take the next batter, outfielder Manny Cortez, despite the boos of the hometown crowd.

"Oh Z," Emma said, tears falling down her face. She remembered now. Yes, Tommy Layton had gotten a nasty head injury, and Zach Hiller, who had been a major pitching superstar, had broken his contract and walked away from the game. Zach Hiller, major pitching superstar for the New York Yankees, was Z. *Her* Z. Her sexy bartender.

She shut the laptop and went to find a tissue, then slumped back down on the couch, leaning her head back and closing her eyes. It fit, all of it. His weird reaction when she said she listened to sports radio. His panic about the word *curveball*. The stress ball.

Tommy Layton had been hurt pretty badly. He'd missed the rest of his rookie year, if she remembered right. He'd suffered from a terrible concussion and ongoing headaches. Z obviously blamed himself. Had he actually tried to hit Layton? Was he feeling guilty because he'd literally gone head-hunting with that pitch? Was there something to really blame him for here?

No, the article had specifically pointed out that spectators could tell Z was saying he didn't mean to hit him.

Besides that, she may not have known Z for very long, but she'd stake her life on the fact that he'd never hurt anyone on purpose. It had just been an accident. Accidents happen. Athletes get hurt all the time. Every single day this or that team was forced to put players on the injured list, and that was true across all sports.

So why couldn't he get past it? What was he doing two years later, serving beer in Dublin and still hiding from the world?

She shook her head in frustration. This just didn't make sense.

Opening her eyes now, she reached for the laptop and opened it again. She wanted to know everything she could about Zach Hiller.

She read article after article about him. He'd been a star athlete in high school. He was heavily scouted and recruited, and he was drafted and signed by the Yankees straight out of high school. That explained why he didn't go to college. And why he'd sort of agreed when she'd asked if he had a trade.

He'd spent a few years in the minor leagues, then he'd been called up to the Majors. He won the Cy Young Award four years ago. He had clearly been a major pitching star. There were even some gossip-mag types of articles linking him romantically to various models and actresses. He'd been a total player in *that* way as well, if those stories could be believed.

She thought about their day together. She'd been yapping the ear off a famous athlete, and she hadn't even known it. He must have died when she was going on and on about the sports talk radio she loved. She laughed at this, then the more she thought about his pale-faced reaction, the harder she laughed. *Poor Z.* She must have given him a heart attack.

"What's so funny?" Tracy asked, walking through the front door and dropping her messenger bag and keys by the closet.

"I did it Trace," Emma said. "I figured it out."

"Get out! You know who Z is?" Tracy kicked off her shoes and flopped down on the couch next to her. "Can you tell me? Did he go on a crime spree? Did he steal millions of dollars? Is he in the Witness Protection Program?"

"Wrong, wrong, wrong," Emma said. "I don't know. I probably shouldn't tell you, but then I probably shouldn't have worked so hard to figure it out. So...if I tell you, can we just keep it between the two of us?"

"Sure, Em. If you want me to keep quiet, then I will. I'm busy doing research all summer anyway, so seriously, who would I tell?"

"Um...librarians?" Emma asked.

"Okay, I swear I won't tell the librarians. So spill it."

"He was a pitcher for the Yankees," Emma said.

"What? Get out! So you know that as a Red Sox fan, that means you have to hate him, right? He's from the evil empire."

"I could seriously never hate him, Yankee or not," Emma said. "That's part of my problem. I like him too much. It's not good."

"Nope, it's not good. Not good at all. It's *great*. So great, Em. I think you should explore your feelings for him while you can." Tracy put her hand up when Emma started to protest. "All right, all right. I know. I'll shut up about it. So what's his name?"

"Zach Hiller."

"Wait, I know that name."

"Yeah, you probably do. He hit another player in the head during a game. I guess it upset him so badly that he walked away for good."

"Holy crap, I think I remember that. It was all over the news in Boston, since it was such a huge blow to the enemy team."

"Yeah, me too. I think I remember all the coverage too." Emma could feel tears threatening to start forming again.

"Hey, Em, are you about to cry?"

"No. Yeah. I don't know, Tracy. I'm just so sad for him. He's clearly still so upset about whatever happened. Whatever emotions he was feeling were bad enough to make him walk away from a fortune. He literally broke a contract that would have paid out like $25 million dollars a year or something. That's crazy. I can't even imagine that kind of money. But he did it. He just…left. And I don't know the rest of the story, and I can't ask him about it because I'm not supposed to know. He's so alone and he's so sad, and I just…I want to help him." Emma started sniffling into the tissue she'd grabbed earlier. "Finding out his secret is…I don't know. It's really devastating. My heart is breaking for him."

"Maybe it's not as sad as all of that, though," Tracy said. "Maybe it's something else. Like maybe he was a big spoiled-brat athlete who just took an easy out or something. You still don't know the whole story."

"No, you're right, I don't. And now I have to be the one keeping a secret and trying to pretend I don't know anything. Oh, and so do you actually," Emma reminded her.

"Why would I have to keep it? Am I ever even going to meet him?" Tracy asked, getting up now and heading to the kitchen.

"I sort of invited him over for dinner tomorrow night," Emma replied, looking sheepish. "I hope you don't mind."

"No, I'd like to meet him. But that's going to be really awkward, given what we know."

"Yeah, well, I invited him before I figured this out. He was trying to push me away. He was giving me some line about how we shouldn't be friends and how it was too hard for him to keep his secret from me. I just couldn't even hear the words. I didn't want to say goodbye to him yet. So I just bulldozed right over his protests and invited him to dinner."

Tracy was laughing now.

"What?" Emma asked.

"That poor guy doesn't stand a chance with you," she said, ducking down to examine the contents of the refrigerator.

"Nope, he doesn't," Emma agreed. "I know he wants nothing more than to push me away so he can stay wrapped up in his lonely little cocoon. But too bad, because I can't leave until I know I've done everything in my power to help him."

"Like I said," Tracy repeated. "He doesn't stand a chance. Not when you've made up your mind about something."

Oh I've definitely made up my mind, Emma thought, comforted for the first time since she'd solved Z's mystery. She was going to help him or die trying.

Chapter 10

WAS THAT THE PHONE RINGING? Zach wondered as he stepped out of the shower.

Maybe it was Emma. He grabbed his towel and hurried down the hall to the living room where he could hear the phone more clearly. *But where is it?*

"Dammit," he grumbled, digging through the junk on his coffee table before finally locating it.

No, it wasn't Emma. He tried not to think about how disappointed he was that his brother was calling. It was perfectly normal to be completely devastated that it wasn't Emma, right? That was a typical "we're just friends" reaction, right?

"Hey, Zeke," he said, wrapping his towel around his waist and trying to hold the phone with his shoulder. Very awkward.

"Hey, Zach. How're you doing?"

"Good. The same, I guess. How are Mom and Dad?" Zach asked, sitting on the couch once he got the towel secured. He set his feet on the coffee table, right on top of the mess. *Man, I need to stop ignoring the mail*, he thought distantly.

"Miserable. So, you know, the same. When are you going to quit torturing them and get your ass back here?" Zeke snapped, his frustration coming through loud and clear. "I'm sick of watching the toll it's taking on them."

"I know, Zeke," Zach said with a sigh. "I know.

I'm trying, I really am. But...I don't know. I just can't seem to work myself around to it. You know I'm not doing this on purpose to hurt them." He leaned his head back on the couch and shut his eyes. As much as he loved his family, he absolutely hated hearing from them. It was always the same questions—*When are you coming home? Why are you doing this to us? What is your problem?* If he knew what his problem was, he never would have tanked his career. And he certainly wouldn't be serving beer to tourists. Did they think this was really how he wanted to be living his life? Honestly?

Zach could hear his brother sigh. It sounded like he was trying to work himself up to saying something. Uh-oh. This couldn't be good.

"What is it, Zeke?" Zach asked. "I know you've got something to say to me. So just say it."

"They didn't want anyone to tell you, but, well, I just couldn't let her blindside you," his brother replied.

"Oh no. Zeke, seriously, tell me what's going on. Who's blindsiding me? Mom?" Zach asked, running his fingers through his wet hair in frustration. What fresh hell was headed his way?

"Nope, not Mom. Zoe. She's coming to see you. She'll be there tomorrow."

"Our sister is coming here to Dublin? Tomorrow?"

"Zach it's been two years. How much longer did you think they were going to leave you alone? If it wasn't Zoe, then it was going to be Mom and Dad. Which would you prefer?"

"Oh no, this is...not good. I don't need this," Zach said.

"Yeah, well, like I said, I couldn't just let them surprise you. So there you have it. Little sis is on her merry way to go save her big brother. You've been warned."

"Zeke, seriously man, thank you. You don't know how much I appreciate the heads up."

"Just do me a favor, okay? In return for this warning, will you promise me to at least listen to her? Try harder than however hard you've been trying up to this point? Please? I'm serious when I say I don't know how much more of this Mom and Dad can take."

"I…yeah, okay," Zach replied. "I will. I promise, okay?"

"Cool. Thanks, Zach."

"Thanks bro. Bye." Zach ended the call and dropped the phone on the couch.

Oh, he was in for it now. And he thought just five minutes ago that his biggest problem was that he'd practically sprinted down the hall, dripping wet and naked, on the off-hand chance that Emma might be calling him. That wasn't a sign that his feelings for her had gotten completely out of control, nooo…. And now his pesky little sister was on her way to use her freckle-faced charm to con him into going back to Houston.

Which would mean leaving Emma.

Wait. What? Why did the thought of leaving Emma pop into his mind before the usual worries and dread about going back and facing his old demons? That was crazy. He'd talked to Emma three times. *Three* times. But suddenly she was on his mind more than the paralyzing fears that had completely ruined his life for two years?

She's engaged…she's engaged…she's engaged….

Zach tried to remind himself of this again. That no matter what he was feeling in this moment, Emma wasn't his. She never could be. There was no point to any of this.

Unless....

Unless he worked to get to know her better and found out where these feelings took them, Jim be damned. Zach was sure she was feeling the chemistry between them, too. It probably wouldn't take much to get her to admit it. And then what? Who knows, maybe she'd actually fall for him. Maybe she'd leave Jim, and then they could....

What? They could what? Live in this dump together while he continued to hide from his former life? Or go back to Houston with him, where she could see everyone who he'd ever known pity him and laugh about how far he'd fallen?

He could not afford to keep forgetting that the problems between them were doubled up. Jim was a problem, and all of his own personal garbage was a problem. It wasn't one or the other, it was both. Emma could never be his for lots of reasons.

Maybe he *should* go back home with Zoe. Just disappear without even saying goodbye to Emma. It would probably kill him, but he was emotionally dead anyway, right? What was one more stake in the heart? Besides, Emma would be so much better off without him and his enormous dumpster full of issues.

No, he couldn't do it. He knew that. He'd promised her he'd come to dinner at seven o'clock this evening, and he knew nothing in the world would stop him from it. Not all his problems. Not Zoe. Not Jim. Not anything.

Great. On top of everything else, he was careening his way toward a broken heart. Terrific. That would really be the cherry on the top of his sundae.

He got up and headed to the bedroom. It was time

to get dressed for dinner. Heaven help him, but he was dying to see her again. Headed for a heartache or not, he absolutely had to go.

Chapter 11

"Z! YAY! YOU CAME!" Emma said as she opened the door. "I'm so happy to see you. I wasn't sure you'd show up."

"I wasn't sure I would either, honestly," Zach replied, handing her a bouquet of wildflowers.

"Thank you!"

"Still not sure how smart it is," he went on. "I meant what I said yesterday about this being too hard. Keeping my secret. Being with you...." He trailed off as he let himself enjoy looking into her smiling face. She was one of those natural beauties—she didn't appear to be wearing a drop of makeup, he noticed—who absolutely took his breath away every time. Tonight her long, wavy hair was falling loose around her shoulders, and he would have given every dime he owned to sink his fingers into it. *Okay, now I'm lost in a lovesick trance, standing here staring*, he told himself. He seriously needed to pull himself together. Get a grip on reality.

"Thank you," Emma said, closing her eyes and dreamily putting the flowers up to her face, "For these—they smell wonderful—and for coming. I really just...I don't know. I'm so happy you're here."

"I'm glad," Zach finally said. "Can I come in?"

"Oh geez, I'm the worst hostess ever. Yes, please do," she said, stepping back to let him enter the small living room.

"The flowers aren't the only things that smell

good. Whatever you're cooking smells like heaven," Zach said as he watched her cross the living room and start opening all the kitchen cabinets, apparently hunting for something.

"Thank you," she replied. "I made a big pot of chili, by the way. It's not the most summery dish, but I'm not exactly a whiz in the kitchen. I only know how to make about five things. Oh, here's what I want!" She pulled a vase out of a bottom cabinet and started filling it with water.

"Chili? Are you serious? You sure know how to make a Texas boy happy," Zach said, watching her arrange the flowers carefully. Who knew a little handful of flowers could bring her so much happiness? If she were his girlfriend, he'd bring her flowers every day.

Okay, where had that thought come from? he wondered. Seriously, he needed to stop this and focus. Remember that this was just a simple meal between acquaintances who could never be anything more than that to each other.

"Where's Tracy?" he asked.

"Oh, she's running late. But she should be here anytime now," Emma said as she finished fussing with the flowers. They looked exactly the same to him as they had two minutes ago, but she seemed thrilled with the results.

He was suddenly feeling very awkward. He hadn't socialized like this with anyone in nearly two years and had clearly forgotten how to do it.

"Z, can I get you something to drink?" Emma asked. "Beer? Wine? Soda?"

"Any of those things is fine, yes."

"Want to sit?" she asked, handing him a beer from the fridge and gesturing toward the couch.

"Sure," he said, exhaling as he sat down. *I can do this*, he thought. He could just have a casual conversation with this woman who absolutely was not setting all his nerve endings on fire. Yep, just an extremely casual talk that totally didn't mean a thing.

"How long do you think you'll be in Dublin?" Emma asked, curling onto the couch next to him like a cat. "Do you have a long-term plan for dealing with...whatever you're dealing with?"

Very casual...very casual...very casual....

Zach was dying to reach over and touch her hair. She was driving him crazy. This was way too hard. What was he doing here? He could feel himself starting to panic. What had she just asked him again?

"Uh, no. No plans. I've just been kind of, I don't know. Winging it, I guess," he said with a shrug.

"Oh. Well how does being here help? Is it something in particular about Dublin? Does it...soothe you somehow?"

"I guess you're going to be asking a lot of questions tonight," Zach said, starting to feel uncomfortable with where this was heading. "I thought you were okay with the fact that there are some things I just can't talk about with you. With anyone."

"Yes, yes, of course. I'm sorry, Z. I'm just really torn. I know you want your privacy, but...." Emma trailed off, looking like she was having a hard time choosing her words. Suddenly she reached over and took his hand.

His senses were already on red alert, so the mere touch of her fingers sent his pulse racing. He wanted to jump right out of his skin. He thought again that he shouldn't be here. He shouldn't be doing this. And yet he couldn't stop himself from gently squeezing back in reply.

"Z, I want to help you," she said, looking into his face now, her eyes sending a pleading message that reached right down to his soul. "I feel like it will always bother me until I know you're okay. If I don't help you, I don't think I'll be able to leave Dublin."

"Emma. I appreciate that you care about me. You have no idea how much I appreciate it. But no one can help me. I'm a total mess. My life is a complete grease fire. Seriously, just enjoy your vacation and go back home to Jim with a clear conscience. There's nothing you can do for me," Zach ached inside as her eyes started to pool with tears. "No, Em, don't do that. Don't cry. Please."

"I'm not. I won't," she said, pulling her hand free and wiping them away quickly. "Better go check on my chili."

She went over to the pot on the stove. Zach took a drink of the beer she'd handed him and then set it on the coaster she'd put down for him, taking no note of the brand or taste. Why was his situation upsetting her so much? he wondered. Really, what was he to her? None of this made any sense. They barely knew each other and yet...he felt it too. This strong sense that they were going to be important to each other for a long time. It was terrifying and exhilarating and painful all at the same time. She couldn't be his. Why was he putting himself through such agony? No one needed a friend this badly. Even him.

Suddenly the door opened, and a petite, studious-looking woman walked in, a messenger bag slung across her chest.

"Trace, you're just in time for supper!" Emma said, giving the chili one more stir before closing the lid and walking over to greet her.

Zach stood up and extended his hand, and Tracy met it with a firm handshake.

"Z, this is Tracy," Emma said before heading back into the kitchen. "My wonderful friend who's letting me crash here all summer. Tracy, this is Zach, Dublin's best bartender from Texas."

Zach.... She just introduced him as Zach. She knew. She had figured out his secret. That's why she was getting so upset earlier and trying to pepper him with questions.

"I'm gonna pop into the bathroom," Emma continued. "You two take a minute to get acquainted, okay?"

Zach met Tracy's eyes. She looked completely freaked out. She'd caught Emma's slip, too. Tracy was in on it. She also knew who he was.

After Emma was gone, they stared at each other a long moment before Tracy nodded at him silently.

"She figured it out," Zach finally managed to sputter. "When?"

"Last night, after you guys got back from the park. She put it together. Listen, go easy on her, okay? Finding out your story really took a toll on her. She cried her eyes out last night. She feels awful for you."

"I...I'm sorry Tracy. I've gotta go. Tell Emma...tell her I'm sorry," he said, his long strides carrying him quickly to the door. He was closing it behind him before Tracy even had a chance to reply.

I'm such an idiot, he thought as he went down the hallway. He should have kept his distance from her. He'd successfully stayed off the entire world's radar for basically two years. Two whole years. Then one week with Emma Crawford, and he dropped so many clues that she put the entire thing together after only three conversations.

His heart was going a million miles a minute. Great, a full-blown panic attack would be the perfect end to a perfect day.

Suddenly he could hear soft footsteps running up behind him. He knew who it was before he even turned around.

"Z! Stop! Come on, Z, please?" Emma said, catching up to him now and putting her hand on his arm.

Zach stopped and turned to face her mutely.

"Z, I'm sorry. I'm so sorry. I know you wanted to protect your privacy but I just...I don't know. I just figured it out, okay? I'm sorry. Please talk to me," she pleaded.

"What was it? What set off the big Scooby Doo reveal?" he asked.

"The stress ball," she said, smiling at his joke. "And you would have gotten away with it, too, if it hadn't been for us meddling kids."

"The stress ball? What do you mean?"

"I was watching you play with that thing all day long, and it was driving me nuts trying to figure out what was familiar about what you were doing with it. I mean, you know, you weren't just squeezing it in the way that a stress ball is typically used. You were putting your fingers on it so particularly, and then last night it hit me—you were setting up pitching grips."

"Okay, I had no idea I was even doing that," Zach said, shaking his head now. "Clearly I've had a complete psychotic break."

"It's probably just muscle memory," Emma said. "Something you've done so many times you don't even have to think about it anymore. So I put Z + *pitcher* into Google, and I found out some truly informative things about water filtration systems. Then I found out Zack Greinke no longer pitches for the Dodgers. And *then* I thought about the two-year timeframe and the fact that you gave me a New York number."

"Dammit. I knew I shouldn't have given you my number," Zach said bitterly.

"Finally I put it all together when I remembered hearing about a pitcher on the Yankees who walked away from a multi-million-dollar contract two years ago," Emma carried on, reaching out to take his hand now. She laced her fingers through his, which had the effect of completely distracting him from his anger. *Well played.* "That's when I knew it was you. You're Zach Hiller, superstar Yankees pitcher."

"Not anymore. But yeah, I used to be," he said, feeling like a dope as tears sprang to his eyes.

"Come here," she said, reaching her arms out and folding him into a hug.

Even though he knew it was the last thing he should do, he felt himself leaning into her. *It feels like home*, Zach thought as he buried his face into her soft hair.

"Why did figuring out who I was upset you?" he asked, talking right into the hair, the sound slightly muffled. "Tracy said you cried."

"I just did," she said. "I felt so awful for everything you've been through and how much pain you're obviously still in. Two years is a long time to suffer in silence, Zach."

"Yeah, well, I'm a big boy. I'll be okay," he said, pulling back from her. If he didn't let go now, he might never do it. "I'll get this figured out eventually. You don't have to worry about me, Emmy."

She smiled at the nickname and sniffed back some emotion that she was trying to hide from him.

"Come back to the apartment with me. You still owe me supper," she pointed out.

"Nah. Listen Em, this is new for me, you knowing and all. I need time to think about it. Okay? Rain check?"

Emma sighed. "Yeah, okay. I understand." She hugged herself now as if suddenly chilled. "I'm really sorry Zach. I am. I didn't set out to upset your solitary confinement. It just...happened."

"Yeah, I know. It's okay. It'll be fine. Go home and eat that chili for me," he said with a smile.

Emma nodded, gave him a final smile, then turned back toward the apartment.

Zach had never felt so alone as he watched her walk away.

Chapter 12

"I AM SUCH AN IDIOT," Emma said, slamming her way back into the apartment moments later.

"You are a lovely idiot who makes a mean pot of chili," Tracy replied. "So where's Zach? You couldn't talk him into coming back with you? Not even for chili?"

"No." Emma flopped onto the couch. "I really blew it this time."

"Oh, I'm sure it's not as bad as all of that. He looked shocked but not devastated. He'll get over it. Now come over here and feed your misery. I'm starving," Tracy nudged Emma's shoe, which was dangling off the edge of the couch.

"I'll join you, but I've pretty much lost my appetite," Emma said with a groan as she climbed off the couch and walked to the table.

Tracy ladled herself a bowl of chili. "Oh cheer up. I think in the end it will help him that you know. If nothing else, he doesn't have to work so hard to be Johnny Mysterious."

"That's Z Mysterious to you," Emma replied, heading to the stove now. She figured she may as well try to eat. "I just wanted to give him a nice dinner with two friendly faces. I get the impression he hasn't had much human contact outside of work. It's like trying to socialize a feral cat at this point."

Tracy laughed. "Oh come on, he's not as bad as all

of that. A feral cat who had the good southern upbringing and manners to think to bring you flowers as a hostess gift. I wouldn't say he's a lost cause."

"No, he's not a lost cause at all," Emma said. "I just want to help him so badly. But part of me is screaming that I need to be careful and think about what I'm really doing here. I'm getting dangerously close to being in the cliché zone."

"What do you mean?" Tracy asked, taking another bite of chili. "Em, this is seriously delicious. Zach doesn't know what he's missing."

"I'm talking about the classic cliché that says women like to pick out men with problems and take them in like strays. You know, try to fix them? I hope that's not what I'm doing here." Emma took her first bite. "Okay, yeah, it's pretty good tonight."

"Hmm, that's an interesting theory," Tracy said. "You made a seriously delicious meal here. Seems like you were working pretty hard to impress your stray. Maybe you *are* trying to fix him."

"Maybe. But I think that…even if I am running the risk of falling into that cliché…I think that maybe…I don't know. I don't know what I'm trying to say here. I think that even if it *is* a cliché, I don't care. For one thing, I'm engaged to someone else. So it's not really the same thing. He's just a friend who, I think, could use my help. That's…totally different from the real cliché—you know, like a woman who starts writing to a guy on death row and ends up marrying him—right?"

"Uh, yeah, duh. It's totally different."

"And the other difference is that he's not a stereotypical bad boy. We're not talking about trying to fix someone who's got a drug problem or is in a gang or something super serious like that. He's just…lost."

Emma was still picturing the distress on Zach's face when they were on the sidewalk earlier. "I still need to find out his side of the story, though. I want to know exactly what happened two years ago. I'm not going to have a moment's peace until I figure this out."

"Then I think you have your answer, Em," Tracy said. "Stop worrying about whether you should be involved and just try to find a few more puzzle pieces. Maybe once you hear the whole story, you'll see that it's just not the big melodrama you're imagining it to be. Maybe you'll be able to walk away from this with a clear conscience."

"Yeah. Maybe," Emma replied, feeling doubtful even though she was agreeing with Tracy's words. She had a sense that she'd never be able to walk away from Zach without some kind of regrets. And wasn't that a weird thing to think about a man she barely knew? She needed to toss this around some more. *Alone.*

"Trace, I'm going to clean up and then lay down in my room. I'm exhausted."

"Nah, I've got the cleanup," Tracy offered. "There's not much anyway. You go rest."

"Really? You're sure? Thanks, Trace. You're a doll." Emma took her dish to the sink and headed to the guest room, which had become hers for the summer. Then she lay down on the twin bed and closed her eyes, thinking again about Zach's reaction to the news that she had figured out his identity.

What was he afraid of? Was he concerned she'd give his secret away to other people? Or that she'd start pressing him for answers that he wouldn't be able to provide? Or the possibility that she was a sports groupie who would only be interested in him because of his money and relative fame? Maybe he was thinking she'd be asking him to sign a bunch of balls that she could sell online, or leaning on him to get her World Series tickets?

She squeezed her eyes tightly shut and massaged her temple. *What was the right thing to do here?*

On the one hand, this seriously wasn't any of her business. He had specifically and repeatedly asked her to stay out of his past. To stay out of his problems. To respect his privacy. And again, she barely knew him. It was beyond a stretch to say a man you'd basically only spent one day with was a close, personal friend. They were acquaintances at best. And as someone with a fiancé, she really had no business getting to know him any better anyway. So that was a pretty strong case in defense of just dropping this and walking away.

She tried to envision what that would look like. Just not showing up at Zach's pub again? Maybe deleting his number from her phone? Would he then take the initiative and reach out to *her*? Should she wait for him to do that? To indicate that it was okay that she had delved into his past and solved the mystery of his identity?

She exhaled and rolled her eyes. She didn't want to play games or run some sort of test. Seriously, he was a big boy. If he didn't like what she'd done, he could just tell her point blank that he wanted to sever ties.

"Hey, Em?" Tracy called, knocking on the door. "Can I come in a sec?"

"Sure, what's up?"

The door opened. "I wanted to mention that I can't come on that bus tour after all," Tracy said. "I'm so sorry. I know you were excited about it. Did you already buy the tickets?"

"Oh, yeah, I did. But don't worry about it," Emma

said, hoping to hide her disappointment. "It's no big deal. I'll just go alone."

"Or you could ask…say….I don't know….an out-of-work Major League pitcher? Do you know any of those?" Tracy smiled and then quickly closed the door again.

"Very funny!" Emma called after her.

Well, that's just great, she thought bitterly. This trip wasn't exactly going the way she planned.

She rolled over and felt around on the floor for her phone, finally locating it in her bag. Then she opened a new text to Zach and started typing.

Send me your address. Can I stop by tomorrow? she wrote before pressing Send. *There*, she told herself. If he didn't want to see her, she'd find out soon enough.

She closed her eyes and thought back to their day in the park. That'd been great. Spending time with him had been so much fun. Maybe she *would* ask him to take the bus tour with her.

Her cell phone vibrated. She opened up the text to find Zach had replied with his address. And he'd added a note: Seems tomorrow's my lucky day. Lots of beautiful women headed my way. So not sure what time is best.

Huh?

She had no idea what that meant. Lots of beautiful women? Wasn't Zach practically a hermit?

Not sure what you mean. Tomorrow's not good? she typed.

Nah, I'll probably need the interference. Come anytime, was his reply a few minutes later.

What in the world was he talking about? Did he even know who he was texting with? His replies made absolutely no sense.

But what the heck, she figured. She was going over there. She absolutely needed to hear the rest of his story, from his perspective. Without knowing what had happened to him two years ago, it was almost impossible to decide how to proceed. Despite everything else, figuring out the rest of the mystery was important. Without the complete picture, walking away from Zach was something she just couldn't do yet.

So tomorrow would be a fact-finding mission, nothing more. Without more information, there was really nothing she could decide.

She felt better having a plan. As usual, coming up with a course of action calmed her. She really did love a good plan.

With a sigh, she set her phone down next to the bed and sat up. Unless she planned to sleep in her clothes, she should probably change.

Chapter 13

ZACH SPENT THE MORNING straightening up his apartment. If nothing else, he was grateful to Zeke for the warning just so Zoe wouldn't be able to report back that he was living like an animal. He didn't need his family to have any more ammunition for why he needed to get his life in order.

As he was putting the finishing touches on the bathroom and washing his hands, the doorbell rang.

Emma. Maybe it's Emma.

He rolled his eyes. Why was she his first thought no matter what else was happening these days?

He dried his hands and headed for the door. It wasn't going to be Emma, he told himself. It was more likely going to be Zoe, his adorably freckle-faced baby sister who could get him to do almost anything with one bat of her baby blues.

He pulled the door open to find…not Emma. And definitely not his adorably freckle-faced baby sister. The creature standing at the door had grown right out of the adorable-little-sister stage and had blossomed into a strikingly beautiful woman. He felt a little choked up as he stared at her. He'd missed so much of her life already. Yet another thing to add to his guilt checklist.

"Zoe-girl!" he said, opening his arms and laughing as she leaped into his embrace. "I practically didn't recognize you! Hi, beautiful!"

"Zachy! Oh I am so happy to see you!" Zoe

squeezed him hard for a long moment, then pulled back to search his face. She put a hand up on his cheek, too, which made him wonder what she was thinking, what she saw when she looked at him. Finally she smiled again, and sniffed back what looked like threatening tears. "I've missed you, big brother."

"I've miss you, too, Zoe. Get in here." He reached down to grab her small suitcase, then stood back to let her enter the apartment.

"You don't seem surprised to see me," she said as she glanced around the living room. "Zeke called, didn't he? I can tell you've been cleaning."

"You could always see right through me, couldn't you, sis?" He reached over to ruffle her hair. "Zozo, I've got to tell you, you have really changed. You grew up in the time I've been gone."

"You've been gone way too *long*, Zach," she said, taking a seat on on the couch. "Of course I didn't stay exactly the same. Time marches on and all that."

He sat down next to her. "Yeah, it does, doesn't it? Okay, well, let's just cut right to it. Go ahead and get it out of the way."

"Get what out of the way?" she asked, giving him an exaggerated look of innocent confusion.

"Oh, save the act. You didn't fly across the ocean to talk about the march of Father Time and apartment cleaning with me. You came here to rake me over the coals. So go ahead, let's have it. Give me your best shot." Zach leaned back and put his feet up on the coffee table.

Zoe sighed. "Okay, so yeah, you got me. I want to know how you're doing. And I want to know why you hardly ever call Mom and Dad. And I also want to know when you're going to come home, at least to visit if not to stay. Oh—and when are you going to start pitching again?"

"Hmm, yeah, those were pretty good shots," Zach said with a smile.

"You asked for it," Zoe said, nudging his leg with her sneakered toe. "So come on. How are you doing?"

"If you had come here a week ago," he began, his head resting on the couch, his gaze on the ceiling, "I would have said absolutely everything was exactly the same as it's always been. I would have said that I haven't taken a single step toward figuring out how to get out of this town. And that I had nothing different to tell you than the last one hundred times you asked me."

"Wait, so does that mean something has changed?" Zoe asked excitedly, putting her hand on his knee. "Maybe even for the better? In the last week? Tell me Zachy or I swear I'll sit on you until you do."

"I don't know, exactly," he replied cautiously. How much did he really want to talk about Emma with his little sister? Not at all, really. And yet he hadn't had a sounding board in a long time. It felt good.

"You must have some idea," she said, sounding dubious.

"Yeah, I do, I guess." He exhaled and looked into her face again. "It's really not that big of a deal. But, well, I actually made a friend."

"You did? Okay, well, that's good, I guess," she said. "But...is this the first friend you've made in two years? That's a little sad. Do you need me to arrange some playdates with the neighborhood boys?"

"Oh, shut up. No, you know, I have acquaintances at work. Neighbors I say hi to. That sort of thing. But this is different. It's an actual *friend* friend. Like, a person I can talk to."

"Okay. And is this person a woman?" Zoe asked, looked unaccountably excited.

"Calm down, Zoe," he said. "It *is* a woman, but it's not what you think. Hey, can I get you a drink, by the way?"

"Nah, I'm too interested in this new woman friend of yours. How is it not what I think, and how do you know what I'm thinking in the first place?"

"Because I know you so well, Zoe," Zach said. "You've already got me married to her in your mind, but I'm telling you, this is different. She's just a friend. She's engaged to someone else, for one thing."

"Oh, bummer. Okay, well, then what makes knowing her change things for you in the last week? I'm lost."

"I don't know sis. Ever since I met her, things feel different. *Better.* I'm not ready to pack my bags and go home yet. But you can go back to Houston and give the report that I'm officially feeling a tad more optimistic about life than I was before. Who knows, maybe I'm actually going to be able to turn things around," Zach said, feeling kind of surprised at the words that were coming out of his mouth. But it was true, wasn't it? Ever since Emma came into his world, things just seemed more…possible.

"You have *got* to tell me this miracle worker's name," Zoe said, looking happier by far than she had when she first arrived. "Mom and Dad are going to want to, like, I don't know, start a scholarship foundation in her honor or something."

"It's Emma," Zach replied. "And she's just a friend, and that's all she can ever be, so don't forget that and please don't oversell it to them. They'll get their hopes too high about what's happening here. Seriously, she's been very kind to me, and for some reason it's made me feel a sliver of happiness when before all I felt was dead. But that's it, okay?"

"Okay, okay. I'll back off. For now. So what are you up to today?"

"Well, I need to take a shower," Zach said. "As you guessed, I spent the morning cleaning. I smell like toilet cleanser."

"Oh, so then you smell like you always smell."

"Very funny. Keep it up, little one," he said, getting up and heading down the hall. "Do you need to use the bathroom before I go in?"

"Nah, I'm good."

Zach closed the door and turned on the shower, thinking about the conversation they'd just had while he waited for the water to heat up. He really hadn't been overselling how Emma made him feel just to get Zoe off his back. Actually, he'd sort of dialed it down to keep Zoe's expectations low.

The truth of the matter, if he was being honest with himself, was that he felt liberated in a way. He'd desperately wanted to keep his secret from Emma. But now that she knew, it kind of felt good. No—it kind of felt *great*. She had been sweet and empathetic and sad for him, but it really hadn't seemed like pity. Or impatience, or even disgust at the pathetic way he'd handled things. She just seemed like she wanted to hear his side of the story. Like she wanted to help him.

But she'd *already* helped him. So he'd told Zoe the truth—when Emma walked into his life, she brought a light and warmth with her that he hadn't felt in years.

And she might be coming by today, he reminded himself as he stood under the water and cleaned off that awful antiseptic smell. Even the chance that he might be seeing her again...he was still smiling at the thought of it as he stepped out moments later and reached for his towel.

Even after a grilling from his sister, it was bound to be a good day.

Chapter 14

THIS WAS IT—the address Zach had texted her. Emma stood outside his door, feeling a little nervous.

Okay, a lot nervous.

She was excited to see him again, but nervous that he was still mad at her for nosing into the truth about his identity.

Yes, he gave out his address, so he must be okay with the idea of her coming over. On the other hand, his other texts had been weird and confusing, so maybe he hadn't even realized it was her on the receiving end. Maybe she wasn't who he'd be expecting at all when he opened the door.

Hmm, yeah, these speculations aren't helping to calm my nerves. Now her heart was thumping in her chest. Geez, it was just a friendly chat with a new buddy. That's what she kept telling herself. That's it, right? No big deal.

She took a deep breath and rang the doorbell.

She smiled as she heard footsteps on the other side of the door and watched happily as it swung open to reveal…an incredibly beautiful woman? No, this couldn't be right. She glanced at the apartment number again. It matched what he'd texted.

"I think I have the wrong address," she finally said. "I'm sorry to have bothered you."

"It depends. Are you looking for Zach?" the woman asked.

"Well, yes…" she replied, stopping when she heard

Zach's voice.

"Zoe, you want to shower now?" Zach called from somewhere inside. Suddenly she could see him come into the room behind the gorgeous creature who was still at the door. His feet were bare, he was in a pair of boxers, and he didn't have a shirt on, the shower water still glistening on his muscles.

Emma felt like she was about to hyperventilate. His chest was a hard plane of chiseled muscles like something out of an underwear ad. Was spontaneous combustion a real thing? Maybe, she thought, as she felt the heat creeping up her face. Not only did Zach have the body of a Hollywood movie star, he'd been using it to frolic in the shower with the ethereal beauty who was still standing at the door. And yet...was that jealousy shooting all through her? *It couldn't be. Ridiculous.* She was the one who was engaged. She had absolutely zero right to be jealous of anything Zach did.

And yet in that moment she wanted to cry. Or die. Maybe both. She shouldn't be here. She shouldn't have seen this.

"I'm so sorry to just show up unannounced," she finally choked out. "You're obviously busy here, and I really have to go."

"Oh. My. God!" the runway model at the door said. "You're Emma, aren't you? Aren't you?"

"Er...yes?" Emma said, confused now. How did this woman know her name? And why did she seem happy to see her? Something wasn't adding up.

"Yes, Zoe, that's Emma," Zach said. "Could you stop gaping at her and open the door so she can come in? I'm sorry, Em. She was raised by wolves."

"I...what?" Emma said, now beyond confused as she walked in. This was *so* uncomfortable. What had she gotten herself into? And would she ever get the vision of Zach's chest out of her mind? It didn't seem likely.

"Emma Crawford, meet Zoe Hiller," Zach started.

Zoe *Hiller*? He said he wasn't married. Now Emma wanted to cry. She felt so stupid. What was she still doing standing there?

"He's making the lamest introduction ever," Zoe said. "To clarify, I'm his sister. His baby sister."

"His…his sister? Oh, yes, of *course*," Emma said, feeling like an idiot now. Of course! Zach had mentioned a brother and a sister before. And now his teasing manner was making more sense. And so did Zoe's familiar blue eyes. Emma saw the resemblance at once.

"I could tell you didn't know I was just his sister," Zoe said, looking apologetic. "I'm sorry. I didn't mean to give you a scare."

"Didn't I tell you my sister was coming?" Zach asked. "I'm sorry Emma. You must have thought I was drunk when I was texting you last night."

"Yeah, I didn't know what you were talking about."

"Zeke had given me the heads up right before I went over to your house for dinner. I guess when we had our…misunderstanding…I, uh…." Zach looked like he was sorry he'd mentioned their dinner in front of Zoe. "Well, whatever, I meant to mention it to you, and I clearly didn't. I'm sorry, Em."

"Emma, please come in and sit down," Zoe said, taking her hand and pulling her toward the couch. "Zach, offer Emma a drink and then go get dressed. We need some girl time. Alone."

"Wait, Zoe—can I talk with you a minute?" he

asked, looking like he wanted to kill her at the same time.

"Nope!" Zoe said. "Don't worry. I won't grill her too much. Just go put some clothes on, you clown."

Zach mouthed a silent *I'm sorry* to Emma before disappearing down the hall. She couldn't help smiling back at him. She could already tell that Zoe was clearly jumping to all kinds of conclusions about their relationship. Pretty much the way *she'd* jumped to conclusions when she got here and found Zach mostly naked with a woman in his apartment. Which, again, totally should not have bothered her. It also shouldn't bother her that Zoe just told him to get dressed. It was a crime to cover that chest up. Or those legs, for that matter.

She'd have to analyze why it completely, one-million percent, bothered her down to her core when she'd thought she'd uncovered a love nest at Zach's apartment. That probably wasn't going to be a fun bit of soul-searching, but she'd put it on the back-burner for now. She needed to be grilled by a little sister first.

"Did Zach just say that your other brother's name is Zeke?" Emma asked. "Your parents named you guys Zach, Zeke, and Zoe?"

"Oh yeah, they are straight-up crazy," Zoe laughed with a nod. "But if it makes you feel slightly better, it's actual Zachary, Ezekiel, and Zoe. It's a pinch less crazy. But, yeah, it's still kind of super nuts."

"You guys are so lucky to have each other, with or without an abundance of Z names," Emma said. "I'm an only child. I always get kind of wistful when I see siblings who obviously adore each other like the two of you clearly do."

"Yeah, we're a close family," Zoe replied. "Which

makes Zach's exile all the more difficult to bear. But, shh, we can't talk about Zach anymore because here he comes."

"Oh shoot, and I was just about to get to the really juicy gossip," Emma said, winking at Zoe.

"Did you two really manage to form an all-girls' club in the two minutes it took me to pull on jeans and a tee shirt?" Zach asked, sitting on the recliner across from the couch.

Emma smiled at him.

He smiled back.

Oh, this is bad, she thought. Just seeing him made her happy.

"Zoe was just telling me what a close family you've got. And I was whining about being an only child, and telling her how jealous I am that you guys have each other," Emma said.

"I don't know how jealous you'd be if you heard the way she was raking me over the coals a few minutes ago," he told her with an affectionate wink at his sister. It was nice seeing him in this family setting. He seemed more comfortable than he had in the entire time she'd known him.

Which, okay, has only been a handful of days. So why does it seem like I've known him forever in some ways?

That was something else she'd need to analyze later. So much to think about here. He stirred up so many questions for her. For some reason, Zach was able to set off an emotional tornado in her without even trying. It was hard to keep track of what she was feeling from moment to moment in the tornado's wake.

"Zach, can you go get us a pizza?" Zoe suddenly asked. "I know it's kind of early, but I'm starving."

"Yeah, my phone's around here somewhere," he

said, standing up again and looking around.

"You're not taking the hint," Zoe told him, flashing a pleading, sugary smile at him. "Please just get out of here so we can have some more girl time."

"No way, I'm not exposing Emma to the same interrogation I just got. No...way...."

"I'll be fine," Emma said, laughing. "I'm a big girl. I'm sure I can take it."

"You say that now, but you have no idea how relentless she can be." Zach looked like he really was going to refuse to go if she gave him any hint that she wanted out of the conversation to come.

"Zach, really, it's okay," Emma said. "Go find Zoe something to eat. She just had a long flight."

"Okay, okay, I can see when I'm outnumbered." Zach walked to the door and slid into a beat-up pair of loafers that were lying there. He wandered around until he found his wallet and phone, and then he finally headed to the door. "All right, you two are getting your way. I'm leaving. Go easy on her, Zozo."

"I will!" Zoe called, swinging back toward Emma as soon as the door closed. "Tell me everything!"

"Everything?" Emma asked, laughing harder now. "Everything about everything? Do I start before the Earth was created, or something more recent?"

"Oh come on, you know what I'm talking about! How did you meet Zach? How long have you two been friends? He said you're engaged. Is that true? Where's your fiancé? Is he here in Dublin?" Zoe rattled off these questions like a machine gun before finally stopping to take a breath.

"Zoe, it's really nothing, so please don't be too excited," Emma replied earnestly. "I walked into Zach's pub about a week ago, and we struck up a conversation.

I like him, and he likes me. As friends. But there's nothing more to it, really. He wouldn't even tell me who he was. I only just figured it out on my own a night or two ago. We haven't even had a chance to talk about it, really. So all I know is that he was a pitcher for the Yankees. He threw the pitch that hit Tommy Layton, ending his rookie year with a long stint on the injured list. And I know what the media had to say about it, that Zach broke his contract and all that. And, of course, I know that he came here. But he didn't tell me any of that, Zoe. We're hardly close confidantes if he wouldn't even tell me his name."

"Oh," Zoe said, looking crestfallen now. "But he said you're helping him. He said he feels better now and that it's because of you."

"That's wonderful that he says he's feeling better," Emma replied. "It really is. I would love nothing more than to see him pull himself out of this funk and go recapture his old life. But it's got nothing to do with me."

"Emma, you may not think you're making a difference, but Zach does. He really thinks you are. Please, whatever you're doing, whatever friendship you've started here, you've got to keep it going. I feel like we're finally onto something here."

"But Zoe, it's true that I'm engaged to my college sweetheart. And I'm only here for a short time. But, yes, I confess I really would like to spend more time getting to know your brother. I'm drawn to him for some reason I can't quite figure out." Emma couldn't believe she was sharing these things with Zach's sister, whom she'd known for a total of perhaps ten minutes. And yet it was nice to get to talk to someone who really knew him. "Tell me about how he was before," she went on. "What was the old Zach like?"

"He was absolutely nothing like the guy you met here," Zoe started. "He was always so confident. He was born with this amazing ability and gift, and he just *owned* it, do you know what I mean? He had the strongest sense of self and purpose of anyone you could possibly meet, even as a little boy in peewee baseball. He knew he was born to be a pitcher, and he always had this single-minded goal. But he didn't really have to work for it. He never struggled really, he just was naturally gifted. There were MLB scouts watching him since junior high, so it was clear that the baseball world was taking notice of him. We all knew he was destined for big things." Zoe shrugged. "And people just flocked to him. I think it was because of his confidence. It just radiated out of him, and it worked like some kind of magnet. He always had an orbit of people around him, drawn to him. He just was…a star. I don't know how else to explain it. You had to have seen it to understand what I mean. But that's why this change in him has been so devastating to watch. In the blink of an eye, he went from being the strongest, most confident person I knew to being a blank, emotionless shell. His old shine is just gone."

"That's so sad," Emma said. "I can't imagine how hard it was for your family to watch."

"I don't think he wanted us to watch, which is why he came here. He's kept us all at arm's length since it happened. He doesn't want to deal with our questions about how long he's going to need to discover his old swagger. He doesn't want to hear it from us. But Emma, for some reason, it seems he's willing to let you in. Please, for my parents' sake, and for Zach's sake, don't turn away from this opportunity you have to reach him. To smack some sense into him."

"I probably won't be smacking sense into him," Emma said, reaching over to give Zoe's hand an affectionate squeeze. "But no, I won't turn my back on him either. I'm here for the summer, and I could use a tour buddy while I'm here. So we'll just see what happens, okay?"

"Yeah, that's great. I'll take it." A look of obvious relief lit up her face. "Emma, my family sent me here to take Zach's mental temperature. I am so happy I'm going to be able to give them a little good news. They need to hear something positive so badly."

"I'm glad he told you he's feeling better," Emma replied. "I was afraid I'd blown it when I figured out his secret. But I think it's going to be better for him now that I know. He won't have to struggle so hard to keep his secret from me. Maybe he'll even be able to talk more about what he's going through. But there are no guarantees, Zoe. He might just shut me down, too."

"Can I get your cell number?" Zoe asked. "Or maybe we could hook up on social media? I really would love to hear from your perspective how he's doing. I worry about him so much. Well, you know that we all do."

"I…sure, we can exchange numbers. But Zoe, I won't spy on him for your family. I'm not going to issue daily status updates on him or whatever. It wouldn't be right."

"No, no of course not. I just thought…" Zoe trailed off. "It's just that we hardly ever hear from him and I thought…well, okay, you know what I thought."

"I'd love to keep in touch with you," Emma said. "And I'll let you know if there's an emergency of some sort. But other than that, it's up to Zach to decide what he does and doesn't tell you, okay? I won't betray his confidence."

"I understand, Emma," Zoe replied as she took out her phone. "Give me your number, please."

Zoe was dialing Emma's number to complete the exchange when Zach walked back in with the pizza.

"Uh-oh, what are you two up to?" he asked, closing the door with his foot and heading to the kitchen. He tossed the pizza box on the counter along with his wallet and phone.

"Nothing at all." Emma stood up. "Well, Zoe, it's been a pleasure to meet you. Have a safe trip home. Oh, wait, when do you leave?"

"First thing Monday morning. This is just a quick weekend thing," Zoe told her, standing up, too.

"Well, enjoy your pizza, you two," Emma said. "I need to get going."

"Stay and eat," Zach said. "There's enough here for all of us."

"No, I really couldn't. But Z, can you walk me to the door? I have a question for you." Emma turned and folded Zoe into a hug. "Bye, Zoe. Thanks for the talk."

"No Emma, thank *you*. Seriously," Zoe said, squeezing her back before letting go.

Zoe wandered off to the kitchen as Zach and Emma went out to the hallway.

"You really are welcome to stay," he said, pulling the door closed behind them.

"I know. But I want you to spend as much time with her as possible. She's not here long, and she is seriously in need of some time and attention from her big brother. Give her a ton of it, okay?"

"Yeah, sure. Of course. Is that what you wanted to ask me?"

"No, actually, it's about Monday. Do you have plans after she leaves?" Emma asked, feeling hopeful.

"No…well, wait. I might be working that day. I can't remember. Why, what's up?"

"I already bought two tickets for a day-long bus trip. It's a guided tour of Northern Ireland. But Tracy can't go now, and I was hoping you'd come instead?" Emma was dying for him to say yes.

"I don't know, Em. I'm not sure if we should be spending that kind of time together," Zach replied.

"Why? I already know your secret, so it's not like you have to spend the day carefully guarding your thoughts and picking out your words. I thought we agreed to be friends? Or are you still mad that I figured out who you are?"

"No, I'm not mad. I think, in a way, I'm actually kind of relieved. But I was serious when I said I hadn't left Dublin in two years." Zach shook his head. "I don't know."

"Just consider it, okay? I really think we'd have fun, and I am absolutely dying to go see Giant's Causeway. Come share it with me, please!" Emma was feeling excited now.

"I don't even know what that is," he replied. "I take it you read all about that in your guidebook?"

"Of course!" Emma said with a laugh. "Well I'm not going to tell you what it is. If you want to find out, then come with me. Just think about it and surprise me. I'll text you the address of the hotel where we're supposed to meet the bus, and I'll send you the meeting time. I'll either go by myself or I'll see you Monday, okay? No big deal either way."

"Okay, yeah, I'll think about it," Zach agreed. "Have a great weekend, Em."

"Thanks. I hope I'll see you Monday."

Emma gave him one last smile before turning to make her way home. She had a lot to think about this weekend, including why she was so deliriously excited at the thought of spending a whole day with him.

Chapter 15

"OOH, ZACH, I just love her," Zoe said as Zach walked back into the apartment.

"Yeah, she's great, right?" Zach replied, joining her in the kitchen.

"Yeah, and as an added bonus, she is totally into you." Zoe took a bite of the pizza.

Zach pulled out a slice for himself. "Shut up, she is not. I told you she's engaged." *Zoe's seeing what she wants to see*, he thought to himself, dismissing her words without letting himself really consider them or believe them.

"Zach, she turned green with jealousy when I opened the door, and the shade of green got even darker when you came wandering out of the shower. I was right here watching the whole thing, so I know. I'm telling you, it gave her the shock of her life when she thought she'd just found you with another woman. Don't forget, she had no idea who I am because you never got around to telling her I was coming."

"Zoe, I'm telling *you* that what you think you saw is absolutely impossible," Zach insisted, opening the refrigerator and pulling out a couple of sodas.

"Zach, shut up and listen to me. I saw it on her face. And when you introduced me as Zoe Hiller?" Zoe said, giggling now. "Oh my gosh. She totally thought you were married. Oh man, it was priceless. Maybe she doesn't even realize it yet, but I'm telling you she looked like she wanted to cry."

"Zoe, seriously, shut up. This teasing is going to get you nowhere." Zach opened one of the soda cans. Little sisters were such a pain.

"And you, you just played it up to perfection didn't you? Strutting out here half naked and showing off your gym muscles? Did you oil your chest first for maximum effect?" Zoe's giggles grew into a full-blown laughing fit now.

"I can see that you don't even want to hear the truth, Zoe. I knew this would happen. I knew you'd overreact about her."

Her giggling died down quickly, although a tiny smile lingered. "I'm sorry, Zach. I don't mean to make you mad. It was just that, well, her reaction was seriously funny. And it was a big reaction, whether you want to admit it to me or not." Zoe grabbed the other soda as she struggled to keep from bursting out again.

"Okay, I don't know why I'm telling you this, but maybe it'll get through your cranium if I just say it. The truth is that, yeah, in another set of circumstances I would totally fall for her. You're right: She's great. And there's a connection between us somehow." He was astonished that he'd just admitted this out loud. "Don't tell Mom any of this stuff, though, okay? Because it can absolutely never go anywhere. Even if she weren't happily engaged to someone she'd dated forever, I've got nothing to offer her. I'm a mess Zoe. You know that. Do you really think it would be fair to try to drag Emma into this pit I'm stuck in? Really?"

"So get out of the pit, you lug nut," Zoe said, looking defiant now. "Emma could be your motivation to solve your problems. Fight for her. You could work at it and prove to her that you want to get better. You can do it if you really make the effort, Zach."

"I don't even know how to *start* making this right, so don't push me, Zoe," Zach warned. He'd had enough of this line of questioning. "Even if I could figure it out, that doesn't solve the problem of the fiancé. So just back off, okay? I love you, but you need to leave me alone on this."

"We *have* left you alone Zach," Zoe said, looking like she was digging in for a long fight. "We gave you space for two years. And don't get me wrong, I'm beyond thrilled that you are feeling a bit better. And, okay, if you say there's no future for you and Emma, then all right. I'll stop teasing you about it. But you told me yourself that spending time with her is helping you. So keep spending time with her. Explore that friendship more. Try to figure out what it is about Emma that makes you feel better. Please, Zach. You've found a little momentum. Don't stop the ball from rolling now."

"Yeah, I know," he agreed. "I'll try. Especially if that means you'll leave me alone about Emma."

"I will, I'll drop it," Zoe said. "If you'll tell me what she wanted to ask you just now?"

Zach shook his head and laughed. He loved his sister, but Monday seemed light years away in that moment. "You are so nosy! Why don't you go to the airport now? You don't want to miss your flight."

"The flight that's not leaving for another two days? That flight? Yeah, I think I'm safe," Zoe shot back.

Zach exhaled, studying her face. She wouldn't stop nagging until he told her, so he may as well just get it over with.

"She has an extra ticket for a bus tour of Northern Ireland. A day trip, on Monday. And she invited me to go," he finally said with a shake of his head. "You're going to make me sorry I told you, aren't you?"

"Oh, Zach, you have to go! Tell me you'll go—promise me!" Zoe made no attempt to hide the complete glee she was obviously feeling.

"I'm not promising you anything," he said, grabbing another slice of pizza. "I still haven't really decided yet if I'm going to go."

"Why not? It's exactly what you need!"

"For one thing, I might have to work that day," he said, taking a bite.

"Oh, come on. That's easily solved. Tell them you need to trade shifts. That's just a McJob anyway. Who cares?"

"And I haven't been out of Dublin in two years. I'm not sure…I don't know if I want to go anywhere." He knew this was just an excuse. He was covering up the real reason he was hesitating. The whole truth was that he wasn't sure he could stand spending that much time with Emma. Because she made him feel things, a lot of things. More than he'd felt about anything or anyone in a really long time. And definitely more than he should be experiencing for a woman who could never return those feelings. So no, he didn't want to be locked in a bus with her all day.

Zoe looked disappointed, and he thought that was the last thing he needed at the moment.

"I'll stop pushing you, Zach," she said, an impish grin on her face. "I won't bring it up again. But just promise me you'll think about it. I think you should be spending as much time with Emma as she'll allow, since she's clearly the Zach Whisperer."

"Ha ha, Zoe. Very funny. Now, are you done eating? Do you want to go walk around and see some of the city?" he offered, hoping she'd agree. He needed to distract her. He couldn't bear any more of her questioning and teasing.

Like everything else in his life right now, it was just too much.

Chapter 16

THE MORE EMMA THOUGHT about the reaction she'd had when Zoe opened the door earlier—where she'd thought for a split-second that Zach was showering and sleeping with another woman—the more upset she became. Because there was no more denying that what she'd experienced was pure jealousy. Zoe had been so beautiful, and Zach had been so sexy and wet and half-naked and muscley and….

Emma slapped her palm to her forehead in frustration. She couldn't lie to herself, not about a reaction that strong. It hadn't been a mild annoyance or a fleeting bit of unreasonable emotion. No, her reaction had been wild and painful, and it had come out of nowhere.

She couldn't deny it to herself anymore. This wasn't just a passing bit of friendly warmth. It also wasn't basic human compassion for someone who needed a friend. And it wasn't a meaningless bit of sizzle for someone with whom she happened to have a lot of chemistry, either.

No. It was perhaps a bit of all of those things. But, in total, it was more than that. She was completely, totally, and quickly falling for him. Hard.

How could that be? she wondered. She'd been with Jim for years now. How could a handful of encounters with a troubled man she barely knew be a threat to what she had built over time with Jim? What they had together was beautiful and rock-solid, right? So how was she letting this happen?

Okay, no.... Emma was kidding herself if she thought there was a single thing she could have done to stop this. From the moment she'd walked into his pub, she had been helpless to stem her rising levels of emotion. He'd made her laugh more and cry more and feel more in the last week than she cumulatively had in, like, the last year. So how was this possible? And what was she going to do about it?

Her phone rang. She shook off her reverie as she pulled it out of her bag and stepped closer to the building she was passing, leaning against it for support. She glanced at the screen; it was Jim. She tried to ignore her disappointment that it wasn't Zach.

"Hey Jim," she said, unable to ignore the fact that he'd called while she was thinking about her feelings for another man. Did he have some kind of radar?

"Hi Em! How's Dublin?" he asked. "It's good to hear your voice, honey. I miss you."

"I...yeah, it's good to hear your voice too," she said, feeling extraordinarily guilty now. Truthfully, she hadn't been pining for him very much. And missing him? No—she'd barely thought about him.

She sighed.

"Em, what's wrong?" he asked. "You sound weird. Like something's on your mind."

"There *is* a lot on my mind, you're right," she said. How much should she admit to him? She didn't know because she really wasn't sure how she was feeling. But there was no need to upset him unnecessarily when she didn't have to. It wasn't like she had already decided to break up with him so she could explore her feelings for Zach.

I haven't decided to do that, right?

Uh, no she hadn't. Okay, she needed to focus.

Why, then, did that idea sound so tantalizing? Yeah, all right, so she had a lot more thinking to do than she realized.

"Emma, seriously, you're starting to worry me now," he pressed. "Is everything okay?"

"No, calm down, Jim, really. It's just, I don't know. I have a lot on my mind, I guess. Tracy hasn't been able to spend much time with me at all, so it's left me to my own devices. Which has pretty much meant that all I do is sit around and think too much."

"About what, Em? Are you…reconsidering our engagement?" he asked.

What was he, a carnival psychic? Honestly.

"Well, yeah, I guess I have been thinking about our engagement a lot. I'm in this transition stage of my life, you know? I'm leaving the college world and heading for a new career, and I'll be getting my own place and…I don't think I want to rush all of that." As the words fell out of her mouth, she realized they were true. Why hadn't she considered this before? She really *did* feel rushed by the engagement. So why hadn't she considered asking him to wait for her?

"Em, there's no rush. We could be engaged for a year or two, if that's what you're asking for. We haven't set a date yet. There's nothing saying we couldn't wait on that for a while."

"Yeah, sure, that sounds good," Emma replied, watching the other pedestrians walking by, all blissfully unaware of the turbulent emotions that were crashing around in her mind.

"Just relax, Em. You're always thinking too much and planning too much," Jim told her, unaware Emma was rolling her eyes in response. "Just lighten up and enjoy Dublin."

"Well, I do have one exciting thing to look forward to. I'm going on a bus tour of Northern Ireland Monday." She was anxious to shift the conversation.

"Great! Tracy's going too, I assume?" he asked.

"Well, she was, but now she can't make it."

Oops.... She hadn't meant to get into this.

"You're not going alone are you? I'm not sure how safe that is," he said, sounding both disapproving and worried. "Maybe you should just cancel."

"No, I'm not going to cancel. I'll be with a bus load of other tourists. Seriously, what's the worst that could happen? I'll get a charlie horse from sitting too much?"

"Why can't you just reschedule and pick a time when Tracy can go?" he continued, sounding annoyed with her now. "It'll be more fun to have a friend along anyway."

"Well, actually, I might have a friend who will come along. I'll have to see if he can make it," she said. Okay, that was stupid. Why had she even brought this up? She couldn't discuss Zach with Jim because she couldn't reveal his identity and break her promise to keep his secret. Plus, it might stir up a whole jealousy thing with Jim that she totally didn't need.

For a moment she seriously considered making the fake static sound and pulling the old, "I think this call is breaking up" thing.

"A guy?" Jim asked. "What guy?"

Okay, yeah, he'd caught that.

"I met a bartender on my first day here. From Texas. Remember? I told you about him."

"I don't remember that," he said, sounding very

suspicious.

"You don't remember because you weren't listening," she reminded him. "A student came into your office, and you brushed me off the phone."

"Well, I'm listening now."

"Okay, well, I made a friend. He's from Texas and it's no big deal. When Tracy said she couldn't come, I offered the ticket to him. He said he'd think about it. Seriously, no biggie." She was trying really hard to sound breezy and not at all like she was covering up anything. Which, of course, she totally was.

"Uh, okay. Emma, I still think you're acting weird. You're sure everything is okay?" he asked again. And he sounded genuinely concerned now, which made her feel terrible.

"Jim, I told you, I've got a lot on my mind and nothing but free time on my hands. I'm on vacation, though. Seriously, what could possibly be wrong? My biggest concern is making sure I don't develop blisters from all the walking I'm doing."

"Okay, whatever you say. I'll drop it, Em. But you know you can talk to me, right? You can always tell me what's on your mind."

"I know that. And I will. If, you know, there's actually anything to tell." She wished they could end this call now. She needed space and time to think about everything that had happened, and everything she was feeling.

"Okay. Well, be careful Monday," Jim said. "Call me when you get back. I'll be worried about you."

"There's nothing to worry about, so please don't," she said, feeling a little annoyed. Honestly, she could take care of herself!

"I'll let you go then. I love you Emma," he told

her.

"You too," she replied. And then, after a pause, she disconnected the call.

She stared at her phone, unseeing for a moment, as she struggled to collect her thoughts. Finally she shoved her phone back in her bag, pushed off from the wall, and continued toward the apartment.

Jim had offered to give her time and space. That's all she needed, right? And she really couldn't make any decisions about her future with him until she saw him again anyway. Being here in Dublin…her thoughts were just too focused on Zach. Thoughts and worries and feelings for him were circling all around her. But it wasn't fair to Jim to assume that any of it meant she no longer loved him or that she no longer had a future with him.

She needed to take the summer to help Zach out and hopefully leave him in a better place than she'd found him. Then she could go home with a clear conscience and give Jim her full attention again. If she got away from this place and freed herself from her ties to Zach—and the idea that she needed to be here helping him—then could she truly figure out what she wanted.

That, then, was the answer, she decided—she couldn't make a single decision about the future until she saw Jim again.

She took a deep breath, feeling lighter than she had since acknowledging her feelings for Zach. She just needed to give both situations—the Jim situation and the Zach situation—some time. Then the answers would reveal themselves.

She was sure of it.

Chapter 17

ZACH HOPPED OUT of the taxi and tossed Euro bills to the driver when they finally reached the hotel. Saying goodbye to Zoe and getting her safely delivered to the airport had taken longer than he realized. But he'd decided he absolutely couldn't pass up the opportunity to spend the day with Emma, stupid idea or not. At the rate he was going, however, he might miss the bus anyway. Emma had texted him the address. He had like a minute to get there.

Luckily, the bus was still parked in front of the hotel. There hadn't been much chance of him not being able to spot it—it was bright green and enormous. It looked like the passengers were already loaded, he realized with mild alarm. The driver—or maybe it was the tour guide—was standing at the door, looking like he was about to climb on, too.

"Wait!" Zach said, jogging over to him. "I'm meeting my friend Emma Crawford here. Did she leave a ticket with you?"

"Oh, yes, you're..." the driver began, looking down at his roster, "...let's see, she told me to cross out the original name and put down Zachary Hiller. That's you?"

"It is," Zach said, pulling out his passport just in case.

"Well, welcome aboard, then!"

The driver stood back to let Zach pass. He

scanned the seats, searching for Emma, and finally spotted her sitting alone near the back, looking anxiously out the window. Was she searching for him? Was she hoping he'd come? He couldn't help being pleased at the thought.

"Is this seat taken?" he asked as he approached.

"Oh!" she said, turning toward him, her brilliant smile sending out rays of happiness that washed over him. "Zach, you came! I'm so happy to see you."

He sat down and looked into her sunny face. *Not show up? I would've walked across burning coals to get here.*

"I wouldn't have missed it for the world," he told her. "I'm dying to know what the Giant Cornball is, and you promised to tell me if I came along today."

"You," she said laughing now. "*You* are the giant cornball. But we, on the other hand, are on our way to see Giant's Causeway. It's going to blow your mind."

"Okay, okay, I give," he said as the bus started to roll forward. "Tell me what we're on our way to see."

"These amazing rock formations on the northeast coastline. It's a World Heritage Site, and I am just dying to see it. It was the thing I got most excited about when I was reading my guidebook and planning my trip." She was bubbling with excitement now.

"Rock formations? It's rock formations that have you this worked up? Formations. Of *rock*," he teased, with a soft smile for her.

"They aren't just any rock formations. They're this series of tiny miracles. They're individual columns all interlocked together. Most of the columns are perfect, neat little hexagons, and the mystery is how were they formed, right? How could nature make something so bizarre and so perfect and so amazing? There are just a ton of them, like…" she paused, pulling out her guidebook to look it up.

Zach smiled down at her as she thumbed through the index to find the description. She was so full of life and excitement over something so simple. It was bubbling out of her in infectious waves. He loved that about her.

"Okay, here it is," she said, unaware of his growing affection. "There are about forty thousand of these little hexagonal columns rising along the edge of the sea. Isn't that amazing?"

She turned away from her book now and was looking up at him expectantly. His breath caught in his throat and his chest tightened. She seemed to be under the same haze of emotion he was feeling, because now they were just gazing at each other. He was entranced, completely under her spell.

"Emma, you should work for the tourism board," he said finally. "I've never heard of this place before, and I already have a feeling it's going to end up being one of my favorite places in the world." His eyes remained locked with hers. He'd been on this bus for less than five minutes and he was already completely lost in her, lost in his feelings for her. This woman had the power to break his heart in a million different ways, yet he was only too happy to let her give it her best try. Because there was no way he'd be able to stay away from her all summer. No use even trying to pretend that was an option.

Unless, of course, she *asked* him to leave her alone...then he'd go without a fight. Because he knew he wasn't good enough for her. Not really. He'd die before he watched her glowing inner light dim in the shadow of all his problems. There was no way he would drag her down with him. *Thank God for Jim*, he thought, and not for the first time.

"We're also going to make a stop in Belfast," she said, breaking their eye contact finally. "We're going to be seeing the political murals on Falls Road. And the site of the Bloody Sunday rebellion."

"You mean like from the U2 song?"

"Yep. Fascinating, right?"

"Really? Wow, okay, that's pretty cool." Zach wondered for the millionth time since Emma had pounced into the middle of his quiet existence why he hadn't bothered to see more of the island up until this point. Would he really have wanted to go home without—as she'd asked him before—seeing a single sheep?

"But we've got a bit of a drive ahead of us before we hit Belfast," she reminded him, "so now you've got all the time in the world to tell me about your story. We haven't talked, we haven't *really* talked, since I put the pieces of the puzzle together and figured out who you were. All I know are the bare facts that I was able to glean from a bunch of news articles online. But what I don't know is what you were thinking and feeling. And what ultimately led you to come to Dublin, of all places." Emma reached over and gave his hand a little squeeze. "So spill it. Tell me everything, okay?"

She went to take her hand back after this innocent bit of gentle encouragement. But Zach, unable to help himself, move fast to thread his fingers through hers. The spark that always burned between them caught into flame in that moment, and she gasped. She looked up at him then, and it seemed to Zach that she was weighing whether or not she should pull away. In the end, however, she squeezed his hand harder than before and laid her head against his shoulder.

"Tell me, Zach," she said quietly. "I have to know."

"Yeah, okay, fine. I don't have any secrets to hold back from you now," he said, even as he realized he couldn't actually tell her about his growing feelings for her. *Anything else but that.* "But you also have to realize that I just don't have answers for some of it, you know? I mean, if I had all the answers, then I wouldn't have gotten myself into this depression, or whatever it is that I'm in."

"Sure, I understand," she replied. "There are limitations to what you can say. Just tell me what you *do* know. Like, start by telling me about that game."

"Well, okay. The thing is, Emma, I was always king of the mountain when I was on that pitching mound, you know? I just absolutely never doubted myself. It's like in all my years of pitching, from the time I was playing tee ball all the way up until that game with the Orioles, it absolutely never even occurred to me to be nervous or to have doubts."

"Zoe told me you were always amazingly confident," she said.

"Yeah, she's right. I was. But it was beyond just confidence I think. It was like I hadn't even thought about the fact that failure was even possible, does that make sense?"

"Sure, I guess so."

"Because of that, I was considered to be really clutch. You must know what that means in the sports world, right Ms. ESPN?"

"Yes, of course. Athletes who are considered clutch are the ones who come up big in the tough moments. The guy who hits a grand slam to win the last game of the World Series. That sort of thing."

He nodded. "Exactly. I was cocky and confident, and because of that, I was totally clutch. I didn't ever let the big moments get to me."

"Okay, I can picture the scene you're setting."

"I was *extra* cocky when Tommy came up to bat that day. Here he was, this rookie who was having this amazing season. He was totally on course to get Rookie of the Year. He was lighting it up every game. And I wanted to show him who was boss, you know? Prove that he still had a lot left to learn if he was going to make it in the Majors. So he came up to bat, and eventually he had worked a 3-2 count, and I decided to teach him a lesson and sweep him back off the plate. So I threw that curveball, but it went wild. It was too high and too fast and he wasn't expecting it, and…I can still hear the thumping sound it made when it connected with his skull. He just…he fell to the ground. And in that moment, it occurred to me he could…well, he might die."

"Z, I'm so sorry," she said, wrapping her other arm around him.

"So that was it. That was the first moment in my life when I realized failure *was* an option. I had just messed up big time. Maybe it was because I'd been so self-important in that moment and so anxious to knock a rookie down a peg that I'd thrown a wild pitch. And maybe, because of my actions and my stupid cockiness, he could die. And Emma, I swear to God, it was like a light switch just shut off in my brain. My confidence just…took off. It left. It abandoned me completely. I was standing there alone on that mound, and the crowd was booing, and my manager Hank was ordering me to take on the next batter and…I just couldn't do it. Not without my confidence to guide me. I didn't feel like myself. It was like I had completely forgotten how to be a competitor."

She squeezed him even harder now, and her empathy was moving through him in waves. It was like being a baby wrapped in a blanket. He also realized that his story wasn't as hard to tell with her holding him like that.

"What happened next?" she prompted.

"I walked off the mound, into the dugout, grabbed all my stuff, and kept going. You know the rest. I broke my contract. Signed the non-competition clause that bars me from pitching for any other team for ten years. I put my stuff in storage. Sold my car. And I just took off. I sort of picked Dublin randomly."

"I'm glad you did," she said, "because it eventually led to me meeting you."

"I'm glad too, Emma. For the first time in a long time, I'm happy about something. I'm happy we're…friends. I'm happy to have met you. It feels good," he admitted, "being able to find a little bit of joy in something finally."

"Well, I'm here to stay, at least for the summer," she told him, pulling back and gently releasing his hand. She reached down to the bag in front of her and pulled out a bottle of water, taking a sip before offering it to him.

He took it, and there seemed to be a certain intimacy in sharing the bottle with her. But then they'd just been holding hands, too, he realized. It was going to take a lot of energy to keep reminding himself she was taken. She wasn't his to be having intimate moments with.

He glanced out the window then and noticed they were traveling past a green meadow dotted with sheep.

"Emma, look! It's the sheep you wanted to see," he said, laughing inwardly that he was so excited to be livestock spotting with her. *Man, I'm sunk*, he thought.

"Ahhh!" she squealed happily. "My first real Irish sheep spotting! Okay, I can die now."

He shook his head and smiled at her. He was glad he came today. And happy he'd told her the ugly details of his story. He was even glad she'd figured out his secret. He was happy about a lot of things these days, which was far more than he would have been able to say even a week ago. He hadn't been lying or even exaggerating when he'd told his sister that being around Emma was helping him.

The real question now, of course, was what effect would it have when she left Ireland to go marry another man? Would it send him even further down into the grips of his panic and depression than he'd already been before? Would it kill him? He didn't know. But nothing, not even the chance that those things could happen in time, could tear him away from Emma in the present. As long as she wanted him around, he was going to be right here by her side.

He'd worry about the future later.

Chapter 18

THE BUS DROPPED them off at the visitor's center, at the top of the steep road that would take them to the Giant's Causeway.

Emma casually took Zach's hand before even considering what she was doing. He laced his fingers with hers and gave her a little smile. It felt so comfortable being with him; holding his hand felt so right.

But it also felt completely wrong, particularly when she thought about Jim. And her guilt ramped up further when she realized thinking about Jim was something she had to make a conscious effort to do. He was far from the top of her mind these days, which totally wasn't fair. It wasn't Jim's fault that he wasn't in Ireland with her. But she had made a promise to him, and she wasn't living up to that promise. She was engaged to him. He trusted her not to be holding hands with someone else. And when she really thought about this, she pulled her hand away from Zach's—even though she didn't really want to.

She could feel Zach studying her profile. The silence between them suddenly felt uncomfortable. What was the right thing to do here? What was the right thing to say? She knew she was leading Zach on, and that wasn't fair, either. She needed to take more care with his feelings. She wasn't available, and it was wrong to act as though she were. Until she saw Jim again and could really figure out how she felt about him and their relationship, she needed to be more careful. More distant. More....

Her internal dialogue screeched to a halt as they rounded the bend and the Giant's Causeway rose spectacularly into view. The columns of rock led from the shore into the water, looking like the interlocking stones of a cottage path. A larger jutting formation was covered with tourists, giving it the busy look of a beehive. To the right, much taller columns spiked into the air, towering above the shore like chimney stacks. It was incredible. All her personal worries and relationship doubts fell away in that moment. Sometimes nature had the power to make her absolutely speechless.

"Oh Z!" she gasped. "It's so amazing!"

"Yeah, it really is," he said, but it seemed like he was looking at her and not the beautiful show nature was putting on in front of them.

She turned and caught his gaze. She was held entranced in that moment. She didn't know if it was the feeling of awe inspired by the scene in front of her or the emotions triggered by this man; emotions she couldn't bring herself to analyze just then. This was such a wonderful day, and she was so grateful to be spending it with Zach. They may not have any sort of future together, but she wasn't going to let her feelings of doubt and guilt about Jim ruin this experience.

"Let's walk out there," she said, battling the urge to take Zach's hand again.

"Okay, sure," he replied, an unidentifiable emotion flickering across his face. Emma wondered what he'd been thinking there.

"Let's go then," she said and started to make her way toward the water. This was easier said than done, though. Each column was a different height, which created an extremely uneven walking surface. In addition to that, the rocks were wet from the water spray. Emma wobbled around until she finally stopped moving and started laughing instead.

"This is crazy hard!" she said. "I feel like I'm going to break my ankle."

"Here, I've got you," Zach replied, reaching over and taking her arm.

She looked up at him quickly, startled as always by the jolt that any small touch from him elicited.

"What are you, part mountain goat?" she asked, trying to cut through the tension that was crackling in the air around them. "How are you not slipping and sliding around, too?"

"Well, I'm a professional athlete. Or, you know, I was," he said softly. "That should give me some sort of added balance, I guess. Here, take my hand."

She hesitated. Hadn't she just finished reminding herself that she was being unfair to *both* Jim and Zach? How did that resolve last less than five minutes? She wanted nothing more than to take his hand. Well, no...that was a lie. She wanted nothing more than to throw her arms around him and kiss him passionately.

Whoa...where did that thought come from?

Straight from her heart, she admitted. She'd already suspected she was developing feelings for Zach. This day was just cementing that truth for her. Tracy had been so right. She should have asked Jim if they could take a break this summer. What had once felt like a happy, comfortable relationship to her now felt like a rope that was holding her back from fully enjoying her time with Zach.

But Zach wasn't really free to explore a

relationship with her, either. Jim was her reason. But Zach had many, and they more complex. He was stuck in the middle of a huge life crisis. Throwing the uncertainty of a new relationship on top of his problems wouldn't be fair at all. Not to either of them.

Zach was still holding out his hand, a quizzical look on his face. Slowly she reached out and took it, letting him pull her toward him.

"Hold onto me," he said, holding her steady. "I'll get you out to that big rock, if that's where you want to go...?"

"Yeah, thanks," she replied, trying to turn off her internal struggle and just enjoy being here. This was an amazing natural wonder that she'd been looking forward to seeing for so long.

They worked together in companionable silence, making their way across the expanse of rocks and then onto the larger stack of columns in the water. When they got to the top, Emma gasped at the view.

"Oh, I need a picture!" she squealed, pulling out her phone and holding it up in the air. "Time for a selfie! Get in the picture, Z! 1…2…3!"

She pulled up the photo then and laughed. She'd managed to take a picture of her ear and Zach's neck.

"You didn't get in the picture, but neither did I. Let's try again," she said, counting off a second time.

On that one, she got her beaming face and nothing of Zach. *For heaven's sake. You can't even tell where I am.*

In the end, she asked another tourist if he'd mind helping out. This time she ended up with a perfect picture of both of them, with the rocks and the water behind them. They both looked so happy in the moment they'd just captured. She gazed at the image for another long moment, blinked back a tear she didn't quite understand, and put her phone away.

Zach was watching her again. She knew she'd been acting weird since they'd gotten off the bus. But how could she explain it to him when she couldn't even explain it to herself?

They made their way back to the shore and wandered toward the towering columns that were a striking contrast to the shorter hexagonal columns they'd been climbing across.

"So explain this place to me," Zach said. "How was it formed and why is it called the Giant's Causeway?"

"There's an old legend that says giants created it as a walkway. I don't remember the details exactly—the story is something about two giants warring with each other and creating a path so they could meet in close quarters and face off. These columns continue under the water, then emerge again on the Scotland side, where one of the other giants supposedly lived." Emma pointed across the water. "So you can see how it must have seemed like a huge walkway to whatever group of people started the legend."

"But how was it really made?"

"Well, if you're just going to pooh-pooh the giants story, it's the result of volcanic activity and the way the lava cooled and contracted," she said. "I think that's what I read in the guidebook."

"Ah, yes, the trusty guidebook," he replied, chuckling.

"Don't mock the powers of the guidebook!" she demanded, feigning outrage. "All the time I spent reading it is what got me interested in this place and ultimately brought us here today, right?"

"Yeah, I guess it did. Want to stop over here and

just look around?"

"Sure," she said, letting him help her over to a dry spot where they could sit.

"So tell me what's going on with you today," he said quietly. "Is everything okay? Have I done something to upset you?"

"What do you mean?" she asked. She wasn't sure which part of her odd behavior he was questioning.

"You pulled back from me as we were walking down here and...I don't know. It just felt like something was up. We're still friends, right?"

"Yes, of course. It just occurred to me that I was sending you all kinds of mixed signals. I'm telling you I'm engaged, but then I'm holding your hand. It just didn't feel like the right thing to be doing to you. Or to Jim."

"I know you're taken, Emma," Zach said, looking out at the water as he talked. "You haven't been unclear about that. In a way, it's a good thing. I'm glad I know that Jim's there between us."

"You are?" Emma wasn't sure if she was feeling relief or heartbreak now.

"I'm a mess, Emma, you know that. I don't have a single thing to offer you right now, and I have no idea if I ever will. But being with you...I don't know how to explain it. It's like you lighten my burden somehow. But I'd be feeling torn and conflicted if you *weren't* taken. I'd be wondering if *I* was the one sending the wrong signals. I'd be afraid I was making promises and implications that I might not ever be able to live up to. This way is perfect, though. You have Jim. And I have your friendship without any added pressures." Zach turned to look over at her now. "But I'd be lying if I said I didn't feel something. I'm not going to pretend about it, not with you. There's a chemistry between us that I think we'd be ridiculous to ignore. And I think it's that chemistry that keeps bringing us both together like magnets."

"Yes, you're right," Emma replied quickly. "I won't lie, either—I feel it too. I think we should probably work to fight it, though. I don't hold hands with my other friends. I don't touch them and actively work to hold myself back from, uh…. Okay, I don't know what I was going to say there."

"I think I probably do, but we can let it remain unsaid," Zach told her. "We both know, Em. Somewhere out there, in another time and place, you could have said it out loud. But right here and right now, all we'll ever have is this summer as friends and friends only. I'll try to respect your wishes and keep better boundaries between us. But please don't say we can't spend more time together. Being with you is like standing in the sunlight for me."

Emma nodded. "I won't push you away, Z. We definitely have this summer. As friends."

"Okay, so we're supposed to use this time to grab lunch," Zach said then, abruptly changing the subject. "Want to go?"

"I don't want to miss a single moment here," she said. "I won't starve to death if I miss a meal."

"All right. Why don't I give you a few more moments alone while I walk ahead and grab us some sandwiches for the road?"

She nodded again. "Here, let me give you some money. I've got to see how many Euros I brought with me."

"Your guidebook might have failed you, Emma," Zach said. "Last I heard, Northern Ireland doesn't use

Euros. I think it might be British pounds here."

"Seriously? Oh no, I don't have any money then." She suddenly felt unbelievably stupid. *How did I not know that?*

"I owe you for the ticket anyway, so it'll be my treat. Just enjoy the view, Emmy," Zach said, reaching over as though he were going to touch her leg. He stopped then, gave her a little shrug, and stood up without making contact.

She felt a deep sense of sadness as she watched him walk away. Their conversation had been a tough one to have, but it had been good for both of them. She wasn't free. He wasn't free. Nothing could ever happen between them.

She stood up then to follow him. The beauty of the scenery had lost its fascination for her.

Chapter 19

"OKAY, SO where are we headed next?" Zach asked after they got back on the bus, and he handed her the bag of sandwiches he'd bought. "Any other stops after Belfast and Giant's Causeway? Back to Dublin?"

He couldn't help hoping there would be more. He wasn't ready for their day to end, even if she *had* basically just told him to keep his hands to himself.

He had wanted to mean those things he'd said, he really did. It *should* be good that she was with Jim. It should be better that there never could be anything more between them. But as much as he knew it was the best thing for Emma—which is why he'd said what he had—he couldn't help but wish things were different. He wished he was his old, confident self. He wished he could just sweep her off her feet and be with her forever. He couldn't lie to himself about these feelings. Every time he saw her, they got deeper and deeper. He was falling hard, like he'd jumped straight off a cliff. But in this particular case, the fall would probably kill him.

She could never be mine. She could never be mine. She could never be mine....

He hoped Jim knew how lucky he was. Emma was amazing. He had adored watching her at the Giant's Causeway. He could see how the natural wonder had moved her. He'd enjoyed her awe-filled reaction even more than he'd enjoyed the scenery, and it had been pretty amazing.

"Next we're going to a rope bridge," she announced, setting aside the sandwich she'd just pulled out and sliding out her guidebook. "It's…called the…okay, here it is. It's called the Carrick-a-Rede rope bridge. For a small extra fee, we can walk out over this crazy bridge suspended high in the air between the mainland and an island. I think it started as a connection to the island for fishermen or something, but now it's a tourist thing. Although maybe fishermen still use it to reach the island? I'm not sure about that part."

"So, in this scenario, we're willingly going to pay someone for the chance to put our lives at risk by walking on a rickety bridge?" he asked. Tourists really paid to do that?

"Yes, that's exactly what we're going to do. Well…at least I want to. I think there's a viewing platform where you can just watch if the bridge itself is not your thing." Emma closed the book and slid it back in her bag.

"Eh, whatever. I'll give it a try," he said, taking the bag back and pulling out his lunch. "So tell me about teaching. You always wanted to be a teacher? Any particular grade?"

"I like the younger grades," she said. "At least I think so, based on my student teaching experience. But anything, really, will make me happy. I just absolutely love kids so much. Jim and I want to have a family. So it's the best of all worlds—I can work full-time with kids, which I love, and then I can have the summers off with my own kids, which will be really important to me. I just always knew this career would fit my life perfectly." She was smiling now.

Okay, he thought, *I'm sorry I brought that topic up.* It had seemed harmless coming out of his mouth, but now he was sitting there picturing Emma and Jim creating a happy home full of children who looked like Emma. The mental picture hurt. A lot. He needed a different topic fast. What would be safe? The weather? Charity work?

Before he could figure out just the right question, however, Emma said, "Do you want them? Kids, that is?"

Only if they have blonde hair and brown eyes, he thought, but he just nodded instead. Topic change. Now. Anything.

"So…what other trips are you scheming up this summer? Are you dragging Tracy all over the island?" There, that was good. Nice, safe topic.

"Oh, I'm glad you asked me that! I've been meaning to see if you're free sometime soon for a road trip? I'm absolutely dying—*dying*—to go to the Cliffs of Moher. But it will be another all-day thing, and I think I want to try doing it via car, which would mean no strict timetables. So, I guess it was the lack of a set itinerary she didn't like—Tracy decided she just couldn't commit to that kind of uncertainty. She's too busy. I guess I could drive it alone, but it'd probably be smarter to have a road-trip buddy along. So what do you think?"

"What's with you and cliffs?" he asked.

"Well, we won't be walking on rope bridges over these particular cliffs, if that's what you're thinking. They're on the northwest coast of Ireland, and the reason I don't want to do the bus trip thing is because I'd kind of like to stop and get some pictures of the landscape. Y'know, be more leisurely about it."

"I can only assume sheep pictures will be

involved?" he teased.

"Of course. You know my obsession with sheep-spotting. So, anyway, no pressure. Just think about it."

"I'd love to," he said, clearly not thinking at all. The chance to spend another day with Emma? There was absolutely no way he could pass that up.

"Oh! Yay! I'm so happy!" she said, her face lighting up. "I'll make all the car rental arrangements and whatever. Just let me know when would be good after you look at your work schedule. It might be smart to pick a time when you have two days off in a row in case we get home late. That way you can sleep in."

"Yeah, sure, I'll check my schedule," he said. "But I kind of think I'm not off again until Sunday. I tend to have Sundays and Mondays off. So that would probably work."

He'd be seeing Emma again next weekend. He couldn't wait. Spending time with her was too enticing to deny himself. But on the other hand, the more time they spent together, the deeper and deeper he was going to fall. He had a feeling this summer would be over before he knew it, and he'd be left standing in Dublin alone, waving goodbye to his heart.

He blinked and tried to shake that thought away. Yes, he knew the day would come, but that didn't mean he had to face it just yet.

The bus stopped then. Great, he thought—they were at the death-defying bridge. He tossed the rest of his sandwich in the bag and gathered up the garbage. It was time to go do this crazy thing.

The hike to get to the bridge was maybe a half mile or so. They went along in silence, and Zach couldn't decide if they'd both run out of topics or if maybe Emma was having to work as hard as he was to not join their hands together. In the end, he shoved his hands in his pockets. Respecting the boundaries she'd set wasn't going to be fun, he reminded himself.

When they finally got to the bridge, they found there was a bit of a line before they could cross. The sky and the water were both clear and blue, and Emma pulled out her phone and snapped some more pictures.

"Are you sure you want to do this?" he asked when he noticed the bridge swaying as each person walked across.

"Oh, it's no big deal. The rope is just for show. It's reinforced with steel, and they tested it to ten tons of pressure or something. So, seriously, baby elephants could walk across."

"Oh, okay, no problem. You totally convinced me with your rock-solid, baby-elephant argument," he said, which made her laugh out loud.

When it was Emma's turn, Zach couldn't believe how brave she was. She set off across the bridge without a moment's hesitation. He loved how strong and independent she was.

She was almost across when the guides told him he could start. *Here goes nothing*, he thought.

He took his first couple steps onto the bridge. The water looked so far away. *Okay, maybe I shouldn't be looking down.* He saw that Emma was just about to step off the other side, but then she seemed to lose her balance. He could feel panic bubbling inside his chest as he watched her wobble and take an awkward half-step to the side as the bridge swayed. He couldn't watch anymore. Before he gave any thought to the wisdom of what he was doing, he sprinted over to her.

She'd just stepped off the bridge and into the grass when he got there.

"Whoa, that was…wait, how'd you get over here so fast?" she asked.

His heart was racing; a thrumming mixture of adrenaline and panic fueling him as he tried to catch his breath.

"Emma…I…" he couldn't say it. He'd thought she was going to fall right in front of him. He had never been so scared in his life.

"Zach, what?" she asked. "Are you okay? Wait, did you think I was going to fall? Did you race across the bridge to save me?"

He still couldn't put words to his feelings, so he just nodded.

"Oh, geez, I really scared you," she said. "I'm sorry, Z. Come here...." She opened her arms wide, and he walked into them without a fight. He didn't even take notice of the other tourists standing around them. She was hugging him tight, her head against his chest. And his arms were wrapped around her shoulders. Thank God she was okay.

Finally, he pulled away just enough to look into her sweet face. He needed to calm down before he did something he'd regret. But he couldn't resist stealing this one moment to look at her.

She was looking back at him just as intently. She seemed to be searching for answers he just wasn't able to give her. He could feel her warm breath on his face as he continued to look into her eyes. But his gaze couldn't help but be drawn down to her mouth. It was so inviting. So close.... He knew he was waging an internal war with himself. *I can't kiss her...I can't.* He really couldn't…but then, suddenly, her lips parted and she leaned even closer. Slowly, gently, she reached up until their lips almost met. One more small movement from either of them and they'd be together. He wanted to kiss her more in that moment than he'd ever wanted anything.

"Emma?" he asked, making his lips barely brush hers. He heard her gasp.

Then their guide announced, "Tour bus is heading out soon. You need to re-cross the bridge now."

Emma froze, looked back into his eyes, and slowly pulled away.

"I'm so sorry," she said.

"No, that was all my fault," he countered, dropping his arms to his sides. "*I'm* sorry." He had been seconds away from kissing her...someone who was engaged to someone else. *What am I doing?*

A couple of teenage boys from their tour group walked up to take their turns for the journey back across the bridge.

"Dude, get a room," one of them said.

Emma laughed then, and the spell between them was finally broken. Zach smiled back at her. They got in the line then and eventually crossed back without further incident.

On the return hike to the bus, Zach felt himself torn. Should he never bring that almost-kiss up again? Or did he owe her an apology? Really, it had been less than an hour or two ago that she'd asked him to respect her personal space. He'd responded by doing absolutely everything *except* leave her alone.

Okay, he decided, he had to say something. As awkward as that conversation might be.

"When you lost your balance back there, I...I don't know," he began, "I lost my mind. I just took off like I'd been shot out of a cannon. If someone had been timing it, I might have just qualified for the

Olympics. Seriously, I...that just shaved about twenty years right off my life."

"It really was nothing, though," she told him. "Honestly, Zach, I just sort of wobbled. But I'm so sorry it scared you."

"I wasn't trying to get you to apologize, I just wanted to explain why I wasn't thinking clearly back there. I'm so sorry, Emma. You just got done asking me to give you space, and there I was trying to...well, you know what I wanted to do." He didn't want to talk specifically about the near-kiss too much. It would just remind him how much he wished he really could have done it, and with no regrets, no interruptions, and no problems between them. He sighed then, not even realizing he'd done so out loud.

"It wasn't all your fault Z," she said. "Please don't think I'm mad. The truth is it felt really good...too good. I wanted it, too. But I am absolutely not doing right by Jim. So I can't let myself...feel..."

Zach didn't say anything more; there was no use. There could never be anything between them. He knew he should stop tempting himself. And yet, even with all that had just happened, he knew there absolutely was no way he'd be the one to back out of the upcoming trip next week.

No way.

Chapter 20

EMMA COULDN'T FALL ASLEEP that night. She had way too many issues battling each other for her attention. The thoughts that seemed to be winning the war were mostly about Zach and the wonderful day they'd spent together—and, of course, the kiss they'd come only half a breath away from sharing.

She thought about how much she loved being with him, and about how right he'd been with the magnet analogy that he'd used earlier. She totally did feel like she was having to fight against invisible forces pulling her toward him. And obviously it was getting harder and harder to keep that fight going and to keep resisting.

She was also thinking about Jim, and about how *little* she'd been thinking about him. She really was suffering from a bad case of "out of sight, out of mind" when it came to her fiancé. And because of that, she knew she was being unfair to him. She might not have been technically unfaithful, but it really was a mere technicality. If there had been nothing standing in between her and Zach, she'd probably be with him right at this moment.

So, okay, how had trying to turn her thoughts to Jim ended in a vision of her spending the night with Zach seconds later? It's like she was the worst fiancée ever.

She needed to work hard to analyze the situation. She figured she should probably start by splitting the worries in two groups—her Zach worries and her Jim worries. She had to remind herself that even if she decided to break up with Jim, that didn't automatically mean she'd be in a relationship with Zach. Not only was it impossible because of the problems he was dealing with right now, but it also wasn't good for her. She'd been with Jim for six years. She needed a little time on her own to rediscover who she was and what she wanted.

So there it was—the Jim issue involved the question of whether or not she still wanted to spend the rest of her life with him. And the Zach issue was less about them being together and more about how she could continue to help him while she was here. Period. They were two separate issues, not at all intertwined with each other. She could control whether she remained engaged to Jim. And she could control whether she was trying to help Zach. What she couldn't control were the other issues; for example, she couldn't "fix" Zach or magically make his problems disappear. Obsessing about why she had so much electricity with Zach wasn't helping his situation, and it certainly wasn't helping her figure out her own life. It was just making the situation more confusing.

Zach.... As hard as it was not to think about him, she needed to. She wanted to keep helping him; maybe even find a way to help him even more. But Jim needed to be her first priority.

It seemed like an actual, physical feat to force Zach out of her mind. She was envisioning the way he had looked when she'd stumbled off the bridge and right into his arms. He looked terrified in that moment. He actually ignored any thoughts of his own safety because he'd been worried about her. He'd flown to her side like Superman outpacing a train. And then she'd felt like the train plowed right into her. She looked up into his face and watched his eyes wander down to her lips. She had been the weak one then, the one to press forward and almost make the kiss a reality. Their lips had even brushed together slightly, like the fluttering of a butterfly's wings. She'd wanted to kiss him then and never let him go.

Dammit! She'd done it again! She attempted to think only about Jim, and this time she'd ended that futile exercise with thoughts of exploring Zach's mouth with her own and….

Okay, okay…obviously she was falling for another man. A man who wasn't her fiancé. She wasn't being fair to *anyone* here. Yes, she'd told herself she couldn't make any decisions about Jim until she saw him again. But the honest truth was becoming clearer with each painful moment that passed—she really didn't want to see Jim again. Certainly not in the way that a fiancée who'd been separated from the man she loved for a whole summer *should*.

At that moment, she reached a decision. She was going to break things off with Jim. And at the end of the summer when she saw him again, she'd give him his ring back. Yes, it'd been six years. She'd spent *six whole years* with him. It almost seemed like a lifetime ago. But she absolutely owed him the courtesy of telling him in person.

She was startled out of her reverie by the sound of her phone vibrating. She glanced at it and saw that it was Jim. *Huh? Now why is he…oh shoot.* She'd forgotten to call when she got home from the bus trip. She'd promised she would.

"Hi, Jim," she said as soon as she answered, feeling even guiltier than she had before. "I am so sorry. I realized when I saw your name on the screen that I never called."

"I was worried about you!" he said. "What happened?"

"Seriously it just slipped my mind. We got back, I went to bed, and I just never even thought about it."

"You said 'we' just then," he pointed out quickly. "Did Tracy change her mind and go with you?"

Oops....

"Uh, no. Remember I told you I had asked my new friend to go with me since Tracy couldn't?" She really, *really* didn't want to be having this conversation. How was she going to act normal with Jim the rest of the summer? She could barely bring herself to talk to him at all without just blurting everything out.

"Emma, what is going on?" Jim replied, sounding exasperated. "Who is this guy? I feel like there's something happening here that you're not telling me."

"Uh, yeah, okay, there is something, but it's just not my secret to tell you. Texas, the, uh, bartender, he's someone who's trying to hide from the public eye." There, that sounded reasonable, right?

"You mean like a drug lord would?" Jim sounded sarcastic now.

"No, I mean like someone who'd gotten a pinch of bad press. Nothing big, really. We were talking and he just sort of confided that in me. Seriously, it is totally not a big deal. But again, it's not my secret to tell. I was able to verify his story online, so I know that I'm totally safe. I'm not striking up a friendship with a crazy psycho who's going to make a bathrobe out of my skin."

"That's all that's going on?" he pressed again. "There's nothing else you want to tell me?"

"No, seriously. I made a friend. I didn't think I needed to send out a formal announcement." She instantly regretted being so snarky with him. None of this was his fault, after all. Why was she acting like it was?

"Okay, fine. So how was the bus trip with the tax evader?"

"He's not…okay, whatever. The bus trip was great. Seeing the political murals in Belfast was so unreal. It was like standing in the middle of a history book. Unbelievably moving." She was thankful to be on safe ground now. "And we walked across a rope bridge, which was just amazing. It's really narrow, and you can see forever from up there. You can also feel the bridge give and sway as you walk. It was like being on the tightrope at a circus."

"That sounds terrifying," Jim said. "Weren't you scared at all?"

"Well, sure, of course," Emma replied, trying to make a casual laughing sound. "I just charged out there and didn't even really think about it until I was halfway across. So yeah, it was a little scary, especially when I lost my balance for a moment at the end. Scared the daylights out of…myself."

"I still think you're hiding something from me Emma," Jim said, his tone increasingly demanding. "Just tell me. I'm a big boy. What is going on? Are you falling for this guy?"

"I like him, Jim. A lot. We had a really fun day today. I haven't even told you yet about my favorite part, the Giant's Causeway. It was amaz—"

"Don't change the subject Emma," Jim said sharply.

"Fine, Jim, yes. Yes. I've been thinking and re-evaluating things. I told you that in our last conversation. I have a lot of free time that I just haven't had since I was a kid. I'm not focused on school anymore, and my thoughts haven't turned to my career yet. So I'm trying to decide where I want to go from here. What you're hearing in my voice is inner turmoil. But it's nothing I want to continue to discuss in the middle of the night over the phone, so back off." She knew her irritation at his line of questioning was beginning to flood out of her now, and she didn't really care all that much. "I just need some time to myself to keep thinking."

"I'm sorry, Emma. I don't mean to attack you here. But it's a little hard to sit back and ignore what's happening. I know you're pulling away from me. I can feel it. You don't call. You don't text. And when we do talk, you're defensive and vague and weird. Every other sentence out of your mouth is about some guy whose name you won't even give me. So I'm sorry if you've caught me in the act of being upset that my fiancée is pushing me away."

"I'm sorry, too, Jim," she said, suddenly weary. "I am. But this isn't a conversation for the phone. Or the middle of the night. I'm exhausted right now and much more likely to say something I don't mean. So please, just say goodnight and let me go."

"Fine, Emma. I'll drop it," he replied. She could hear the same weariness in his voice that she was feeling in herself. "Goodnight."

"Goodnight."

She ended the call and put the phone back on the

bedside table.

Well, gee, that went well. Clearly she hadn't gotten her master's degree in professional lying. She'd now succeeded in putting Jim on full red alert. She'd wanted to break up with him in person, but maybe dragging this out over the rest of the summer was even crueler than ending it long distance. She needed to think about that some more, too.

She wished she could talk to Zach right now. Talking to him was so easy. But obviously he wouldn't hold the answers about how to best break Jim's heart. No, this was a road she was going to have to travel alone. And when it was all over, that's exactly what she'd be—alone.

And despite dreading how she was going to hurt her fiancé, she couldn't help but be happy that she'd have some time on her own. She hadn't been lying about that to Jim. This was a huge transition for her. She needed a bit of time to concentrate on her career and how she wanted the rest of her life to play out. The thought of standing alone and deciding on her future without any outside influences was liberating. She'd been part of a couple for a really long time. Being alone for a while might be just what she needed.

She rolled over then and looked at her phone again. It was just after two-thirty. She needed to find a way to turn her brain off or she wasn't going to get any sleep at all.

She laid down, settled the covers over her arms, and tried to push all of these swirling thoughts out of her mind. Nothing could be settled tonight. Getting rest was the most important priority in the moment.

She finally drifted off, but visions of Zach floated and fluttered through her dreams. Those magnetic forces Zach had talked about were working on her again.

Even when she was asleep, it seemed, her mind couldn't push him away.

Chapter 21

THE WEEK HAD DRAGGED BY so slowly, but Zach kept firm in his resolve to respect Emma's wishes and stay away from her. She needed to be focusing on her fiancé and having fun on her vacation. What she didn't need was to figure out the extent of his feelings for her. It would just make her feel sorry for him.

Because he'd finally admitted the full truth to himself—he wasn't just falling for Emma. He'd already *fallen*, past tense. He loved her. He was totally, completely, goofily in love with her. He wanted to write her sappy poems and send her mixtapes.

He was pathetic. Right smack in the middle of all his problems, he chose now to fall in love harder than he'd ever fallen before. And with a woman he could never have. That was some seriously great timing.

But who knew how his mind was working lately anyway? Maybe he'd fallen for her *because* she was completely out of his reach. Maybe it was just another in a long line of ways he was finding to torture himself these days. Maybe it didn't have a thing to do with how beautiful she was. Or how smart and independent and funny and brave and….

Okay, okay, so it wasn't just his mind playing tricks on him. He loved Emma for exactly who she was. He loved her because she was the kind of woman who'd happily dive into a summer-long adventure even if it meant exploring a whole country alone. He loved her because she found more joy in a pile of weirdly shaped rocks than he had found in anything since he'd left baseball. He just loved *her*. And he wanted desperately to tell her all of these things.

He let that last thought roll around in his brain for a while. What would such a moment look like? What would happen if he just bared his soul to her? She already knew the really bad stuff about him. So she'd know precisely what she'd be getting if she took a chance on him. And there was no getting around the fact that it *would* be a risk for her. He couldn't promise her that he'd ever be able to reclaim his old life.

But maybe she'd want to stay here with him and help him try. Maybe she already loved him back. Or at least maybe she *could*, one day. He'd never know for sure if he didn't take a chance, right?

So…what? Was he actually pondering the idea of laying his heart out in front of her?

Yeah, he was. Maybe she'd leave Jim for him. Crazier things had happened, right? And, really, what was the absolutely worst reaction she could have? She could laugh at him, he guessed. Or give him a really sad, pitying look. She could ask him to please leave and never come back. That would rip his heart right out of his chest. But that's what would happen at the end of the summer anyway if he said nothing. She'd pack up, probably give him a sweet little pep-talk about working to solve his problems, then go back to Jim, and that would be the end of it.

So either way, he was facing having his heart smashed. He may as well tell her how he felt and give himself a tiny chance at happiness. It was probably about a one-percent chance at best. But still, it was a chance. He certainly couldn't let her leave without trying. That much he knew for certain.

He grabbed his phone, wallet, and keys. *Maybe a jacket, too, in case this trip actually happens.* Emma had never said what time he should come over this morning for their drive to the west coast, but it was already almost nine. Surely she wanted to get moving soon. She had texted him earlier in the week about the car rental, but he hadn't heard anything since.

Okay, so he was doing this. He'd go over there, lay his cards out on the table, and then, with any luck, he'd find out she shared his feelings. Either way, the trip would probably get cancelled. But he didn't care. Now that he'd made the decision to tell her, he wanted to do it as soon as possible. He'd never be able to sit in the car silently, all day long, without blurting it out. May as well give her the chance to back out of the trip and run away screaming before they got too far down the road.

He was so excited at the thought of seeing her again, he actually jogged to her apartment. It would take everything inside to rein back his feelings the minute she opened the door. It had been a long week without seeing her. More than anything, he just plain missed her company. He couldn't wait.

By the time he reached the apartment, he had worked himself into a giddy, lovesick cloud. And still he wondered—why? Hadn't he estimated that the odds of walking away with his heart still beating in his chest were extremely low?

No—even that thought didn't wipe the silly smile off his face as he knocked on the door. He absolutely couldn't wait a moment longer. He heard her footsteps approaching the door. This was it, this was it, this was....

A man.

Yes, a man had answered the door and was now staring back at him, a piercing gaze studying Zach from behind thick black glasses. He was a few inches shorter, and his brown hair and short beard were both neatly combed. And Zach felt exactly the way Emma likely felt when she met Zoe, not knowing she was just his sister. In that instant, the goofy smile fell off his face.

"Oh, you must be the tax-evading drug mule," the man said.

Huh?

"You're...Jim?" Zach asked.

"Nailed it on the first try," Jim said, not offering to let him come in.

"Who is it?" Emma said, walking up behind him. The shock in her face was obvious when she realized who it was.

"Z!" she said. "What are you doing here?"

"Uh...." he started, feeling like the world's biggest fool now. Had he really been all but skipping his way over here to tell her he loved her? And she wasn't exactly looking thrilled to see him, he couldn't help notice. At all. "I thought you wanted...."

"It's Sunday, isn't it?" Emma interrupted. "I totally forgot. Oh, speaking of which, Jim this is my friend Z, the one I was telling you about."

"No, the one you *weren't* telling me about," Jim said. *Okay, so what's going on here?* Zach wondered as his mind swirled. He'd just been served a big plate of uncomfortable with a side of awkward sauce.

"Z, I'm sorry, I totally lost track of the day. I meant to text you and tell you that my plans had changed. Jim surprised me yesterday out of the blue." She sounded a little weird. Overly chipper or something. Well, that probably made sense. The love of her life had surprised her with an unexpected visit. Of course she'd lost track of the time. They'd probably been having nonstop sex since Jim arrived.

Zach wanted to kick himself now. Thoughts like that were just going to add to his pain. Considering he was drowning in nothing but despair at the moment, he didn't need to pile on any extra layers.

"Oh geez, that's my phone," Emma suddenly announced. "Jim, do you mind checking who it is? I'll just say goodbye to Z."

Jim gave Zach a hard look before walking back into the apartment.

"Zach, I am so sorry," Emma said quietly. Her super-happy look was gone, and in its place was one of complete torture. It was like he was having a conversation with the comedy and tragedy masks. "He just showed up, and he and I have a lot to talk about. So I lost track of what day it was. Obviously, I never went to pick up the rental. I'm so sorry. Can I get a rain check?"

"I...yeah, of course. Enjoy your visit with your fiancé," he managed to choke out. How could she not hear the sound of his heart shattering, too? It was roaring in *his* ears.

"It's Tracy," Jim called out, then returned with the phone. "She wants to talk to you."

"Oh, sure, okay," Emma said awkwardly, taking the phone from him. "See ya, Z."

"Yeah, see ya," he replied, trying to match her breezy tone as she walked away. Then he turned to leave, but Jim's words stopped him.

"I don't know what's going on here," Jim said while Zach remained frozen with his back turned. "But she's taken. She's my fiancée and she's going to be my wife. But even if that weren't true, she's too good for you. She won't tell me what your big secret is, but I know you're hiding out from something bad that you've done. Emma is pure and beautiful and good. She doesn't need a criminal in her life. She deserves better."

Zach turned back slowly.

"You got it half right," Zach said, nodding. "I'm not a criminal. I represent no danger to Emma at all."

"So which part did I get right?" Jim asked. "The part where I deduced you're trying to be with her?"

"No, the part where you said I'm not good enough for her."

Jim closed the door without saying anything further.

Great, Zach thought as he walked away. He'd managed to miss an option when he'd been listing off the worst-case scenarios earlier today, but he *had* managed to walk right into it. Not only was Emma never going to be his, but now she was getting to spend time here in Dublin with her future husband. The one-day father to all those kids she wanted so desperately to have. And on top of everything else, the guy was kind of a jerk.

Then again, he probably wasn't being totally fair. If Emma was in his life, he wouldn't be thrilled to have some other guy show up at her door, either. Jim had reacted exactly the way a man would react if he felt threatened. But he didn't need to worry about it. Zach was no real threat to Jim and his relationship with Emma.

As he walked home, he thought again about how he'd been planning to pour his pathetic heart out to her. Really, what had he been thinking? Emma was bright, happy sunshine, and he was in a dark, bottomless pit. How could he be so selfish? He couldn't drag her down here with him. Never. Not unless he figured out a way to get over his fears and issues on his own. And since he hadn't managed to get anywhere with that goal in the past two years, things weren't looking so great for his future, either.

It was over, he admitted to himself. The silly little fairytale he'd been dreaming up for himself and Emma was nothing but an illusion. A trick of his depressed mind. Emma was marrying Professor Jim. Even if she wasn't, she deserved better than him and all his problems.

So there, now everything is back where it should be, he told himself. Emma had Jim, and Zach had…Dublin. He had a couple days off and then he'd have a week of shifts at the pub. That was his life now, and that was his future.

When he got back to his apartment, he locked the door tight behind him. His biggest immediate concern now was whether he should spend the next two days laying on the couch or on the bed. He had a broken heart to deal with, and he knew he was in for a bumpy ride.

Couch first, then the bed, he thought as he flopped down on the former, letting his shoes fall onto the floor.

He missed her already. It was going to be a really long week.

Chapter 22

"SO THAT WAS HIM, huh? Your super close friend?" Jim asked, making air quotes around the last word the moment Emma was off the phone.

"Yeah, Z's my friend. We had fun on the bus trip. There, is that what you came here to find out? Did you show up because you decided you missed me or because you wanted to check up on me and fact-check my story?"

She was so torn. When Jim showed up on her doorstep, her first emotion had been irritation—which was a pretty good sign that she'd made the right decision about wanting to break things off with him. She hadn't been happy to see him or eager to show him around Dublin. She'd just been annoyed. Because it felt precisely like he *was* checking up on her. They had gone out for dinner, and then she'd made a flimsy excuse about not wanting Tracy to worry about her just to get out of going back to Jim's hotel with him. The timing hadn't seemed right, to just dump him the minute she saw him. But now she was tied into knots, not knowing when the best time was.

Then Zach showed up at her door, looking so…what? What had she seen on his face? She wasn't sure. He certainly looked like he was in pain, seeing her there with Jim. But hadn't he gotten done telling her, just a few days ago, that knowing she had Jim in her life was helping him? That it was actually a *good* thing?

Maybe saying that and actually seeing her and Jim together were two different things. She knew she owed Zach a huge apology after Jim finally left town. She couldn't believe she'd forgotten to text him and warn him not to come, either. That had been so awkward and painful. And since she was the world's worst actress, both men had surely seen right through her attempt at breezy cheerfulness.

"I miss you, Emma," Jim was saying as she tried to unravel everything in her mind. "I love you. I want to spend the rest of my life with you. But I'm standing here looking at a woman who didn't seem all that thrilled to see me. A woman who isn't wearing my ring on her finger. A woman who refused to come to my hotel and spend the night with me. We're obviously in the middle of some sort of relationship crisis. Just tell me what I'm fighting against here. I'm completely in the dark. You've got to open up to me."

Emma nodded. "Okay, yes, you're right. I will. Let's sit down." She set herself on the couch sideways so she could face him. *This is it,* she realized. *The perfect time to do this is now.* "It's exactly like I've been telling you on the phone. I've had a lot on my mind since I got here. It's like coming here and having this opportunity to stand apart from my life has given me the ability to view it better. I was just too close to it. But here in Dublin, clear across the ocean, I can see what I couldn't see before."

"And what's that?" Jim asked. "What are you seeing?"

"I'm seeing that I feel rushed by the engagement."

"We dated six years. Tectonic plates move faster," Jim countered. "Seriously, how is that rushing?"

"I went from being a kid living in my parents'

house to being a kid living at college and exclusively dating you. Now we're talking about getting married. So I'd be going from my parents' house to the dorm to my married home. I want some time in between those things."

"I'm not trying to sound sarcastic here, but hello? You're spending a whole summer alone. Isn't that feeding your need for space?" He sounded exasperated and more than a little patronizing.

"Not to be sarcastic back, but how much space are you giving me right now?" Emma asked, trying unsuccessfully to dial back her snippy tone. She didn't deal well with condescension. Or being nudged, for that matter. "Pressuring me on the phone wasn't quite enough, so you had to come do it in person?"

"I'm sorry, Emma," Jim said, taking her hand. "I can see now that I made a huge mistake in coming here. I didn't do it to be a jerk, though. I did it because the woman I love is going through something I don't understand. You wouldn't open up to me about it, so I got on a plane. I had to know what was going on."

"You're right, I have been shutting you out. But not on purpose and not to hurt you. I've just been trying to decide the right path for me to take. And the good news, I guess, is that I've finally reached some decisions."

"It's okay, I'll wait for you," Jim told her. "I'll give you the space you need. Take this summer, and I'll back off. I just want you to be happy."

"I don't think that's fair to you, Jim. I don't want to leave you hanging on the line like that."

"Don't do this, Emma. I know what you're about to say, and I...I just don't want to hear it."

"Jim, I'm sorry, but I have to. I have to be fair to

you. I want you to know that I loved you, I really did. But sometimes people just grow apart. I think that happened for me. I just…went off in a direction I never expected. And now I need to be alone the rest of this summer and to figure out what's right for me."

"You're saying you don't love me at all anymore?" he said, dropping her hand. "You want to be with that low-life, don't you? That's really what this is all about, right? That guy. I can see in your eyes that I'm right. You're falling for the tax evader." He stood up and went to the other side of the room.

"Yes, I'm attracted to him. But I'm not just walking into a relationship here. Have you heard nothing I just got done saying? I'm going to spend the summer unattached. I need to figure out where my head's at. I need to know how I could go from saying yes to your proposal all the way to wanting to end things in the span of just a few weeks. How did it get to this?" Emma felt the first tickle of tears forming, making her voice catch. "I didn't set out to hurt you, Jim. I didn't. I shouldn't have accepted your proposal, but it just seemed easy and natural, and I never sat down and asked myself if it was what I really wanted. I guess this time alone showed me that I should have asked those questions first. I'm sorry."

"Don't cry, Emma," Jim said, coming back and sitting down again. "Come here."

She leaned into his arms then and cried. She wasn't even sure exactly what she was crying about. Mourning the death of a relationship that had been part of her life for a really long time? That she could never have those things with Zach? Maybe a little of both?

When her tears finally subsided, the silence heavily blanketed the room and highlighted the distance between them. She wasn't sure what was left to say.

"When's your flight home?" she asked finally.

"Can't wait to get rid of me?" he said, a sad but teasing tone to his voice.

"No, of course not. Would you like to see some of Dublin while you're here? Or would that be too hard? I'm not sure what the right thing to do is anymore," she confessed.

"You could say you've changed your mind again. You could say this can just be a temporary break and not a permanent split."

"No, I'm sorry, Jim. I don't want to drag things out or have to put either one of us through this conversation again. It's too hard, and I'm convinced that this is the right thing for me."

"I guess I just want to say goodbye, then," Jim said. "Pretending to enjoy myself while sightseeing would be too painful."

"Sure, of course. Will you stay on or are you going to change your flight?"

"I don't know, Emma. But don't worry about it. I can take care of myself."

"I know you can," she said, nodding. "And I know you're going to be okay with all of this eventually. One day you'll look back and see that I did the right thing here. We weren't supposed to be together forever. You'll agree with me someday."

"Can I have your promise on that?" he said, a weak smile on his face as he stood up again. "So this is goodbye forever, I guess."

"No," Emma replied, standing up too. "I have to give the ring back when I get home."

"Just do it now," he said, perplexed.

"I didn't bring it here. I was afraid to travel with it.

It's back with the rest of my stuff in my parents' house."

"That tells me a lot, Emma," he said. "It kind of makes it seem like you knew before you ever got here that you didn't want to be wearing it. And in a funny way it almost helps, knowing that. It makes this all seem less out of the blue to me. Less about the bartender."

"I don't want to talk about him or any of this anymore," she told him, feeling more frustrated than ever. Why couldn't he just accept her reasons at face value? "I'll call you when I get back. I promise."

"Sure. Great," he said, walking to the door and opening it. "Goodbye, Emma. Enjoy the rest of your summer."

"Goodbye," she said softly.

She locked the door as soon as he was gone and then collapsed on the couch, completely drained.

Breakups were never fun, but that one had been especially painful. It was extra bad partly because they'd been together for so long, and the memories of him would always be inextricably tied together with her college years. Closing the door on your first serious adult love was extremely bittersweet. It was also bad because he'd seen through the lies she'd been telling, both to him and to herself. Yes the breakup was something she wanted just for herself. But yes, it also had something to do with Zach. She couldn't lie about that anymore.

She was falling in love with Zach. Or maybe she was done falling and was fully there. And now that she was single, she had an overwhelming desire to see him. Maybe even to tell him.

She tried calling, but his phone was off. So she sent him a text instead.

Sorry about before. **Call me**, she wrote before setting the phone back down.

She leaned back and closed her eyes. *There, I've done it.* She'd broken up with Jim. She wasn't being hit by any huge doubts or crashing waves of remorse. Maybe she'd feel differently after a night of sleep, but as of right now, all she felt was relief. It felt *right*. Breaking up had been incredibly painful, but mostly because she knew she was hurting him. Not because she had any regrets about doing it.

She glanced at her phone, but it was still dark and silent. Where was Zach? She wanted to see him. She wanted to make plans to reschedule their trip. She wanted to apologize to him for cancelling it at the last minute.

And mostly, she wanted to tell him she was free.

Then she sighed—because she knew she couldn't do that. She could never do that. Zach had specifically said he didn't know if they could be friends if she became single again. He'd said knowing she was available would make their friendship impossible. And she couldn't let that happen. With the time she had left in Dublin, she wanted to do absolutely everything in her power to help Zach. But she couldn't do anything at all for him if he pushed her away.

Okay, so that was it. As far as Zach could know, she and Jim were still happily engaged and planning their future together. Fine. But if she was really going to pull off this ruse, she needed to be strategic about it. And she needed to find actual ways to help him. Walking away at some point would be impossible if she hadn't first done everything she could to help him heal.

She glanced back at her phone again. Still silent. This was going to be incredibly difficult to pull off, but

she had to do it.
 It was all she could do for Zach now.

Chapter 23

ZACH WAS NOT doing well. And that was a kind way of putting it. He'd been spiraling deeper and deeper into a self-pitying paralysis ever since he'd gone over to Emma's...and found out Jim was in town.

It shouldn't have been a huge shocker that she was with her fiancé that day. She hadn't exactly been lying to him about her future. No, he'd known from the very start of their friendship that she was completely unavailable.

He was the dummy who'd let himself forget that vital piece of information. He allowed himself to spend more and more time with her, even though he'd known he was getting far too close. He'd known fairly early on that it was driving a tanker truck off a cliff when it came to the way he felt about her and the very miniscule possibility that it could end well.

So he'd known this day was coming—but knowing and having it actually open the door and kick you in the teeth were two different things.

What he had now was just an average, mopey, run-of-the-mill case of heartache, right? Well, okay...maybe it was an unusually severe case. But his real problem was that it was so much more. The heartache was igniting a firestorm of self-doubt and worry and anxiety. It was all the things he'd been suffering through for two years, only someone had dumped gasoline on those feelings and then lit a match. The net result was that he was feeling as bad as he'd felt when the Curveball Incident first happened, times infinity.

Pity Party, table for one, please.

The cherry on top was that he was bogged down with an extra layer of regret and what-ifs. Like, what if he could have gotten his act together any time during the last two years? Maybe he would have been strong enough to sweep Emma off her feet. He felt like he was sitting inside a prison cell of his own making. And his sentence was to sit helplessly while the woman he loved happily married another man without seriously considering him as an alternative. Because, honestly, in his current situation he was absolutely no one's good alternative to anything.

Yeah, he was a super great catch. He'd barely gotten out of bed all week. He'd turned on his phone long enough to call the pub and tell them he needed the week off. Since he'd never taken a day for anything in two years, they didn't have any problem with the short notice. He told them he was sick. Which was sort of true. He was sick of feeling like this.

He'd noticed he had some texts, but he assumed they were from his family. He'd call them back soon enough. Just one or two more days of swimming around in his big bowl of heartbreak soup, and then he'd get back to them and head back to the pub. Even he was tired of listening to his brain complain about his problems. Just a little longer and he figured he could force himself out into the world again.

There was a knock at the door just then.

Okay, he seriously hadn't thought the world was going to come to *him*. He couldn't even remember the last time he'd showered. He looked—and smelled—like a wild animal. He ignored the knock. Probably just the mailman or something.

"Zach? Are you there? It's Emma."

He froze with indecision. Should he wait for her to go away?

"Zach please! If you're there, just answer the door." She sounded frantic. "I'm so worried about you. Please. Open this door or I swear I'm getting an axe."

For heaven's sake.... He walked over to the door but didn't open it.

"Em, please don't chop my door down," he called to her. "I'll never get my security deposit back."

"Oh please, you're loaded," she said, sounding relieved. "You could light cigars with hundred-dollar bills. Please just open the door, Zach. I need to see that you're okay."

"I'm alive, Emma," he replied, then opened the door a crack. He knew he looked like reanimated death right now. His unshaven scruff was taking over his face and his hair was kind of greasy. Plus, all he was wearing was a low-slung pair of old sweats.

"Oh, Zach," Emma said, her eyes filling with emotion. "I have been so worried about you. Please let me come in."

"I'm not fit for human interaction, Em. I can't remember the last time I showered or shaved, for one thing." He self-consciously ran a hand over his prickly chin. "I look like a Chia pet. Seriously, go. Save yourself."

"No way. Not until I find out what this—" Emma waved her hand up and down in his general direction "—is all about."

"News bulletin: Zach Hiller is depressed," he said. "Details at ten. It's the same old, same old. You've heard my sob story before. Really. Flee while you can."

"Zachary Hiller, let me in right now," she commanded. He wasn't sure if that was actual anger or a joke. Either way it worked, because he opened the door.

"Suit yourself, but seriously, you've been warned."

Emma walked in and surveyed him.

"Have you lost weight?" she asked. "Are you even eating?"

"Yeah, it's no big deal. You know how guys are. Just the act of deciding to switch to diet soda makes us lose twenty pounds."

"Whatever. Seriously, Z, what's the story? Now I'm more worried than ever."

Zach studied her face a moment. She did not have the look of a woman who was going to be talked into leaving without a struggle.

He sighed. "Have a seat then. Can I get you anything?" he asked, his Southern manners deeply ingrained even in the middle of a funk.

"Yeah, some answers," she said, plopping herself down in the recliner.

He sighed again and flopped back down on the couch, then leaned his head back.

"I don't know what you want to hear, Emma. I told you from the start that I'm a mess. Are you just now hearing what I said? Surprise! I meant it."

"You're hilarious," she told him. "But stop lying, because I know this represents a change. When I met you, you were working at the pub. You were interacting with the human race. You returned my calls and my texts. You bathed. I didn't have to come racing over here frantic that maybe you were sick or injured or…"

"I'm depressed and a little whiny right now, not suicidal," he replied, looking away from the ceiling to lock his gaze with her worried eyes. "I never was."

"Good. I'm glad to…I, I'm sorry, Z. I just had never asked that before. I don't know the exact parameters of what you've experienced in the past two years, and since you apparently never sought any help for it, well…yeah, I didn't know. I'm sorry to come racing over here, ready to huff and puff my way in. But you wouldn't return my calls or texts, and they said at the pub that you were sick for the first time since you'd started there, and no one had seen or heard from you in days."

"Emma, I am so sorry." Zach felt like a complete jerk now. "I haven't turned my phone on in days, so I didn't realize you were getting frantic. As far as I knew, you were hanging out with your almost-husband. I seriously didn't think that you'd be looking for me. Again, I'm so sorry Emmy. Forgive me. This having-a-friend-in-Dublin thing is new for me."

"Just tell me what's going on," she said, her eyes shimmering with the tears that she'd been struggling to bottle up.

"Seeing you and Jim together…it hit me like a cement truck. I mean, sure, I knew you were taken. I knew our time here was going to come to an end. And then I'd be left without my…my friend. But then we had such a great time together on the bus trip. We connected in a way I haven't connected to another person in…I don't know. Ever? And our chemistry was ratcheting up to all-time highs. We almost kissed, remember? We would have if we hadn't been interrupted. I know we would have." He stopped to take a breath.

Emma nodded at him slowly. She wasn't denying the truth of his last statement.

"So there I was, floating up in the clouds, happy with this connection we'd found. Happiness is a rare emotion for me these days, so I was really floating high. And so I went over to your house to go on another trip and enjoy more time with you, then *bam!* Frying pan to the face. There you were having an even closer connection with another man, the one you *actually* love. And he sort of politely reminded me of a few things I'd forgotten." Zach shook his head now. "I can't believe I'm telling you all of this. But, anyway, I came home, shut the door, and haven't been outside since. I'd been so happy lately, so I had farther to fall, you know? And maybe in my recent happiness I'd been pushing back a bunch of bad stuff that then had the opportunity to swallow me up again."

"What did Jim say to you?" Emma asked, a look of complete outrage darkening her features.

"Don't worry about it, Em. I'm a big boy, and frankly everything he said was the truth anyway."

"Just tell me. Don't make me threaten to get an axe again." She looked so serious and determined that he didn't know if he should laugh or scream.

"Geez Em, you're relentless. He said you were going to be his wife, and that I should remember that. And I should also remember that you deserve better than me. That I'm not good enough for you."

"Really? And you accepted the word of a man who doesn't even know your name and nothing about you? You just agreed with his assessment and gave up?" Emma's beautiful brown eyes flashed with indignation. "He had no right to say those things, and you had no right to accept them as truth. Prove him wrong. Work to get your life back. Show him how terribly off the mark he is about everything!"

"Emma, seriously, he's not wrong," Zach said, with a shrug. "You're way too good for me."

"I can't take this, Zach. Please, you've got to fight to get your life back and to recover your old confidence. I can't take the defeated attitude."

"Not to pull an I-told-you-so here, but when you came to the door, I told you I wasn't feeling so great. Don't say it's fine and then beat me over the head with how not fine it is. I wasn't exactly up to entertaining company."

"I'm not company, I'm your friend. The same friend who wants you to shower, shave, and come road tripping with me like you promised."

"I don't think it's smart for us to spend any more time together," Zach told her then. "It's just going to make things even harder on me when you leave."

"You promised you'd come," she reminded him, looking completely obstinate now. "Either you come with me or I'm going to drive across the country all by myself, on the opposite side of the car than I'm used to, and on the opposite side of the road than I'm used to. I will be seriously lucky to live through the first ten minutes of it. You're going to just stand back and let me die alone and friendless in a field of cows?"

"You don't fight fair," he said, his first genuine smile in days cracking across his unshaven face.

"Get yourself together, Zach," she replied. "I am on a mission now. You and I are going to figure out how to get you better. Step one, get out of the house. Road trip. Sunday, okay?"

"How are you even free to do this?" he asked. "Jim's gone?"

"Yes, he's gone."

Zach stared at her for a long moment. He

shouldn't spend even a second more with this woman. Being with her, but not really being with her, was breaking his heart.

But, in the end, he was powerless to say no to her. Like usual.

"Okay, Emma. You win," he said, shaking his head at her in resignation. "I'll be there."

Chapter 24

EMMA WAS FURIOUS with Jim. *Furious.*

How dare he say those things to Zach? How dare he kick Zach further into depression and deeper into whatever other issues he'd been battling? Zach had been doing really well and he was making a lot of progress, she just knew it. He'd even told his sister Zoe that he was doing better. And then Jim came along and decided to mark his territory and undo all of it.

If she hadn't already broken up with him, she definitely would have now. She was almost inclined to call Jim anyway and rip into him about it. But in the end, that wouldn't really help anyone. Sure, it would temporarily make her feel better, but it wouldn't get Zach moving forward again. And it wouldn't undo the harm Jim had done.

She was walking back to her apartment now, fueled by so much frustration, anger, and relief. There seemed to be about a dozen emotions battling for supremacy inside of her. But she was mostly relieved that Zach was physically all right. Well, okay, he was a shower and a shave and a couple big meals away from being physically *fine*. But her imagination had spiraled so far out of control the longer she didn't hear from him that she'd shown up at his apartment completely terrified about what she was going to find there.

She was frustrated with Zach, though, too. She wasn't a professional therapist by far, so she wasn't sure how to proceed with getting him on the road to recovery. But she had to try. And *he* had to try too. That was what frustrated her. It kind of seemed like he'd given up trying to get better. What was the right thing to say or do? Should she tell him she'd broken up with Jim? Would that be the incentive he needed?

No.... She dismissed this idea almost as soon as it floated across her mind. She really didn't want to dangle the promise of a relationship between them like a carrot on a stick. That didn't feel like the right way to start something new. And until Zach was better inside, he couldn't even be in a healthy relationship in the first place. She couldn't fix him, either. He had to do it himself.

So she wasn't going to tell him about Jim. There—she'd made one decision.

Suddenly she realized she was back at the apartment. She had absolutely no memory of the walk home. Her exploding emotions had fueled her trip home like a jet pack, apparently.

"Trace? You here?" Emma called as she walked inside. She had barely seen Tracy at all in weeks.

"Hey, stranger," Tracy said, walking out of her bedroom. "What had you out of the house so early?"

"Zach," she replied, sitting on the couch. She brought her knees up and hugged her legs like a security blanket. "Do you have a few minutes? I really need someone to talk to."

"Sure, I was planning to leave soon, but it's not urgent." Tracy sat at the other end and picked up a throw pillow to idly play with. "What's up?"

"My world is exploding," Emma told her. "I feel like it's fluttering all around me like little pieces of confetti. And it's like my entire future depends on my ability to reach out and grab exactly the right piece. Everything's completely chaotic and random and out of my control and, I don't know...."

"Uh, can you talk in specifics? I'm not sure the confetti analogy has gotten me completely up to speed," Tracy said.

"Ugh, okay yeah, I know I'm not being crystal clear. First things first—I broke up with Jim when he was here before."

"Wow, really? Spur of the moment or planned?"

"Planned. I'd made up my mind already, but I was waiting for the end of the summer when I saw him again. Then he sort of did me the favor of showing up, so I took advantage of the opportunity."

"I'm…sorry? Are *you* sorry?" Tracy asked.

"No. I mean, yes, I'm sad to say goodbye to my first serious love," Emma said. "Of course. But it was the right thing to do. I didn't want to be with him forever, not really."

"Okay, good, that makes me happy that you realized how you felt and took action. So keep going. What else happened?"

"Zach stopped by when Jim was here. When I walked out of the room to take your phone call, apparently Jim took the opportunity to say some nasty stuff to him. He was posturing, naturally. I guess he felt threatened. But he told Zach to back off and that he isn't good enough for me," Emma shook her head. "I'm so mad at Jim right now. Part of me wants to get back together with him just so I can dump him again."

"Emma!" Tracy said, laughing. "That's terrible."

"Yeah, well, he'd pretty much deserve it. His words set Zach off in a downward spiral. He'd been feeling better, and then he just went off the deep end. I basically had to force my way into his apartment this morning to do a welfare check on him. He wasn't answering my calls or texts, and he wasn't showing up at the pub for work. I got so worried about him."

"So he's fine, and he told you what Jim said?"

Emma nodded. "Yes."

"Okay. Did you tell him you broke things off with Jim?"

"No, and we're coming up on the part I need your help with. I don't think I should tell Zach that I'm free. I think he has to get better on his own, do you know what I mean? If I said I was free and we started a relationship, I'd always be wondering if he'd ever actually healed completely. I think I'd spend my life waiting for him to unravel again. Does that make sense?"

Tracy shrugged. "Yeah, I guess so. I mean, neither of us are mental health professionals, but it seems reasonable that he shouldn't be jumping into anything in his current frame of mind."

"That's another thing I need to tell you," Emma said, biting her bottom lip now. "I finally acknowledged my full feelings here. Well, only to myself. I love Zach. I'm totally in love with him."

"Wow...Emma! How long have I been buried in my research and out of touch? I feel like Rumplestiltskin here. Did I sleep through a hundred years?"

"I know, I know. A lot changed really fast. I broke up with Jim, and I acknowledged to myself that I love Zach. But those two things don't automatically go together. I didn't only break up with Jim so I could be with Zach. For one thing, I want some time to be alone and single. But of course there's also the issue of whether Zach is ever going to regain his self-confidence and take back his old life."

"I get it. So, what did you want to bounce off me?" Tracy asked. "I still feel like I'm not getting the point here."

"I want to get strategic about helping Zach. This is hard to admit to myself, and even harder to say out loud, but...well, I don't really think Zach and I can ever be together. I just don't think it's going to be in the cards for us. There's too much that would have to happen. Too many stars that would have to align. But the one thing I can control is whether or not I do absolutely everything I can to help him before I leave."

"What kinds of things do you have in mind?"

"*That* is where I need your help," Emma said. "Can we brainstorm a little bit?"

"Sure. Maybe you could ask his family for ideas. You're in touch with his sister, right?"

"Yeah, I've got her cell, and she friended me on Facebook. But I don't think I want to start there. They've been through a lot where Zach's concerned. I don't want to put them through even more if I don't need to. Like what if I got their hopes up too high or something?"

"Okay, yeah, I see what you're saying. Umm, let's see.... What was the story again? He was pitching in a game, and he threw the ball that hit that guy…I don't know. Did the guy ever forgive him? Is needing forgiveness part of this issue?"

"Ooh, yeah, okay, I think you're onto something there." Emma's eyes flashed with excitement. "I wonder if I could get a message to Tommy Layton. Ask him to talk to Z? Something like that?"

"Did Layton recover enough to return to

baseball?" Tracy asked. "He'll be harder to find if he's a private citizen now."

"I'll do a little research on Tommy right now," Emma said, grabbing her laptop from the coffee table. "In the meantime, keep the ideas coming."

"Okay, well, let's see…so he threw the pitch, Tommy got hurt, and what happened next?" Tracy asked.

"Hank Wilson, Zach's manager, ordered him to take on the next batter, but Zach refused. Hank was clearly trying to use the 'get back on the horse that just threw you' reasoning, but Zach just couldn't do it. That's when he walked away. He never threw another—wait! That's it! I need to get him to start throwing again! Maybe we could go to the park and he could throw some pitches to me!"

"I kind of think he's not going to want to hurl fastballs at your head," Tracy told her, skepticism written all over her face. "That'll just make him nervous and worried."

"Any kind of throwing would work, I'd think," Emma said. "We'll set up cans like a carnival game. I think this could be good."

Tracy nodded in agreement. "Yeah, I like it,"

"Okay, here it is…." Emma was reading from the laptop now. "Tommy Layton's been back in baseball for a while. He came back the year after he got hurt, so he missed the end of his rookie season."

"Huh, okay. Well, that helps. Maybe you could contact the PR people for the team he's on. Who does he play with now?"

"Looks like he's still the rightfielder for the Orioles. But I can't imagine the team would take a random call or email from a stranger and hook me up with one of their players."

"Fan letter? Direct message on Twitter?"

"Nah, you can't send a direct message on Twitter unless that person follows you, and I doubt seriously that Tommy Layton will follow me, if he's even on Twitter." Emma brought up the Twitter home page and searched for his name. "It looks like @RealTLayton is him. There is a bunch of baseball and Orioles stuff on his home page."

"So just send him a tweet. Who knows, maybe he'll reply. Nothing to lose, right?"

"I guess," Emma said. "What should I say though? Absolutely none of this is his fault. I don't want to say something that could be interpreted as a guilt trip."

"What do you basically want to know from him?"

"I just want to know if he forgave Z. Or whether he'd be willing to, I guess. That would help Z, right?"

"You'd think. Okay, maybe write something like, 'Hey, Do you still hate Z Hiller?' What do you think? It's simple and direct."

"Seems too random and out of the blue, though. Maybe I should butter him up first. Something about being a huge fan."

"Yeah, whatever. Chances are he won't tweet a reply anyway, but just try it."

"Okay," Emma said, typing. "Here's what I have: **@RealTLayton** Big fan! One question: Do you still hate Z Hiller?"

"Perfect. Hit send before you chicken out."

Emma wavered. *Should I do this? Will it make Zach mad?* Her finger hovered over the Enter key a moment more, then she hit it.

"There," she said.

"Okay, so you're going to try to get him throwing

balls in the park, and with any luck, you'll find out that Tommy forgave him, and you'll be able to tell him that. Anything else?" Tracy asked.

"Not right now," Emma said, closing her laptop. "This is a good start, I think. Well, actually, I'm also going to keep dragging him out of the apartment. Being with me was helping him before Jim opened his big yap. So hopefully being with me can help again. Seriously, Trace, thanks for listening and helping."

Tracy nodded and got up. "I'll keep thinking, too. Maybe I'll have a big inspiration."

"Yeah, same here. I'm not leaving Dublin without knowing I did absolutely everything I possibly could."

"Good luck," Tracy said, gathering her things. "Listen, I'm about to take off for a bit. You're going to be okay?"

"Yeah, thanks," Emma replied, the wheels in her mind turning furiously as she watched Tracy leave.

She hadn't been exaggerating. She was completely, one-hundred percent committed to using absolutely every tool she had to help him with his recovery. But it was still going to come down to how much he wanted this for himself. She couldn't do the work for him.

And she thought again that she loved him so much. If he was suffering, then she was suffering, too. Seeing him today had been incredibly hard. He'd been right, in a way. It was one thing to hear someone tell you they'd been battling through personal issues. But it was another to see that person actually in the middle of it and actively suffering. He wasn't showering, he wasn't eating, and she doubted he'd been sleeping much, either, given the dark circles under his eyes. Part of her had wanted to hold him and comfort him and make him some chicken soup.

But the other part of her had wanted to shake him. Why wasn't he in therapy? She wasn't a professional, but he could definitely use the advice of one. If she pushed him too hard, maybe she would end up doing more harm than good.

Okay, so getting him to go into counseling would be part of the plan of attack.

Zach was about to feel the force of exactly how much she loved him. Sometimes it had to be demonstrated in the form of tough love—and this, unfortunately, was going to be one of those times.

Chapter 25

I WONDER WHY Emma wants to have dinner with me, Zach thought. She'd suggested meeting after his shift at the pub Saturday, which was weird. They were already supposed to be spending all of Sunday together.

Unless she was backing out?

Yeah, that was probably it. She likely had thought more about what a head case he was after she came to his apartment and caught him mid-heartbreak. She probably realized she really didn't have any place in her life for him and all his problems. And seriously, who could blame her?

So now, as he walked into the restaurant—American themed, with menu items like burgers and fries—he fully expected Emma to tell him to get lost. At least there'd be some comfort food involved. A taste of home was nice once in a while, even if it wasn't spot-on authentic.

"Hey, Z!" she called. She'd already been seated at a booth. He slid in across from her and had to quickly place his order when the waitress descended on them. Then Zach leaned back and gave Emma his full attention.

"Okay, so what's this about?" he asked. "We were supposed to see each other tomorrow. I'm assuming that's off now?"

"No, it's n—" Emma started, but Zach kept going.

"Is this the part where you tell me I freaked you

out the last time you saw me? It's all too much for you, isn't it? What pushed you over the edge? It was the crazy Chia facial hair, wasn't it?"

"Seriously, Z, shut up a minute and let me talk," Emma said with a laugh. "First thing, our trip is still on. Be at my apartment as early as you can roll yourself out of bed. I want to hit the road and get moving."

"Oh…okay," Zach replied. "So what's up then? I seriously thought you were going to tell me to disappear."

"No, I'm not," Emma said. "I'm sorry if I gave you a scare. I just wanted to have a conversation now and get it out of the way so we can have fun tomorrow and not be weighed down with all this heavy stuff."

"Oh, sure, no problem. Hit me with your heavy stuff, then. You can say anything to me." Zach was still stuck in the part where she said she wasn't turning away from him. *Unbelievable.* Emma was the strongest person he knew.

"Well, first I wanted to say that I'm sick of worrying about everything when I spend time with you. We worry about Jim and we worry about your future and we worry that we're getting too close and…it just sucks after a while."

"The easy solution to that, of course, is for you to tell me to take a hike," Zach pointed out.

"Nah, I never jump in with the easy solutions. Where's the challenge in that?" She smiled at him as she absentmindedly folded and unfolded her napkin. "And, really, I don't see much that would be easy about walking away from this…uh, friendship, we've formed. You've become incredibly important to me, Zach. Not sure how or why it's happened, but in the short time we've known each other, it's just…magnetic. It's like you said, we're magnets."

"You know, I agree. You've become a great friend," Zach told her, trying to make sure he kept his full feelings hidden. She had become beyond important to him. And he desperately wished they could be more than just friends.

"Okay, so what I'm trying to say," she went on, "and not very well, is that I want us to have one completely fun, carefree, happy day. None of our usual angst. Just you, me, and the Cliffs of Moher. No issues."

"*You, Me, and the Cliffs of Moher* would make a great book title," Zach said.

Emma smiled and seemed to be studying his face, looking for some sort of answers. He wondered what she saw when she looked at him.

"What?" he finally asked. "Something else you want to say or tell me?"

"Yeah, there is. But first, you're good with tomorrow being completely stress- and issue-free? Really?"

"Sure. It might be easier said than done, though. We're still going to have to be working hard to actively fight the magnetic forces. We still have boundaries to think about." He wasn't really convinced her idea would actually work. How could he forget about the vast pile of issues that lay in between them, even for a day? It would be impossible.

"Well, let's just try," she said. "It'll be good for both of us. Before we close the book on our issues and open up the worry-free zone, is there anything you'd like to talk about? How are you doing? I see you shaved and got dressed."

"Yeah, I'm up and around," he said with a shrug.

"Went back to work. I'm okay. Everyone gets down now and then, Emmy. You can't be up constantly."

"No, no you can't. Well I'm glad you're feeling better."

The waitress came then and gave them their plates, stacked high with burgers and crispy little shoestring French fries. Zach poured out a pool of ketchup.

"How did things go with Jim?" he asked. "He surprised you, huh? That must have been so great for you. Did you get to show him much of the city?"

"Uh, no, not really," Emma said as she took a bite of her burger, pausing to chew before finishing her response. "We went to dinner once, though."

They only managed to leave the apartment once? That made Zach think they totally had a weekend of marathon sex. Not that he blamed Jim one bit, but he needed to mentally bleach that vision out of his brain. Fast.

"He just stayed for the weekend," Emma said.

A whole weekend in bed, Zach thought. The vision of how Jim had looked when he was telling Zach to back off and go be a loser around someone else's fiancée flashed through his head then.

Change the subject. Change the subject. Change the subject.

"It's the ketchup," he blurted out. Oh great, that was smooth.

"Huh?" Emma asked.

"Oh, uh, sorry. You had to be inside my head to make that conversational shift," Zach said, glad she couldn't *actually* look inside his head right now. "I've been trying to figure out why this place never quite tastes like home, no matter much they hope to. And I've decided it's the ketchup."

"Let me try," she said, dipping one of her fries into

it. "Yeah, you're right. That's not quite ketchup. Or at least it's not the kind we know back in the States."

"Exactly. The recipe is different, so that makes everything else taste weird."

"Okay," Emma said, looking at him like he was nuts. "You've given this far too much thought."

"Yeah, ketchup is going to be a chapter in that Cliffs of Moher book I'm working on," he said, winking at her while she laughed.

"That sounds fascinating," she said. "Really."

"Okay, Emma," he said, feeling awkward now. "Cards on the table: I just wanted to get the conversation off the romantic weekend you spent with Jim. I know I was the dummy who asked, but then I decided I didn't really want to know."

"It was whirlwind, Z, not romantic. And honestly it mostly just annoyed me, okay? He definitely was checking up on me."

"Oh. Sorry Em. Really, it's none of my business. So…do you want to hear more of my condiment theories?"

She laughed and took another bite while shaking her head no.

"Fine, your loss. So we cleared the air and agreed not to whine about our problems tomorrow. But I think you said you had more you wanted to talk about."

"Yeah, I do. I had a small idea about something we could try. Later, after our trip. Maybe next week sometime."

"Really? An idea about what?" he asked.

"I was thinking that maybe—and I'm sorry if this seems like I'm pushing here—but maybe you need to try throwing the ball again." She looked a little nervous now, like she was afraid what his reaction would be.

"Why don't we go to the park again? You could pitch to me. I think you need to get that feel again, but not with a dopey lightweight stress ball. Let's go buy an actual baseball and get it in your hand again. What do you say?"

She looked so excited and hopeful. If he hadn't already fallen in love with her, that sweet, optimistic look she was giving him would have pushed him right off the edge. She wasn't just saying it to be nice; she really did care. She was honestly trying to find concrete ways to help him. He couldn't help but be touched and honored.

"Emmy, you are the most beautiful, kind-hearted person I've ever met. I am so touched that you're willing to do that with me." And he meant it—he felt like his heart was expanding in his chest with a big sloppy burst of love. She was turning him into such a sap, he knew. But he didn't care. Emma absolutely held his heart in her hand. "But if you think I'm going to take the William Tell approach to solving my problems, you are straight-up nuts. Trust me when I say I value your head too much to risk knocking it off your shoulders with a wild pitch. I haven't thrown in two years, and the last time I did, I almost killed someone. So, thank you, Em. I am honestly never going to forget that you were willing to do that for me. But no way. Never."

She was nodding already. "Yeah, okay, it was worth a shot, but I figured you'd say that. So my backup idea is cans. Like a carnival game. We could set up a series of cans on the ground and let you try to knock them over. I was going to suggest we try to put a target on a tree, but that would probably get us arrested or fined or something."

"Trying to hit a small target on the ground isn't the best way to simulate a pitching throw," he said. "We're trying to keep it out of the dirt, not in it."

"Yeah, okay, I know it's not perfect. But it seems important for you to take that first throw. Come on, at least think about it?" she asked.

"Sure, I'll think about it," he replied. "And we won't even have to go buy a baseball. I don't know why, but I brought one with me."

"You did?" She looked pleased and even more excited than before. "Ooh, I think I know why! I think your subconscious mind knew full well that you'd be going back to the game one day."

"I hope that's true. That would be…nice, I guess. Nice to think I still had faith when I first came here, even if it's been buried deep all this time."

"Even if it's *not* true, I have enough faith right now for both of us," Emma told him, looking triumphant. "This is going to work. I can feel it."

Zach smiled at her and took a bite of his burger. Her excitement really was infectious.

"I'm onto you, Emma," he said. "I think you've been planning again, haven't you? I'm about to face the full-strength power of an Emma plan, aren't I?"

"Yes, I confess I've been doing a little scheming. As you know, my time here is getting shorter and shorter. It won't be long before I'm saying goodbye and getting on a plane. So I know we're fighting the clock. But you've told both Zoe and me that being with me helps you somehow, right?"

"Yeah, you know it does."

"So then I started thinking and scheming and trying to get super strategic about this so we can use the time we have left more efficiently. I hope knowing this doesn't bug you, but I was brainstorming with Tracy about it, looking for ideas that might help. If ever a situation needed a big old well-thought-out plan wedged into the middle of it, it's this one." She sat back now; before, she'd been hunched over the table and thumping it for emphasis with her finger. "And you know how much I love to figure out plans anyway. It's like a puzzle for me. I try to look at every angle of a situation and figure out the best course of action for getting through it. It's like doing a daily crossword or Sudoku."

"What else are you scheming up?" he asked, narrowing his eyes at her. "Should I be afraid?"

"Nah, don't be afraid. But let's just take this one step at a time. Step one was getting you out of the house, which you did all on your own. Step two will be decompressing. We're going to enjoy our time together tomorrow or we're going to die trying."

"I still think you should work for the tourism board," Zach teased. "Ireland: Have fun or die trying."

"And step three," she continued as though he hadn't spoken, although she cracked a smile, "is getting you to throw the ball again, even just one pitch. Let's just see how all of that goes, and then we can see where the other steps take us. Deal?"

"Deal," he said, nodding.

He couldn't believe it, but her plan wasn't freaking him out or making him feel crowded or pressured. Just the opposite, really. Sitting there, in that booth, and listening to her explain her strategy was actually exciting. Exhilarating, even.

He smiled at her again, marveling once more at just how much he loved her. He couldn't wait for tomorrow. The road trip was going to be a lot of fun, even if they ended up circling the airport all day after they picked up the car. When he was with her, he realized in that moment, *everything* seemed fun.

And everything seemed possible.

Chapter 26

BY THE TIME they picked up the rental car at the airport the next morning—and then spent a little time trying to get the feel of driving a stick shift on both the opposite side of the car *and* the opposite side of the road—it was well after eleven.

"Oh no!" Emma said, forgetting that Zach was trying to split his focus between driving, listening to the GPS, and talking.

"What? Did I take a wrong turn already?"

"No, I was just doing the math. It's about three hours from Dublin to the Cliffs of Moher, give or take, and that's with no lunch, no bathroom breaks, no traffic or bad weather, and no wrong turns. Picking up the car and getting the feel of driving it took longer than I was counting on."

"So we'll drive home late," Zach said with a shrug. "No big deal."

"Do you really want to be driving in the dark in an unfamiliar country while you're still getting used to this opposite-side stuff?" she asked, looking doubtful.

"Well, I know you well enough to be fairly certain you're not suggesting we give up and turn back. So what are you saying? Stay overnight? That's not a problem for me, if you don't mind. Actually, if you can book the rooms on your phone now, I'll treat."

"Yeah, okay. I guess that sounds good. You focus on driving, and I'll focus on finding rooms," she said, pulling out her guidebook. "Looks like the closest town to the Cliffs of Moher is Lahinch. I'll start there. This might be tough, though. We're right in the middle of the tourist season."

"Well, look at it this way," Zach replied. "Maybe by the time we get there, the crowds will have thinned out. The tour buses will have to get in and out if they're going to bring people back to Dublin or wherever they originated."

"Hmm...yeah," she said. "True. But that only addresses the crowds at the actual site, not in the hotels. I wonder if I should just start calling places, or even try to do it online? What do you think?"

"I'd probably attempt booking online first. Do you have one of those hotel apps on your phone?"

"No, but good idea," she said, opening the app store. Maybe if she kept busy enough trying to figure this out, she wouldn't let her mind start wandering to topics like not pouncing on Zach during an overnight stay in a hotel. She could barely keep her hands off him under normal circumstances.

Yeah, okay, so nothing is going to keep those thoughts at bay for long, she knew. And she had a feeling she was going to get precisely zero minutes of sleep. So she may as well just try to sleep in the backseat of this tiny car.

Or in Zach's arms....

What was wrong with her? She needed to focus. On...the...wait, what was she supposed to be focusing on?

Oh yeah. Finding a hotel-booking app. For the hotel. *For tonight. With Zach....*

Yeah, this was useless.

"Okay, it's definitely tourist season," she said after unsuccessfully finding anything available near the Cliffs of Moher. "I located a single room with two double beds in Shannon, but it was crazy expensive."

"Oh, just book it," Zach told her. "We can make the single room work. I'll remember the boundaries, Em. I promise, it'll be no big deal."

No big deal for him, maybe. But she was already fighting their chemistry, and they'd barely been in the car an hour. It was only because he needed to focus on the road that she hadn't reached for his hand already. How was she going to keep from blurting out that she and Jim broke up? Especially when she knew Zach was right there in the bed across from her tonight?

Zero. Absolutely, one hundred percent—she was going to get zero minutes of sleep.

"Okay, fine," she said finally. "I'll hold the room with my card, and then we'll figure it out when we get there."

"Great," he said. "So where's Shannon?"

"Let's see...." She pulled out the map in her guidebook. "What highway are we on? The N7? Looks like we stay on the N7 until Limerick, then…we take the N18 to Shannon. We can check in, then make decisions about whether we should attempt to go to the cliffs tonight or in the morning."

"And we're okay with the car for more than one day?" he asked.

"Yeah, I reserved it for three days. I figured you never know what might happen."

"And that's why you're good at making plans," he said, smiling over at her before looking back at the road.

Oh yeah, I'm a genius at it. That's why she had stumbled into this situation where she was going to be tortured all night by being so close to Zach, yet completely unable to tell him she was free to be with him. But it was all for his sake, she kept reminding herself. He needed to focus on himself and rebuilding his old life. What he didn't need was to leap into a messy new relationship full of problems. And she knew that if anything happened between them while they were on this trip, there'd be no turning back. She'd never be able to deny herself from staying with him once she had crossed that line.

Yes, this was for Zach. She was doing what was best for him. And honestly, she needed time, too. Zach was too important to her to become Transition Guy as she worked to move past her breakup with Jim.

Okay, so there it was. She had a whole fistful of reasons why she needed to keep things light and friendly tonight. Particularly while they were alone together in a hotel room. Those stupid magnetic forces were going to be torturing her, she just knew it. But this was how it had to be....

Now let's lighten things up a bit....

"Trivia time!" she announced out of the blue. "When's your birthday?"

"July 23rd," Zach said. "Which is a bummer because it's right in the middle of the baseball season, so I always end up celebrating alone in some nameless city with room service. It's just sad. How about you?"

"What, we missed your birthday? Why didn't you tell me?"

"I don't know. Didn't seem like a big deal, I guess."

"How old did you just turn?"

"I'm 28. I should be right in the prime of my pitching years," he added, looking rueful.

"I'll be 26 on November 30th," she replied.

"Nice. End of November is perfect. That's after the baseball season, so I…okay, I don't know where I was going with that."

"So you could…spend my birthday with me each year? That's what you almost said?" Emma asked, feeling a pang of regret for all those birthdays they would never actually get to spend together.

"I guess. Hey, I'm sorry. I know that's not going to happen. The words started walking out of my mouth before I could catch them," he said.

"Yeah, no problem," she said, although an almost tangible air of sadness had seeped into the car. "So, anyway, more trivia. What's your number? On your uniform, I mean?"

"I was always number three, all the way through high school. It was a nod to Babe Ruth."

"Oh, right, because he started as a pitcher."

Zach nodded. "Right. But his number is retired with the Yankees. Actually, every single-digit number is retired for the Yankees. So, when I got called up to the Majors, I sort of randomly picked 56. It was available and, I don't know. It seemed like a good number."

"Have they given it away to anyone else since you left?"

"I don't think so. But I'm honestly not sure."

"So you haven't been in touch with any of your old teammates or coaches?" she asked. "Or anyone from the team?"

"The few people who tried to keep in touch at first gradually gave up. It's just been my family since I got to Dublin basically," Zach glanced at her again. "Until you showed up."

She smiled at him but fell silent then, thinking about the weight of what he'd just said. Her plan was to do everything she could for him until her time in Dublin was up. That was less than two weeks away. After that, she'd be yet another person who was giving up on him and walking away.

How was she going to do it? she wondered now. And really, *should* she even do it? Was she positive she was making the right choices here? And why wasn't she willing to give him a say in any of this?

Maybe what she really should do was reveal everything. Tell him about her feelings for him. Tell him that her engagement was over, and that she was free now. And maybe tell him that she wanted to do absolutely all she could to help him heal.

But even if they were together, what if he still wanted to stay locked in his Dublin apartment with her forever? What if revealing her feelings gave him an easy excuse for never proactively doing something to get out of his rut? And how did she even know he actually wanted to be with her in the first place? She didn't know if he could ever love her back.

What was the right thing to do?

She looked at him and thought maybe she should just grab this chance to spend the night together. Maybe this trip and this night in a Shannon hotel was the only bit of happiness that they were ever going to have together.

She could feel the heat crawling up her face as she pictured herself walking into his arms and spending the entire night loving him.

The vision was so clear and so enticing she almost gasped. She could easily picture how that would feel. Wonderful, at first. Perfect even. But first she'd have to tell him that she'd broken up with Jim. And then, if Zach still refused to leave Dublin, what would she do?

Stay here? Would she be strong enough to leave him after letting things get that far?

She was so torn, and she just didn't think telling Zach about any of this would ultimately help him. It might even set him back further.

She tried—unsuccessfully—to make some sort of decision during the rest of the drive to the hotel. They stopped for lunch and gas, and still she didn't know what to do. She took a turn driving, then, which only served to distract her temporarily. Focusing on the road and the feel of the car helped push the worries out of her mind a bit, but when they got to the hotel, she was even more torn than before. What should she do? What was right? What was best?

She tried to make light conversation over dinner, and then during a stroll around a few blocks near their hotel. But she couldn't really focus. She was so upset with her indecision that she almost blurted out everything, just to be done with it.

But something was holding her back. Deep down, she knew that telling him everything wasn't the right approach. So she continued to agonize as she got ready for bed. She was practically in tears by the time she walked out of the bathroom. Zach was laying there, still in his jeans and tee shirt. They didn't have anything to change into since they hadn't planned on staying over.

"Emma, please talk to me," he said, getting up and swinging around so he was on the edge of the bed. "Here, sit and tell me what's on your mind."

"Wha..what makes you think something's on my mind?" she asked, nervously settling down on the bed across from him.

"Because you've been distracted and ready to jump out of your skin all day," he said. "You billed this as the carefree day, but, at the moment, you're about the least carefree person I've ever seen. And this is coming from me so, you know, that's really bad."

"It's nothing," she told him.

"You're not going to tell me, huh? Well, my best guess is that you're torn about whether or not you should tell Jim that we stayed here together, right? You're feeling all guilty and unfaithful and secretive. But Emma, nothing's going to happen, so please stop worrying. You won't have anything to hide from him."

"Yeah, you know, this is sort of a weird situation we find ourselves in," Emma replied, not sure how to defuse the situation without straight-up lying. "But trust me when I say I'm not worried about Jim right now."

"Oh, then you're worried about me, aren't you?"

"How do you mean?" She didn't want to fill in the truth if he was just casting around with vague suspicions.

"You're worried I'm getting too attached, aren't you? You're sitting there thinking that I'm going to read too much into our time together. You're thinking that you've told me a hundred different ways that you're not in love with me and are very much in love with someone else. Hey, I get it. I hear you, Emma. You're not leading me on. You can climb right on that plane in a couple weeks and not have a thing to feel guilty about. You'll never have to give me another thought. I understand where your heart's at. Is that what this is?"

"Not exactly," Emma replied, feeling sadder by the minute as she realized she was terrible at staging a carefree day. "You're vaguely circling around what I'm thinking and feeling, but since I can't even really vocalize my thoughts, I can't expect you to."

"Please honey, you look so sad," Zach said,

looking worried now. "What can I do? Can I make it better? Would you like me to go sleep in the car so you don't have to lie to Jim about this whole hotel thing?"

"No," she said, with a hiccupy laugh. "I do not want you to sleep in the car."

"On the floor? In the bathtub? Under the desk? In the hall?" he asked, clearly teasing.

"I just feel sad and overwhelmed and…I don't know. Sad again, I guess. What I want and what I should do are two different things."

"Okay, then I don't know. You lost me. Tell me what you want me to do, and I'll do it. Anything to get that look out of your eyes. Anything."

"Can you just…let me lie next to you tonight?" she asked. "I feel like we are about to be separated forever, and I think I just miss you already. We're both fully clothed, so it's not like it's anything I, uh, need to confess to Jim."

Zach looked at her a long moment, then he reached out his hand and just held it there in the space between them. Emma looked at it and then back into his eyes, where emotions she couldn't interpret were swirling.

Slowly she lifted one hand off the bed and gently placed it into Zach's. He gave it a soft kiss and then pulled her up and onto the bed next to him.

"You're right," he said. "We are about to be separated forever. When you leave, that'll be it. I'll have to delete your number from my phone in order to make it permanent. I can't be…I don't know…trading recipes with you on Pinterest or whatever after you marry Jim. It'll be too hard. But you have to know I wish things were different between us."

"I do, too," she admitted.

"But there's nothing for you to be sad about, Emma. You have shown a lost soul more kindness than he ever could have expected. You've given me hope, and I know I'll be getting out of town soon. I don't know how or when, but it's going to happen. So it's going to be okay. Go have your wonderful life. Teach all those kids and start that family. Go and don't look back."

Emma could feel tears start to tickle at her eyes.

Okay, this was officially the lamest fun-filled, carefree day ever, she thought as she wiped impatiently at the tears before they started rolling down her cheeks.

"I'm sorry for getting so melancholy," she said. "I don't know what's come over me."

"Listen, let's just try to sleep. We'll attempt to have our carefree day tomorrow, okay? Today was more the fun-filled reflective and somber day," he said, standing then and pulling back the covers. He got in and lay down. "Your choice, Emma. I'd be happy to hold you all night if that would help. But if it would just make things worse, well…again, you decide."

She chewed her lip in indecision. She was no closer to seeing the right path than she had been before. But in the end, she just couldn't resist climbing into bed next to him. He settled the covers over them and pulled her into his arms. Her head was on his arm, and she had an arm wrapped around his waist.

It felt so right being there. She never wanted to leave this room. Maybe they could just stay here and forget about the problems waiting for them back in Dublin.

"I'm laying on your pitching arm," she said finally, also realizing his fingers had begun playing with her hair. "This is officially my first million-dollar pillow."

"That's a multi-million-dollar pillow, missy," he corrected.

She smiled and closed her eyes. Being with Zach in this very intimate way all night long might not make it any easier when the time came to walk away from him. But at this moment, there was absolutely nowhere else in the world she wanted to be.

Chapter 27

ZACH WAS SO HAPPY. He and Emma were finally together. She was in his arms, and that was exactly where she was going to stay.

He trailed his free hand down her sweet face, her brown eyes looking at him with so much love and trust.

"My sweet Emma," he said, leaning forward to kiss her. Closer, closer now to her beautiful lips...

"Zach?" Emma replied in a faraway voice. "Zach, I think you're dreaming."

Huh? What?

He opened his eyes then. *Wait...where am I?* A moment of disorientation fluttered through him as he looked around, then down into Emma's face again. The fog of the dream he'd just been having was still swirling around his brain. What was real?

"Em?"

"We're in the hotel in Shannon, remember?" she said, talking to him like he was a child.

"I'm...you're...." he spluttered, still foggy.

"You were dreaming I think. But nothing happened. You held me all night and helped me feel less sad. That's all."

He stared into her brown eyes a moment longer as reality locked back into place in his mind. Harsh truth number one—he shouldn't be laying on top of her, no matter how amazing it felt.

"I'm sorry," he said, pulling away. "You probably

can't breathe."

"No, you're right, I can't breathe, but it's not because you're lying on top of me." Her voice was filled with emotion as she grabbed his arms, apparently signaling she didn't want him to move yet. "Zach, I want to be very, very selfish right now, just for a minute. Extremely selfish. I suppose I'll eventually regret this but I don't care. Please, Zach, just one kiss?"

He couldn't believe what she'd just asked him. A wave of happiness mixed with disbelief sloshed around inside him.

"You're sure, honey? I don't want to do something you'll feel guilty about. And I promised you I'd be a gentleman."

"I know. Just one tiny kiss. To complete the one we almost shared at the rope bridge. But we have to promise each other that we'll stop there though, okay? If we go any further, I won't be able to stop myself, and then I really will feel guilty."

"One tiny kiss?" he asked again, slowly lowering his face to hers, just like in the dream.

"Yes. Just one, tiny, itty-bitty...." Emma trailed off.

Their lips brushed together softly, a light, hesitant touch as he closed his mouth gently across her top lip before pulling back.

"Like that?" he asked, watching her bite her bottom lip. She was going to kill him if she kept doing that.

"No," she finally answered. "More like this."

She leaned up and caught his mouth in a longer, more insistent fashion. He could feel the heat radiating between them, like an electrical current had been sparked as the intensity of their connection burned even hotter.

He pulled back then and sat up on the bed, running his hands over his face. *Gotta stop now.*

"I'm sorry Z," she said, sounding a little dazed. "My fault. I told you I was being selfish."

"We can't do that again," he said. "As much as it hurts me to say that, we have to get ourselves right back into the friends-only zone. Like, immediately."

"Yeah, I know," she said, regret evident all over her face. "I'm so sorry. I don't know what I was thinking. You were just so cute talking in your sleep, and then when you woke up all confused, and…I don't know, I just couldn't resist and…okay, this isn't helping."

"Uh, no, I guess it's not," Zach replied, still feeling a little off. What had just happened? She was acting really weird for a woman who claimed to be fully committed to her fiancé. Something strange was going on here.

"Unless…did you…." he started, trying to figure out what to say until he realized she was asking him something. "You first."

"Do you want to quick use the bathroom before I take a shower?" she repeated.

"Yeah, okay," Zach said then, climbing off the bed. "Sure."

He was about to ask her if she was considering leaving Jim. He was glad she hadn't noticed that he'd left a sentence hanging in the air. He needed to think about it more.

He propellered his arms in circles trying to get the kinks worked out as he walked to the bathroom. When he was finished, he washed his hands and brushed his teeth with one of the toothbrushes they'd given him at the desk. Then he splashed cold water on his face and studied his reflection in the mirror while drying off with a towel. He looked as lost and confused as he felt.

He just didn't know what to make of all this. Emma's mood had been all over the place since they'd left Dublin. She'd seemed reluctant and guilty about getting the hotel room at first, then she asked to sleep in his arms all night. Emma was also the one who'd pressed for the kiss. It was like road-tripping with a caffeinated pendulum. He just couldn't keep up with her, and he had no idea what she was thinking and feeling from one moment to the next. What was motivating her right now? Guilt about him and his situation? Regret that she would be leaving soon? Or was it guilt about Jim? Sadness? Remorse?

Or had the surge of hope he'd felt earlier been right—could Emma really be tossing around the idea of leaving Jim?

No, that didn't seem likely. The two of them had been together forever. And Zach was still too much of a mess. There was no way Emma would walk away from a secure and happy relationship for a crazy-small chance of an uncertain future with him.

He had to stop thinking about these things. It was already incredibly painful knowing Emma was leaving soon. Pumping himself up with false hopes about the future they could maybe have together? No, he didn't need the added heartache that the false hope would give him. He needed only to focus on making this trip nice for her. With all her mood swings and their late start yesterday, she hadn't gotten her fun, carefree day that she'd wanted so badly. They hadn't even seen the cliffs yet.

As he headed back into the room, he thought again that he didn't know what else she needed. But he knew for sure that she wanted a fun, worry-free day. And to see those cliffs she was so wound up about. So he was going to give her those things. Her happiness was all he cared about. He wasn't going to mention the kiss or start another pointless conversation about the sad end to their friendship…which was barreling toward them like a freight train.

No worries. No problems. And no talk of kisses that never should have happened.

"Zach," Emma started when he walked out of the bathroom, "I am so…."

"Oh no you don't," Zach interrupted. "Bathroom's yours, and then we're going to grab our free breakfast downstairs before we find those cliffs. You wanted one carefree cliff day. Let's do it. Get carefree. Stat."

"Okay, great, but I absolutely owe you…" she began again. He was still sure she was trying to apologize for the kiss.

"Emma, please don't," Zach pleaded. "I can't talk about it. I can't. I'm enacting the carefree fun day zone. Now."

"You can't just demand that carefree fun appear," she said, a cautious smile creeping onto her face now.

"Oh, yes I can," he replied, turning a lopsided smile back at her. "Now let's go have some fun, dammit. We've been doing too much moping."

"Yeah, sure, okay." She got up and shuffled into the bathroom, closing the door behind her. A moment later, he could hear the water for the shower begin running.

He'd done the right thing. They couldn't keep hashing over the same pointless topics. She was leaving. She was marrying someone else. And their time together would soon be nothing more than a memory.

Okay, that isn't helping me have carefree fun. He was glad when Emma was ready to go on their little journey. Being left alone with his own thoughts was dangerous these days.

A short time later they were back in the car heading toward the visitors' center. Zach found he was so distracted by his attempts to push the kiss out of his mind that he was having trouble remembering which side of the road to drive on. Add the mechanics of the stick shift on top of that, and it was a lot to juggle.

After they parked, they bypassed the visitors' center and started the short hike to the viewing platforms. The wind was whipping off the water as they climbed to the top level and tried to figure out where to get the best views. The crowds weren't terribly thick yet. They seemed to have beaten the big tourist buses there.

Zach noticed there were signs posted along the guard rails cautioning people not to climb over and get too close to the edge.

"Tourists have fallen over before," Emma said into his ear since the wind was so strong. "Or that's what the guidebook said."

"They don't have to tell me twice to stand back," Zach tried to reply, but talking was basically useless. Breathing wasn't any easier. It felt like he had to battle to yank each breath back out of the wind. Standing high above the towering cliffs made him feel sort of puny and powerless; nature was definitely in control here.

He watched Emma for a long minute as her hair whipped around in the air. She looked as awed as he felt by the sight of the massive cliffs that rose high above the crashing waves on either side of them. He loved how much she enjoyed seeing these kinds of things. If she was his wife, he'd take her to every national forest, historical marker, natural wonder, and tourist trap she could dream of or find in any guidebook.

Oops.... He'd just violated his carefree fun zone again. Torturing himself with visions of a future they could never have was definitely the opposite of carefree fun.

"Picture?" Emma was mouthing at him now as she held up her phone. He reached for it, but she shook her head and leaned in to his ear again. "I want one of *you*."

Oh geez, why would she want a picture of him? That didn't seem like something Jim was going to love.

Then he decided okay, he didn't care at all what Jim thought.

Zach was terrible at posing for pictures, but he managed to smile, and she seemed happy with the result. *I should get a picture of her, too*, he thought. Soon it would be all he had left. He pulled his phone out then and gestured for her to get into place. She looked surprised but attempted to pull her hair to the side so it wasn't flapping in her face. Then she smiled. He pressed the button on his screen and got a good shot. Even in a windstorm, she was the most beautiful person he'd ever seen. He put his phone back in his pocket and smiled back at her.

She took some pictures of the cliffs, then they headed back to the visitor center to warm up. The wind was just too strong to stay there long.

"Oh! That was so beautiful, Z!" Emma said when they got inside. "It was absolutely amazing! Thank you so much for coming here with me!"

"Would you call it both carefree and fun?" he teased.

"Of course!" she replied with a laugh.

They walked around then. Emma became interested in an exhibit called "The Cliffs of Moher Experience" while Zach made his way to the gift shop. There were all kinds of Irish-themed items, like linens, jewelry, and sweaters. Plus, they had aisle after aisle of cheaper souvenirs like coffee cups, magnets, tee shirts, and pens. Zach didn't know what he was looking for exactly, but he decided he'd like to give Emma a little present. Something to remember him by.

Jewelry seemed maybe too personal to give to a woman who was marrying someone else. And he didn't want something goofy and cheap like oven mitts, salt-and-pepper shakers, or any of the countless items that seemed to either feature green clovers or sheep.

He was looking at a collection of hand-carved figurines made from locally mined marble when he saw it—there in the glass case was a little green turtle figurine. He laughed out loud.

It was perfect. It would remind her of their day in Phoenix Park. And maybe it would also remind her that someone out there knew and understood that she didn't have her life all planned out. That there was nothing wrong with not having all the answers. He sure didn't.

He had just finished paying for it when Emma reappeared.

"Hey, did you find something you want to buy?"

"Yeah, actually, I did," he said, handing her the bag. "For you."

She gave him a cute, quizzical look.

"Keep your expectations nice and low," he told her.

She smiled at him, then opened the bag, pulled out the tuft of tissue paper, and peeled it away to reveal the little turtle. The burst of laughter that followed shot its way into Zach's heart like an arrow. She'd been so sad for the entire trip, and now he'd made her smile.

"You bought me a turtle!" she said, holding it in her palm as she examined the little lines carved into the rounded shell.

"It's made of Connemara marble," said the cashier. "A green marble only found in this region."

"Oh, that's wonderful," Emma said to the woman before turning back to Zach. "Thank you, Z. You know, I don't actually collect turtles. But seriously this little guy makes me want to start. He is the cutest thing I've ever seen. Thank you so much; I'm going to treasure it forever."

Zach nodded. "Yeah, I thought you'd like it. When I saw it, I thought of you instantly. And, you know, I also thought, just maybe, it would make you think of me once in a while when you go home."

"I won't need it to remember you, Z. I'll never be...um....." Emma paused, trying to find the right words. She also looked like she was tearing up again.

"Emma, I don't think *carefree* means what you think it means," Zach said, trying to tease her out of another mood swing. *Is she ever going to tell me what's really wrong?* he wondered.

She smiled at him then, blinked away the tears, and tucked the turtle back inside its tissue-paper nest.

"I won't forget," she said. "Ever. Now let's get going."

Zach decided then that he wouldn't push her. If there was something she wanted him to know, she'd tell him eventually.

They walked out of the gift shop and got into the car. It was time to head back to Dublin.

Chapter 28

EMMA KNEW SHE HAD BEEN impossibly emotional the entire trip and was probably driving Zach crazy. She just wanted to give him a lighthearted day away from his troubles. But instead she'd manage to practically attack him, confuse him and, no doubt, hurt him further.

Really, a job well done.

What should she do now? She still didn't know, and she was running out of time. It was like a large clock was following her wherever she went, loudly ticking away the minutes they had left together.

Okay, I need to regroup, she thought as she watched the rolling green farmland through the car window. Her plan had been to get strategic about his issues. She still wanted to do everything she could to help him, and then she'd have to sacrifice her own happiness and walk away. He had to reclaim his life without her shoving him into decisions and choices that maybe weren't right for him—or at least weren't right for him *yet*.

Once she got back to the apartment that night, she'd check her Twitter account to see if Tommy had responded. So that was one thing she could do.

Her other idea had been to get Zach pitching again. She needed to focus on that. He seemed somewhat open to it, so she'd definitely work on that angle.

She glanced over at him. He turned and smiled at

her.

"What are you thinking about so seriously, Emmy?"

"The same thing I'm always thinking about," she replied somewhat mysteriously. So should she just tell him how much he was on her mind? Maybe what he needed was a push like that. Just a little well-meaning pressure to get him moving. "You. You are what I'm thinking about."

"Me? What about me?"

"I'm really excited about you throwing some pitches again. So excited. Why don't we stop the car right now? You know I want to take some pictures of the scenery anyway. We could find somewhere to pull off, and I could snap a few shots, and you could, I don't know…pick up a rock and throw it. I really feel like the key is to get you moving that arm again."

"I appreciate how much thought you've put into this, I really do," he said slowly, like he was trying to pick out his words with care. "But I really don't think throwing a rock into an empty field is going to be the career-igniter that you think it will."

"I'm not saying you should look into the world of professional rock hurling," she snapped, feeling a little annoyed now. *Why not just try it for heaven's sake?* "I'm talking about one pitch. One single pitch to get the feeling back."

"It would have to be quite a rock in order for me to actually position my hands on it. I don't think we're supposed to be driving past a rock quarry today. This isn't *The Flintstones*." Okay, it sounded like he was annoyed now, too. Well…good. Maybe he needed some anger to spark forward movement.

"I don't care about finger positions. I'm not at all

worried about whether you throw a cutter or a slider or a fastball. The sheep don't carry radar guns, so no one will know how fast it is, either. Just make a throw!" She was practically yelling now.

"Emma, I need to do it right. I can't risk some sort of damage to my arm. With my luck, I'd end up needing Tommy John surgery, which is a guaranteed one-year recovery at least. If I'm going to throw, I need to get into the gym, warm my arm up, and do it right."

"Okay, so my rock idea was dumb," she said. "So let's do that instead, then. Let's go get your arm warmed up. We could do it tomorrow. Let's get you straight into the gym, and then we'll go to the park and work on throwing. This is it, I can feel it."

"Emma, again, I appreciate that you want to spend your few remaining days doing something as boring as making sure I warm up my pitching arm, really. But I've got to work tomorrow."

"Call in sick," she said, snapping again. Why wouldn't he just agree to take this small step? Why couldn't he see their time was running out here?

"Emma, what's really going on here?" Zach demanded, his usual easygoing patience peeling away. "You've been all over the map this entire trip. Come on, talk to me!"

"I told you, Zach, but you're not hearing me. I want to *help* you! I don't have much time left. I want to get strategic about it. Methodical. Let's just try some tangible things that might actually make a difference. Or do you not really want to get better? Is that what's going on here? Do you want to be left alone in Dublin forever?"

"Of course not. You know I don't. But you running out of time here doesn't automatically mean everything is going to be perfect," he told her. "I appreciate everything you've done, and I love how much you care. Really, Em. And I meant it when I said I feel better. I do. I feel close. Like maybe things are about to change. But you can't just push me off the cliff and hope I can fly, you know?"

"Is this about forgiveness?" she asked suddenly, remembering her tweet to Tommy.

"What do you mean?"

"Do you still blame yourself that Tommy got hurt? Would talking to him and getting forgiveness from him help? Because that's another idea Tracy and I were batting around. Like maybe if you knew Tommy had forgiven you, maybe that would help somehow."

"It's not the issue," he said.

"Well, maybe it is and you don't even realize it," she pressed. "Which is why I reached out to him already."

"You what?! Emma, what the hell?"

"I told you, I was looking for tangible ways to help. So I tweeted him the other day, asking if he was still angry. I was hoping he might reply and say something nice that I could bring to you as proof that if Tommy forgave you, that *you* should be able to forgive you."

"Emma, you're off-base with this one. You should have talked to me about it first and not gone behind my back." He looked mad now. "It wasn't your call to make."

"I'm sorry, Zach. But it's not like I mentioned our connection or anything. There's only so much backstory you can give in 280 characters." She was feeling defensive now. "He won't know you've got anything to do with it."

"But I *didn't* have anything to do with it, did I?

Because you didn't talk to me about it first, like you really should have. This is *my* mess, Emma. My mess, my career, my mistakes, and my life! And for what it's worth, he forgave me right after it happened."

"He did?" she asked, startled. "You never told me that."

"Yeah, well, who knew you'd jump in the middle of it? I went to the hospital where they took him. His family was there, and they were kind to me and his mom even said she would be praying for me. They couldn't have been more forgiving. It helped, of course it did. But I was still stuck, still suffering, and still lost."

"I'm sorry, Zach," she said.

"And I'm sorry I jumped down your throat about it," Zach replied. "I know you just want to help."

An uneasy silence fell between them then. She didn't know which emotion to process first. She was a little mad, a little hurt, and a lot frustrated. But it was painfully obvious that there really wasn't a thing in the world she could do about any of it.

She couldn't bulldoze him to where he needed to go; that much was very clear now. She'd been telling herself all this time that he needed to be the one to help himself, but she hadn't been able to resist trying to do it for him anyway.

So she was done trying. Done pushing. And done hoping, unfortunately. All she could do now was just say goodbye and walk away.

Should she tell him everything first, though? Should she tell him that she and Jim were over and wouldn't be getting back together? Should she finally admit that she was free? And after that, could she then say the rest of it, too? Like about how crazy she was about him, and even about how much she wanted to spend her life with him? Or would that set him back? Would it make him ask her to stay with him in Dublin? Would it give him a reason to never really make himself want to leave?

She didn't know. She'd been wildly off the mark with every other idea she'd had about helping him move forward. So she didn't know if she could really trust her feelings and instincts now. Maybe he didn't even feel the same way about her. With the terrible way she'd been reading the situation lately, there was a chance his feelings weren't as deep as hers were.

Maybe this was just chemistry between two personalities and nothing more. Just because she loved him deeply didn't mean his feelings were the same. She might be agonizing over a man who would never be able to love her back.

She tried shifting her focus to the scenery. Maybe if she pushed away all these warring thoughts, the solution would present itself. Sometimes your mind could solve puzzles for you when you weren't consciously focusing on them. That might work in this situation. Because agonizing about it nonstop throughout the summer sure hadn't gotten her anywhere. All she'd managed to do was make Zach furious.

She looked over at him then. He glanced back and gave her a tiny smile.

"Emmy, I'm such a jerk," he said, reaching his hand over like he was going to take hers. Then he paused for a second before putting it back on the wheel. "I'm sorry for getting mad before. Here I have this beautiful angel who's trying to take time out of her life to help me, and I'm getting angry about it. I really am sorry, honey."

She desperately wanted to take the hand he'd almost offered her, but she was worried about sending him more crazy mixed signals. Navigating this situation was getting harder by the minute.

Finally, she took a deep breath and jumped in with an apology of her own—"No Zach, I'm the one who should be sorry here. You're right, this is your life, and I can see now that having me blindly tromping around in your business isn't really solving anything. So I'm going to back off now. No forcing you at gunpoint to throw the ball in the park. No rocks, I promise. And no more ill-advised tweets. Okay? I'm done, really. And again, *I'm* sorry."

Zach gave her a little smile, then turned back to the road. Her words hung in the renewed silence that filled the car now. They didn't talk much more for the rest of the drive back to Dublin.

Because really, what was left to say?

Chapter 29

THAT NIGHT, Zach found sleep impossible. He kept tossing and turning as he tried to get the tense conversation with Emma out of his mind.

He knew all she wanted to do was to help him. That much was very clear. She'd quite obviously been cooking up all kinds of plans in the hopes that one of them would be the key to unlocking the prison cell he was in. He absolutely understood her reasoning, her motivations, and even her methods. Trying a little bit of everything they could possibly try totally made sense. Attacking the problem from all different sides made sense.

But the part about throwing...she clearly didn't understand the mechanics of it. She didn't know the complicated world that revolved around keeping a pitcher's arm in top form. She'd never been privy to the massages, the whirlpools, the ice and heat wraps, the lifting, the stretching. There was also the complicated issue of timing. The world of a Major League pitcher was *all* about timing. Days of rest. Throwing days. Game days. It was all carefully counted and measured and watched.

A pitcher's arm was his entire world. Some guys even insured their arms. Teams carefully monitored any sort of pull or twinge the pitcher might experience. The managers would carefully count how many pitches they'd thrown in a game and then pull the guy out once the pitch count got too high, no matter the stakes. It was very scientific. It was calculated and measured and very cautious. Teams had millions of dollars riding on the arms of their starting pitchers. They took great pains to make sure those arms stayed loose and limber.

What they *didn't* do was shove their pitching aces into a field and tell them to hurl rocks while their muscles were cold. So she'd been well-meaning. Cute, even, in her desperation to get him to take that first throw.

But since there was a part of him that thought he could maybe go back to the game one day, and since the team trainers hadn't been in the back seat of the car making sure Zach's arm was taken care of, that had left him to be the one to say no. If he was going to pitch again professionally, he had to take care of his arm.

Still, the core of her idea was a good one. He needed to throw again. In a no-pressure environment, he needed to get the feel of the leather in his hand and remind himself why lining up those red seams perfectly in his grip was a part of his life that he didn't want to live without any longer. Baseball was in his soul. And he'd turned his back on it far too long.

One pitch.... Emma was right. He needed to do that. But he also needed to make sure he did it right. He needed to do it cautiously. Warm up, limber up, and be very careful about it.

The more he thought about this, the more he liked it.

Maybe he could do it alone, then surprise Emma with the news. She'd probably be thrilled. Well, she'd be thrilled if she ever agreed to talk to him again, that is. He came down on her way too hard about the tweet to Tommy. She was probably feeling annoyed with him and delighted that she'd be free of him soon. He didn't want their dwindling time together to end with a tense confrontation as their last memory.

So this would be perfect. He'd go to the park after work, warm up, take a few practice throws, and then call her. They could meet somewhere, he'd tell her about his progress, and she'd be happy again.

Everything about his time with her had helped peel back the layers of his depression and troubles. Each time he saw her, he felt lighter and more fulfilled than he had in years. He wanted her to know how much she'd helped him. If he got his life back one day, it would be almost entirely thanks to her. He certainly owed her the courtesy of making sure she knew that. He couldn't do much more for her, but he could certainly make sure she didn't leave town feeling like she'd let him down.

No, he definitely couldn't leave things the way they were between the two of them currently.

Okay, so the first step was get the morning shift at work out of the way. Which he did—he went to the pub and stepped through the familiar routine. His mind was on his plans for later, of course. He had the itch to hold the ball again. And he knew it had never gone away. Hadn't Emma told him that he spent their entire trip to Phoenix Park practicing the grips for ghost pitches he was never intending to throw?

Yeah—baseball was more deeply ingrained in his soul than he'd ever even realized. Maybe suppressing that was what had held him back. You can only fight your heart for so long. He was born to play baseball. So why was he battling it so hard?

By the time his shift was over, and he got back to his apartment, it was late afternoon. He was ready to head to Phoenix Park when it occurred to him that he should look for an actual baseball diamond. Surely there was one somewhere in Dublin. Standing on a mound and pitching the ball toward home plate would feel better than zinging balls at nothing in a park and hoping no one got hit.

He got out his laptop and went to Google. It seemed that the only place to find a baseball diamond was in West Dublin at Corkagh Park. He'd never even heard of it before. It was too far to walk, so he decided to take a cab.

When it stopped at the entrance of the park, it occurred to Zach that finding another to go back to the city wouldn't be easy. So he gave the driver several large bills and told him he'd double it if the guy came back for him in an hour. The cabbie happily agreed.

As he walked into the park and looked for the baseball diamond, he started slowly stretching his arm. There were two diamonds, as it turned out—one for kids and one for adults. The former was hosting a game between two little-league teams, but he was relieved to see that the larger one was empty.

Perfect.

He continued stretching and loosening his arm. He'd been through these exercises a million times. They felt like coming home every bit as much as walking toward the empty mound.

He approached from the left side of the outfield. He swung his arm in slow circles as he stared at the mound. He drew closer and wondered how many hours had he spent in his life standing on mounds just like this one? It was probably a huge number, measurable in years if strung end-to-end.

He kept staring at it as he made his final approach

and, finally, his ascent.

Then he was there, standing on a mound again with a baseball in his hand. He stretched the arm a few more times. It felt okay. The muscles were loose. He was ready.

He looked toward home plate. The empty field around him slowly receded until it felt like he was back in Yankee Stadium again, surrounded by thousands of fans. He could practically smell the peanuts and the popcorn and the hot dogs. It came back so easily, the feel of it all. He could hear the music of the organ and the sound of the announcer's voice calling out the name of the next batter. He was focused. He was *there*.

He twirled the ball in his hand, feeling the leather and the seams. He lined his fingers up. Then he went into his wind-up, his stride, and finally his release. The ball zoomed forward, veering to the right over the plate at the last minute. Finally, it struck the backstop with a rattle and fell to the ground.

He stood up and watched it as it lay there in the dirt.

He'd done it. And Emma had been completely right—the simple act of standing on this mound and throwing that ball made him want to do it again. This was what he should be doing. Pitching that little leather ball was what he was *born* to do. Why had he been wasting his time listing off which beers they had on tap for tourist after tourist, day after day, for two years? *Seriously, what the hell am I still doing here?* He was wasting his talents and his time. He had poured so much energy into dodging his fears.

He thought about what to do next as he walked over and retrieved the ball. He looked at the scuff of dirt on the side. It was like a badge of honor. He laughed, tossed the ball up in the air, caught it, and turned to head back to the mound. He threw again, this time a fastball. He wondered how fast he could throw now. He'd probably never hit 98 miles per hour again. The older a pitcher got, the slower his fastball became. *But I'll bet I can still put some fire behind it,* he thought.

He glanced at his watch. Maybe he should head back to where the cab would be waiting. Hopefully the driver would return like he'd agreed.

He went to the park entrance and sat on a bench. Then he looked at the ball again as he rolled it around in his hand.

Was he really ready to leave yet? He didn't know. Maybe not. He still didn't know how a person went about reclaiming their life. He was pretty sure that if he did go back home, he'd attempt to get back into the game. But because of the non-compete clause he'd signed, the only team he could play for would be the Yankees. Unless maybe they agreed to release him from the terms of the agreement. That might be a possibility, too.

But what if no team wanted him? Or what if a team took a chance on him but he couldn't recapture the level of skill he'd demonstrated before?

No, I could survive that, he told himself. That wouldn't be the end of the world. He could stay in baseball somehow. He could be a pitching coach or maybe even manage someday.

It was a lot to consider. He'd be taking all sorts of risks. What if he tried, got his family's hopes ratcheted up high, then failed? What if he just couldn't face another batter? Throwing at an empty plate was a bit different from throwing to a person. What if he hit someone again? What effect would *that* have on him?

Maybe he should stay in Dublin until Emma was married. Being an easy car ride away from her, but knowing he couldn't ever see her again...that would be so hard. And she was a baseball fan. What would it do to him to look up in the stands one day at Fenway Park and find himself looking at Emma and Jim with their children all around them? He'd probably pass out with grief.

Yeah, there were still too many unknowns, too many variables. He couldn't rush into a decision like this. He'd take his time, think it through, and figure out the right course. Other than the fact that a Major League pitcher only had so many years before age caught up with him, there wasn't any timetable here. Once Emma left, the frantic feeling of urgency that seemed to be swirling around her would go, too. Then he could calmly figure this out.

In the meantime, he could call her, maybe make plans to see her tomorrow or whenever she was free. He could tell her that he came here and threw that first pitch, the one she'd wanted him to make so badly. She'd be thrilled when she heard how much it really had helped, and that he was closer than ever before to making some decisions. He smiled just thinking about the giddy response he'd get from her.

He stood as the cab pulled up, then thanked the cabbie as he got in. He felt good. He'd thrown the ball again, his confidence was starting to creep back, and he had the feeling that it wouldn't be much longer before he could make some concrete plans.

Yeah—he absolutely couldn't wait to tell Emma.

Chapter 30

EMMA WAS TRYING—unsuccessfully—to get Zach off her mind now. She'd decided to see some more of Dublin, thinking that some quality time with her guidebook was exactly what she needed to wipe him right out of her thoughts.

But it wasn't working. At all.

She was wandering around St. Patrick's Cathedral when she felt her phone vibrate. She pulled it out of her pocket and glanced at the screen.

Zach.... So much for not thinking about him.

She hesitated. She hadn't talked to him since the trip to the Cliffs of Moher the day before. She wasn't sure she was ready yet. She still had so many decisions to make. She didn't know what she should even say to him at this point.

Emma stared at the screen and watched as the call went to voicemail. She just couldn't talk to him at the moment.

He'd made it very clear that she was pushing him too hard and too fast. He didn't need to hear about forgiveness from Tommy. He wasn't ready to pitch yet. It wasn't time for him to leave Dublin. All he needed was for Emma to back off.

So she was out of options. Her strategic approach to picking apart his issues and solving them one by one had failed spectacularly. And so that was it. She was going to have to give up and just walk away.

How will I be able to do that?

Emma sat in the back pew of the cathedral and let her mind go over everything some more. Seriously, should she tell Zach that she'd broken up with Jim? Now that she was definitely on her way out of town, it hardly mattered anymore whether Zach knew or not. Nothing else she'd done had made any difference. Why should that?

Okay, she was getting absolutely nowhere with this. And she could barely focus on the beauty of the Gothic architecture and stained glass that was all around her.

This is pointless.... Emma stood up then and walked out of the cathedral. She pulled out her phone as she made her way down the steps. Zach had left her a message—*Em, it's Z. Hey, listen, I know I was a big jerk to you yesterday in the car, and I'm so sorry. I know you're just trying to help me before you go, and I really do appreciate that you're trying so hard. And, actually, I have something to tell you about that. Can we meet tomorrow? Maybe we could walk around Temple Bar or grab something to eat? Let me know. Bye...*

She listened to the message again and then saved it. She had a feeling she'd want to hear his voice again once she was back home.

So he wanted to meet tomorrow? That might be perfect. Yeah, okay, so maybe this would be the opportunity to cut ties with Zach and walk away. He needed to help himself, and he wasn't ready to do it. She couldn't spend the rest of her life banging her head against a wall while trying to make him see the light. She would have to feel out how the conversation went, though, before deciding whether she should tell him about the situation with Jim. But, honestly, she was pretty sure she would.

There, I've made a decision. Yes, she was going to do it. She'd just lay everything out in front of him and walk away before she gave herself a chance to change her mind.

She pulled out her phone again and started a new text to Zach—**Sure, tomorrow sounds good. Em**.

Short and to the point. Perfect.

It felt good to have a plan of action, but it also felt somewhat painful. She loved Zach so much. Why couldn't things have worked out differently for them? Parts of their friendship had been so wonderful. Being with him had helped her see that she was mindlessly walking into a marriage she didn't really want. She'd always be grateful to Zach for that.

But why hadn't being with her given *him* the same kind of clarity? How had she gotten out of her bad situation, but Zach seemed absolutely no closer to getting out of his own? The future they could have had together was right there in front of them, yet still never within their reach.

Emma thought then about how being with Zach made her feel—so happy and electric and alive.

Laying in his arms all night in the Shannon hotel had felt so right. That's why she hadn't been able to resist asking for a kiss. And if Zach hadn't been the one to pull back, they'd still be in that bed together. She had absolutely no willpower at all when it came to him. That chemistry between them was exactly why walking away tomorrow was going to be so hard. Any small word or look or touch from him was going to break her heart…and possibly her resolve.

She had to be strong, though. This wasn't for her. It wasn't *about* her. It was about Zach and what he needed, and she absolutely had to put his needs ahead of her own.

And who knew? Maybe someday Zach would be able to regain his old life. Maybe she'd turn on the radio and hear the sports chatter about how the Yankees got their pitching ace back. If that happened, she would definitely reach out to him and congratulate him on his recovery. When the Yankees came to Boston, she could drive in for a game and...who knows? Maybe then they could even arrange a late dinner or something. That could certainly happen.

Anything was possible if Zach just had the opportunity to make those choices on his own.

The vision in her head of Zach making his way back to his team and pitching a game at Fenway made her feel better and stronger in her resolve. *This can work.* Anything was possible, and it didn't have to be the absolute end of the line for them. There was still a glimmer of hope. Maybe one day they'd be together again.

She stopped at a busy corner and waited for the light to change. The buses and cars were busily moving past, once again startling her as they came from the "wrong" direction. Then the light changed, and she moved forward with the crowd.

She'd enjoyed her time in Dublin so much. The sightseeing, the sounds, the smells, the foods…all of it. She was so glad she'd made the decision to come here. It had changed her life. She'd made the decision to break up with Jim, and she'd found Zach, who she would love and miss for the rest of her life.

I've changed, she thought. She felt stronger and happier in some ways than she'd ever been. But in some ways, she was also sadder than she'd ever been, too.

Still...she could do this. She could leave Dublin. She was ready.

Chapter 31

THE CROWDS WERE surprisingly light, Emma thought, as she and Zach walked past the bars and cafés of the touristy Temple Bar section of Dublin. It wasn't far from the pub where Zach worked, and, of course, where she'd first met him. The tourists were probably tucked inside to avoid the weather, she figured. It looked like it was about to downpour.

She was bitterly dreading talking to Zach today. She'd moved up her flight. She was leaving Dublin tomorrow, so this was it. It was really happening. Their time was just about over, and she had to find the right way to say goodbye to him.

So how do you just walk away from someone you love when you know they're hurting so much? she wondered. Where would she find the strength to cut all ties and contact and just melt away?

She didn't know. But it was what she was going to do. What—she was still convinced—she *needed* to do.

"I'm so glad you agreed to meet today," he said. "I wasn't sure you'd ever want to talk to me again after our fight in the car."

"No, I understand," she replied. "And it was my fault anyway. I was out of line. I was pushing too much and too fast, and you just reminded me that it's none of my business."

"But you *were* right, and that's what I wanted to talk to you about."

"No, I wasn't right. Not at all. This is your life, and I need to step away and let you live it. Lucky for you, I'm leaving and going home."

"Lucky? You think I'm happy that you're going home and back to Jim? Really?" Zach looked frustrated now.

"No, actually I'm not," she said before she realized the words were coming out of her mouth.

"You're not what? Leaving?"

"No, I'm not going back to Jim," she said, biting her lip nervously. She really hadn't decided whether it was smart to get into this with him. It might make saying goodbye even harder. And yet, suddenly, the words were tumbling out of her mouth anyway. "The truth, actually, is that Jim and I broke up."

Zach stopped and turned to face her. "What? When?"

"When he was here. When he came to see me."

"That long ago? And you didn't tell me? Why?"

"Because you seemed to like knowing that I wasn't free, that I wasn't an option for you. You told me once that if it weren't for Jim, you didn't think we'd be able to be friends. So…I don't know. I wanted to be friends with you. So I didn't mention it."

"I…but this is great news, Em! This changes everything!" An excited smile creased its way across his face. She wished she'd been able to see that smile more often during their time together. He'd spent far too much time being unhappy.

"Nope, it really doesn't, Z," Emma said, shaking her head slowly. "Not at all. You're still here, refusing to help yourself, and I'm still going home."

"Refusing to help myself?" Zach asked, his smile quickly vanishing. "Is that what you think is going on?"

"I think a lot of things, Zach, a *lot* of things," Emma said, feeling herself growing inexplicably angry as the rain finally started to fall. "For starters, I think you should have been in therapy for the last two years."

"Emma, honestly! It wasn't that I didn't *want* to get help."

"Really? Because you never saw anyone, so you never got a diagnosis, and therefore you don't even know what you're up against here. Is it a panic disorder? Is it depression? Maybe you could have been on medications to help you all this time. But you refused to take that step and even investigate the possibilities."

"That's because I was afraid they'd give me something from the banned-substance list. Baseball has a ton of rules about things you can't take. I didn't want to go back to the game one day and end up failing the drug tests."

"Oh stop it, that's a lame argument," Emma fired back immediately. "You could have consulted with team doctors and gotten all your medications approved by them."

"Really? Okay, and what else have you determined, Dr. Crawford?" Zach asked, matching her angry tone note for note.

"You really want to know? All right, I'll tell you. I think your whole situation started out as pure, simple regret that you'd hurt someone. And then it built into a fear that it might happen again if you were to throw another pitch. So then you had regret as the foundation with fear as the house." Emma was struggling to dial back her anger as she chose her words. She needed to go about it cautiously, and she had to say it just right. This would probably be her one last chance to break down Zach's walls, and she didn't want to waste it.

Zach was just watching her now...but was he truly listening or was he just blind with rage? She couldn't tell. But he was still there. She felt encouraged. Emboldened. She could do this.

"Those two emotions started growing around you, building and strengthening their grip on you. And I think that you sailed through your entire life up to that point based solely on your amazing talent. You never had to work and struggle like the rest of us. You never had a wall you couldn't go around before. Some guys have to play baseball in college, then struggle and fight and claw to get into an MLB farm system. After that they spend years—*years*—on single-A teams, where they sacrifice and work and make almost no money and have to give everything they've got in the hope of making it to double A or triple A, and all of that without any guarantee whatsoever that they'll ever get called to the Majors. But not you, Zach. For you it was all very easy. Too easy, perhaps...." Emma paused to take a breath.

"Keep going," Zach snapped back immediately. "It seems like you've got this all figured out."

Okay, yeah, that's anger, she thought. But oh well; she'd come too far now to stop. She had to say goodbye to him anyway; she may as well go all the way with this.

"No, I don't have it all figured out," Emma said, her voice getting louder now as her anger started to ramp up to match his. "Not at all. Because there's no easy solution here, obviously. But you know what? At least I'm *trying* to figure it out, which is more than I can say for you."

Zach just stared at her. He looked shocked by what she'd said. Shocked and hurt.

The rain was starting to fall harder, and they were both already soaked. Her timing for this talk could have been better, she thought as the drops streamed down her face.

"That's what you really think?" Zach asked finally. "You think I'm not trying? You think I want to live here, alone, for the rest of my life?"

"No, I don't think that. But I do think it's time for you to make some sort of plan for getting out of here. You've sat here letting all your problems freeze you in place for long enough. You know, it's pretty ironic that a man who is known for never being able to stay still has been caught in a state of total paralysis for two years. Help yourself, Zach! Free yourself!" Emma was practically shouting now as the rain drove down with a fury.

"Why do you even care, Emma, huh?" Zach demanded, his anger moving into full-blown fury. "What is any of this to you? You're heading back to Massachusetts anyway. How does my plan, or rather my lack of a plan, affect *you*?"

"Why? Why? Do you really have to ask me that?" Tears started pouring down her face, mingling with the relentless rainfall. "Because I *love you*, you big moron! I adore you! I can't *stand* seeing you in this much pain! And I don't want to live the rest of my—"

Zach reached out then and grabbed her, pulling her into a blistering kiss. All the anger and emotion that had been building between them and the chemistry that they'd both been working so hard to ignore came together in the heat of that moment like a cymbal crash, rocking Emma to her core. She threw her arms around him in response and matched the intensity of his kiss with her own.

All her fears and worries for him came to the surface, and she kissed him with more passion than she ever imagined she possessed. She couldn't get close enough to him, couldn't make the crescendo of emotion stop. She pulled her right hand from around his neck and slid it under his wet shirt, sliding her hand over the hard muscles of his back.

Zach finally tore himself away and took a step backward. "Oh my God, Emma, you are absolutely driving me crazy. I can't…I want…."

She watched him try to gather his thoughts as she gasped for air, her chest still heaving with all the wild feelings that were now stirred up inside.

"Come with me. To my apartment. I…I need you," he finally said.

"I need you too, Zach," she replied.

"And I love you, too," he said. "So much. I've been dead inside for so long, but then you came and pulled me out of my little prison and completely turned my life around. Please stay with me. Don't leave. Don't go back to Massachusetts. You could get a teaching job here. Or not. Whatever you want to do. Just stay and we'll figure this out together. Because I absolutely adore you, and I don't want to live another second of my life without you in it."

Emma smiled and tried to sniff away the tears that were still pouring down her face. This was not how she thought this conversation was going to go. She thought walking away from him was going to be hard before. But now that she knew he returned her feelings? It was going to destroy her.

"I can't, Zach."

"Sure you can. Just…just *stay*," he said, reaching for her hand.

"No, I can't," Emma said, squeezing his fingers and then pulling back.

"What are you talking about? We found each other. You're not with Jim anymore. And I'm feeling better than I have in a long time. This is right. This is what's supposed to happen, right?" A look of confusion stole across his face.

"Zach, it's *because* I love you that I can't stay," Emma told him. "I can't be your crutch. I can't be your solution or your cure. I can't…fix you. I don't want to be the kind of woman who falls for guys with huge issues and then tries to patch them up and mold them into the men they want them to be."

"You just said that you care about me," Zach countered. "You're just helping me. There's nothing wrong with you being the one to…I don't know, light my way out of the darkness."

"No, Zach, I can't. You have to figure this out for yourself. Make a plan and act on it. Face your past. Apologize to the people you've wronged. Face the old teammates you abandoned. Have the tough conversations that you never had the first time around. Then go do whatever it is that will make you whole again. Get a job as a pitching coach. Or you could pick a field of study that interests you and go to college. Or you could call the Steinbrenner family and beg to get your spot on the team back. Try to get a minor-league contract and crawl your way out of the system the hard way. I don't care which, Zach, I really don't. But *you* have to do it. You have to actually, actively *decide*. Life isn't just going to magically pave a golden path for you. Not this time." Emma took another step backward to help her resist her urge to hug him. He looked so sad now. It was breaking her heart.

"I can do those things if you're by my side, Emma," he told her. "There's nothing wrong with us facing them together, as a team."

"I can't do anything to risk this for you, Zach," she replied, shaking her head. "If I stay here with you, there's a real chance that just remaining here in Dublin would suddenly seem right and easy to you. But it's not right. You will never be whole again until you face your demons. And you have to face them alone."

After studying her face and seeing how serious she was, he asked, "Will you wait for me? It's not going to be long. That's what I was trying to tell you."

"We'll see what happens. Don't worry about that now. I'm not going to put some kind of time limit on your recovery. But I'm also not going to put my own life on hold, either. What if you need another two years to figure this out? Five? Ten? I'm not going to tie you or me to any kind of promises." Emma was feeling stronger now. She could do this. She could actually walk away and not look back. She had to, for Zach's sake. And her own.

"You're not hearing me," Zach replied, almost pleading. "It's not going to be that long. I feel it. So don't do this Emma. There's another way, there has to be. Stay with me. I love you. You love me. That should be enough for us to build a future."

"No promises, Zach. Nothing is tying you down to me. You've got infinite choices in front of you and almost no limitations. Now you just have to figure out which path is best for you. Yes, I love you. Please believe that. I'll always love you. And it's because I love you this much that I'm choosing to walk away. Goodbye, Zach. And good luck. You can do this. I believe in you."

The rain continued to pool around them as Emma stood there, drinking in one last long look at him, memorizing his sorrow-filled face. He didn't say anything else as she turned and walked away, her tears now pouring out as hard and fast as the rain itself.

She'd done it. She'd left him. Now she just had to pack her bags and leave town before she lost her resolve the way she'd just lost her heart.

Chapter 32

ZACH COULDN'T BEAR IT. His heart was breaking into a million pieces as he watched Emma walk away from him. He stood there, rooted in his stunned sorrow, until he could no longer pick her out in the distance.

She'd left him. That was it. She was going home without any promise to wait for him. She could fall right back into Jim's arms for all he knew. Jim had to know he was crazy to let Emma go the first time. This would be his chance to get her back. Zach knew if he ever was given a real chance at keeping Emma in his life, he'd hold on and never let go. And Jim didn't strike him as dumb. Emma would be adrift when she got back, looking for a full-time job and a fresh start to her life. How long would she take to move on?

Zach couldn't believe he was even thinking this way. *Emma*.... His beautiful Emma actually loved him back. It was a miracle. He had been so happy when she said those words! Like someone had finally lifted some of the weight that had been holding him down for so long. He could do anything in the world as long as he knew that she'd be there in his life.

Emma loves me.

But then she'd shut him down and walked away. How could one person's emotions go from such heights to such lows in that short a span of time? She'd given him all the hope in the world, then she'd crushed it just as fast. What was he going to do? How was he going to live without her?

As the rain finally starting to slow down, he realized he was a wet mess. He needed to go home and take a shower. *There, I've made a plan*, he thought somewhat sarcastically. But hey, it was a first step.

He walked back to his apartment as Emma's words continued to bounce and spin around in his head.

"You have to figure this out for yourself. Make a plan and act on it. Face your past. Apologize to the people you wronged."

It all seemed so easy when she said it. So clear.

"You will never be whole again until you face your demons. And you have to face them alone."

Sure, but how? How was he finally going to face those demons? She was right that he'd been putting this off for too long. And she wasn't the first person to say those things to him. His parents had said variations of those very same ideas. Zeke and Zoe had each taken turns leveling their whacks at him. His manager and his agent had tried to talk sense into him back when it all happened. But aside from his family, most people had given up and written him off. So Emma's was the first fresh voice coming into the "get yourself together" chorus in a long time.

It especially hurt to hear those things from *her*, which seemed ridiculous since she didn't know him before. She didn't fully understand how far he had fallen or how much this whole situation had changed him. His confidence was gone, along with his sense of self and his sense of worth. All of that had taken a beating, and Emma just couldn't possibly understand what she was really asking of him.

But then she wasn't really asking anything at all, was she? She hadn't asked him to fix himself for her.

And she hadn't made any real demands or expectations for how he could win her back. She just told him what she thought he needed to do, and then she walked away.

Zach got to his apartment and slogged down the hall, unmindful of the soggy trail of rain and dirt he was leaving in his wake. He went into the bathroom, kicked off his shoes, and pulled off his wet tee shirt. Then he leaned over to turn on the shower before unbuttoning his soaked jeans and slowly peeling them off. He was miserable inside and out, he thought as he yanked on the heavy wet material that was clinging to his legs.

Finally free of his soggy clothes, he left them all over the floor of the bathroom and stepped into the hot shower. The water pelted his face as he stood there, lost in the memories that were twisting all around. He remembered seeing Emma walk into the pub that first day he met her, when she sat down and ordered a beer and struck up a conversation with him. He remembered taking her hand and pulling her off the bus at Phoenix Park, lost in the electricity of that innocent touch. He thought of how she'd cried when she learned his secret. He thought about the trips they'd taken together. The sizzling kiss they'd shared today in the rain. He thought about all of it, all their time together. All the smiles and the touches and the little moments that ultimately had come together to create their beautiful love story.

Those moments were what was important to him. That's what he had to work to save.

He had thrown away his entire career over stupid fears and regrets. He'd walked away from his teammates, his contract, his family, everything. He'd thrown away absolutely everything. He'd lost every single thing that ever meant anything to him, including his pride. But he wasn't going to make those mistakes again.

He wasn't going to lose Emma.

She was his line in the sand, and this was as far as he was going to let his fears and his problems take him. He'd figured out a way to deal with losing his talents, his career, his earning potential, his friends, and his family. But he would die before he let Emma walk out of his life.

All of this ridiculousness was over. He was going to walk into the pub tomorrow and quit. He felt like he owed the owner the respect of giving him notice. If it wasn't for the kindness that man had shown him over these years, he wouldn't even bother going back in and getting his last check. But no, he was going to do this the right way. He'd burned enough bridges.

Okay, so that's step one. Quit the job at the pub. Step two would be to pack his suitcase and give up the apartment. It had come furnished, and he hadn't really acquired much over the past two years. So he could be packed and ready to go pretty fast.

But go where? This is where the plan got murky and tough.

Should he go straight to the Bronx and talk to the Yankees? Apologize for breaking his contract and beg for anything, even a position as a bat boy? Or maybe he should call Hank first and feel out the general sentiment there. As manager, Hank would probably get a sense of how he might be received if he showed up.

Zach stepped out of the shower and grabbed a towel, then he walked to the bedroom and pulled on a pair of sweats. He scrubbed the towel over his hair as he wandered around looking for his phone, which turned out to be tucked between the couch cushions.

Okay, he thought, step two probably needed to include hiring a maid service to clean the apartment. It was a mess.

He unlocked the phone and pulled up his contact list. Would Hank have the same number? Was he still the manager in the first place? Zach honestly didn't know.

He hit Send before he could overthink what he was doing. If he didn't just jump into this, it was never going to happen.

"Wilson speaking," Hank said, his familiar gruffness making Zach smile.

"Hank? Hi, it's Zach Hiller," he said.

"Z? Wow, I never thought I'd hear your voice again. Where are you?"

"I'm in Dublin, actually, but I'm finally ready to get over my…fears…and, uh…" Zach said, rolling his eyes. He was such an idiot. He should have thought about what he wanted to say before he called. This was so awkward.

"You're ready to come back home, son?" Hank asked, a soft kindness in his voice that Zach had never heard before.

"I want to figure out whether baseball has any use for me anymore," Zach started. "But first I have some amends to make. Coach, I'm so sorry I quit on you. I quit on the Yankees and my teammates and I left you high and dry. I was only thinking about how upset I was about what happened to Tommy. I didn't…I didn't care, I guess, what the repercussions would be for everyone else."

"It takes a big man to admit when he's wrong, son. I'm glad you called."

"Well, a better man wouldn't have walked away or

let two years go by. But I'm finally ready to get my life together. Do you think that the Yankees would ever consider taking me back? Is there even room on the roster?"

"You're forgetting what time of year it is, Z. We're past the trade deadline. The team is set for this year," Hank said. "But I have no idea whether they'd be open to talking to you about next year. You burned a lot of bridges, Z. And it won't be easy to convince them that two years away from the game wasn't too long. Do you still have your stuff? Is the arm still there? The velocity?"

"I stayed in basic good shape and went to the gym all the time, but no, I haven't been throwing," Zach admitted. "I'm not sure what to do here."

"Talk to the Yankees. They might want you to prove yourself. Maybe spend some time in the minors or in Japan. But talk to them the way you just talked to me, and I'm sure you can get them to listen. At the end of the day, a pitching ace is too hard to find for them to stand on too high a moral ground."

Zach laughed, relieved to hear Hank's thoughts on his situation. Taking the next step suddenly seemed possible.

"I've got to reach out to my agent and the players' union," he went on. Even talking about the baseball world again felt exhilarating. How had it taken him this long to make this call? He was such an idiot. "Make sure I go through the right channels. But yeah, I'll do whatever they want me to do. I'll sell peanuts at the stadium if that'll help."

"Good luck, Z," Hank said. "I'm rooting for you, really. Let me know if I can do anything else to help."

"Thanks, Coach. This has helped me more than

you'll ever know," Zach told him before saying goodbye and ending the call.

That felt great, he realized. This was so right.

Time to call his agent and keep those apologies rolling.

Chapter 33

FOR A GUY WHO had watched the love of his life walk away the day before, Zach was feeling pretty great when he woke up the next morning.

The kindness and encouraging words from Hank had helped Zach get past his fears about how people would react to his apologies. If Hank—the man who he'd directly defied when he walked off the mound and left the game—could forgive him, then maybe some of the other people he'd wronged could do the same.

His next call was to Scott Burrell, his agent. Scott had lost money with the broken contract, so that was another tough conversation. But Scott seemed happy to hear from him and more than willing to set up a meeting with the Yankees in a couple weeks. Zach couldn't request that it happen right away, even though he'd love to get it over with. He still needed to give notice at the pub and tell the landlords he was breaking his lease on the apartment. He'd happily pay for the months he wouldn't be there. Whatever it took to keep his recovery momentum rolling.

I am doing this...I really am. He was really leaving Dublin and going home to reclaim his old life. Even thinking about the possibilities filled him with excitement and joy. What had seemed absolutely impossible for so long now seemed surprisingly easy. *This is amazing....*

Seriously, why had he struggled for so long to get

to this point?

There was no use, he decided ultimately, in continuing to beat himself up about it. He'd suffered in a private hell for a good long time. Now he was emerging victorious on the other side. The important parts weren't about why it took so long or why it had happened. All he needed to focus on now was that it was really over. He'd made his breakthrough, and nothing could stop him from doing absolutely everything he could to make things right again.

He couldn't wait to tell Emma. She was going to be shocked, probably, that he'd taken the first steps toward getting his life back. But she'd be happy, right? Maybe she'd even be willing to stay with him these last couple weeks. Spending two weeks in bed with her sounded like the right way to launch their new life together, he thought, laughing when he noticed the dopey, lovesick smile on his face when he padded into the bathroom.

Emma. Yeah...he absolutely had to see her. As soon as possible.

He pulled on his jeans and tee shirt; brushed his teeth; found his wallet, keys, and phone; and was happily walking out the door minutes later.

Emma...Emma loves me....

It seemed unreal. A miracle. It was almost more than he ever could have dared to wish for. And yet she'd said those words to him in the rain just yesterday.

What had her exact words been?

"I love you, you big moron! I adore you! I can't stand seeing you in this much pain."

He *was* a moron for having caused her so much worry. She was so concerned about his recovery that she'd walked away from him so she could try to spur him along.

But it had worked, right? He was getting better now! He *was*. He'd made those first tough phone calls, and now his agent was working to set up a meeting with the Yankees. This was it. It was happening. All his uncertainty and pain and fear and regret and loneliness…it was over. All he'd needed was a push from Emma and the promise of a lifetime of loving her. The sight of her walking away had been more painful than any of the days he'd spent after the Curveball Incident. Losing Emma would be the real tragedy.

Thoughts of their future together kept flowing through his mind, then curling and weaving their way into his heart. He pictured marrying her. Buying a home with her. Having kids with her. Then her sitting in the stands with the rest of the Yankees' wives and families, cheering him on. Loving him back.

It wasn't just a dream though. It was going to be his reality. He could feel it. All those wispy visions were right there, ready for him to step forward and claim them, make them his truth and his future. And it would all start today when he saw her again.

His excitement had built up to a crashing wave inside him by the time he knocked on Tracy's apartment door. Hopefully they weren't trying to sleep in. It was midmorning, but Emma *was* on vacation after all. He wondered briefly if he should have called first, but then he heard footsteps on the other side of the door.

Emma…!

This was it. He couldn't wait to touch her and hold her one more time, tell her once more how much he loved her. Hopefully she'd say those words back again.

He was smiling broadly when the door finally

swung open, and he saw…Tracy standing there. Okay, he'd had a fifty-percent chance of getting either Emma or Tracy. He tried to shake off the immediate stab of disappointment of the unfortunate mathematics in action.

"Hi, Tracy," he started, noticing she looked uncomfortable. *She probably doesn't want to feel like she's being put in the middle of the break-up Emma initiated yesterday*, he thought. "Where's Em? I'm sorry to come by so early, but I'm really anxious to see her and work some things out between us."

"Hey, Z," Tracy replied. "Listen, I'm so sorry to be the one to have to say this, but you missed her."

"Oh, what, she's out for a walk or something? Is there a single thing in town she hasn't already seen?"

"No, Zach, she left," Tracy told him. "Like, *left* left. I'm so sorry."

"Wait, what do you mean, she *left* left?"

"Let me give you the details, Zach," she said, her face awash with compassion. "Come on in."

He mutely followed her into the apartment, then obediently sat down when she gestured toward the couch.

"Can I get you something to drink?" she said, sitting next to him.

He shook his head. "Where is she, Tracy?"

"Her flight left first thing this morning, Zach. She's somewhere over the Atlantic drinking her complimentary soft drink as we speak."

"No, she wasn't supposed to leave yet," Zach said, feeling like a child who thought he could get his way if he just held onto the denial long enough. "I thought it was later this week?"

"She paid the fee to change it. The situation

between the two of you was too hard for her, Zach," Tracy said, looking as upset as he was feeling. "She couldn't take it anymore. She had to go."

"I thought…I thought I could come here and tell her," Zach replied, knowing he wasn't making much sense at the moment. "I wanted her to know."

"To know what?"

"To know that she did it," he said. "She got through my thick skull. Her words yesterday…it finally caused the spark I needed to get moving. I called my old manager and agent and set a few things in motion. I'm trying to get a meeting with the Yankees set up. I wanted to tell her."

"Zach, oh, but that's wonderful!" Tracy said, clearly excited for him now. "Those are exactly the words she'll want to hear! You can still tell her. In fact, text her right now. When she lands, your news will be the first thing she sees. Seriously, Zach, she'll be thrilled."

"I can't believe she left," he said, barely registering Tracy's enthusiasm. "She really thought I was a hopeless case, didn't she…."

"No, shut up, she absolutely thought the opposite. She always thought you had it in you to get your old life back. She never doubted it for one second. Really."

"No, I don't think so. She never told me that she and Jim broke up, and she wouldn't stay here with me and help me once we both finally told each other about our feelings. She just…she walked away and took the first flight out of town without looking back. She's probably on her way to beg Jim to take her back." Zach was already regretting dumping all this on Tracy, but he couldn't help it.

"No, she's not. Zach, she didn't break up with Jim

to be with you. She broke up with Jim because that relationship had inherent problems. I was nagging her to break up with him before she even met you."

"Really?" Zach looked shocked. "I figured all her friends would be running the Professor Jim fan club. He's everything that she needs—stable, smart, no two-year panic attack…."

Tracy laughed. "Then maybe *you* can marry him."

"Okay, sure, tease me when I'm down," Zach said, winking at her as he ran his fingers through his hair. "You know, I really don't know anything about their relationship. I just assumed that since I had so many problems, it was obvious that he'd be the better man for her."

"First off, everyone has problems. Second, Jim was her only serious adult relationship. They had a nice thing for sure. It wasn't hugely flawed or anything. Jim wasn't abusive or unfaithful or anything like that. But, I don't know…sometimes you just grow beyond your first love. And it was pretty obvious to me that that's what happened for Emma."

Zach shook his head. "I can't believe she didn't tell me they'd broken up, though. It would have changed everything."

"That was your fault, you big dummy."

"*My* fault? How?"

"She broke up with Jim, and her first instinct was to tell you right away and to confess that she'd fallen in love with you. But she remembered that you'd been yapping about how it really helped you to know she had Jim in her life, and how you weren't sure if you'd still be able to be friends with her if Jim wasn't around. Or something like that."

"Yeah, yeah, okay, that's all true. I was trying to be

selfless and not reveal how much I loved her. I thought she deserved better than me."

"Yeah, well, good plan. That was when Emma launched her own brilliant plan to sacrifice her happiness for *you*. You two could have avoided a lot of pain if you'd just talked more."

"We talked constantly, Tracy. Just not about the right things, I guess." Zach suddenly became lost in the memories of his time with Emma. "But...wait, what do you mean she decided to sacrifice her own happiness for me?"

"She came home one day and told me that she could never reveal her feelings to you or tell you she wasn't engaged anymore. She said that if she did that, she'd run the risk of interrupting your healing and recovery. You know how that girl likes to plan, right?" Tracy asked with a conspiratorial smile. "Well, she launched this huge scheme to do whatever she could to help you. That's when she tweeted Tommy Layton, not that she ever got a reply. But her plan from that moment forward was to put you first, get you on the road to recovery, and then go home and cry her eyes out knowing she could never be with you."

"You're exaggerating," Zach replied. "No one would put themselves through that much misery for me."

"Emma did, and she did it willingly. Zach, you need to believe her when she says she loves you. She absolutely does, body and soul. I know, because you are literally all I've heard about all summer long." Tracy laughed and nudged his leg with her foot. "Seriously, I've had enough of hearing about you for a lifetime."

"I am such an idiot," Zach said, slinging his arm over his eyes as he slouched back on the couch. "I can't believe I put her through so much this summer. Here she was, selflessly trying to help me. And I seriously gave her hell for tweeting Tommy."

"Eh, don't worry about. I'm not saying every single part of her plan was so brilliant. She was definitely sticking her nose into something private, something you obviously wanted to keep to yourself. And I'm not trying to add to your guilt or oversell what Emma's done. You know, I'm not exactly saying she's Mother Theresa here."

Zach laughed. "I get your point, basically."

"Yeah, you know, I'm just saying that her leaving this morning wasn't a spur-of-the-moment thing," Tracy went on. "She'd been planning to do what she could and then to walk away for quite a while. That's the honest truth. The fact that you two revealed your feelings to each other yesterday...that was the part she wasn't counting on. It caught her off guard. And it made leaving you here even harder than it would have been before. She cried a river last night, and she looked like a convicted felon walking down death row when she left this morning. It's not the biggest stretch in history when I say I think she'll happily see you and listen to what you have to say if you show up on her doorstep. Seriously Zach, it's not the end of the world that she left this morning. Maybe it'll give you all the more incentive to get out of here."

"Oh, I'm definitely leaving," he told her. "I wasn't kidding when I said I had good news to give her this morning. I'm quitting the pub today and breaking the lease on my apartment and everything. It's really happening. Anyway, thank you so much for telling me all of this. You've been a good friend to Emma, and a good friend to me."

Tracy smiled. "I'm just happy to see Emma heading down a path that seems like it's going to make her happy. She deserves it."

Zach nodded. "Can I give you my number, Trace? And could you text me Emma's address in Massachusetts? If I'm going to show up on her door and beg her to take me back, I kind of need to know where to look for her. And finally, if you don't mind, could we keep this conversation between us? I'd like to tell her all of this in my own way and in my own time."

She agreed to keep his confidence, and they exchanged numbers. Tracy also promised to send him Emma's address, and then they said their goodbyes. He gave her a hug and a kiss on the cheek. As he headed toward the pub moments later, he thought about how kind she'd been to him all along.

Okay, so I need to make a slight change of plans, he thought, because Emma wouldn't be at his side when he left Dublin after all. *Not the end of the world, though, just like Tracy said....*

And that was because he'd be seeing her very soon. That thought made him smile. Hopefully the Yankees would agree to a meeting, too. Once he had the date and time, he could make arrangements for all the other flights he'd need to take on his apology tour. And going to Emma's house would be the final stop.

He'd save the best for last.

Chapter 34

ZACH HADN'T WORN a suit in over two years. The tie cinched around his neck felt alien and constricting. He'd worn almost nothing that wasn't jeans, shorts, or sweats since the day he arrived in Dublin.

When he had landed in the New York area and rented a car the day before, one of his first stops had been to his storage unit in New Jersey. That's where he'd found the suit. Good thing it still fit. A quick run to a dry cleaner to get it pressed was all he'd really needed to do to finish the prep for his meeting with the Yankees.

The rest of the evening was spent at a hotel, missing Emma and wondering what she was doing...how she was feeling...and whether she missed him as badly as he missed her.

But now he was focused on the task at hand. He knew this meeting, tough though it could potentially be, was something he had to face before he could see Emma again. So that morning he put the suit on, got into the rental car, and drove to the Bronx.

The Yankee organization and the Steinbrenner family demanded a certain formality from their players. They were to arrive and depart the stadium on game days in suits. They had to remain clean-shaven for the duration of their contract. And with the tradition of winning that this team embodied, most guys had no problem following these rules. Now it was expected. By the owners. By the fans. By the media.

His years with the organization came flooding back as he drove to the stadium. It was his first time back since he'd broken his contract. He parked the rental, then took a few moments to walk around the perimeter, soaking in the blue signage and familiar white façade.

It really does feel good to be back, he thought. He was relieved more than anything else. He hadn't been sure how he'd feel when he actually got here. It was one thing to set up a meeting, entirely another to come face-to-face with almost every ghost that had been haunting him, and all in one building.

But no, this didn't feel overwhelming. Panic wasn't coursing through his veins like it had been before. Baseball had been his life for a long time. Being at the stadium felt like coming home.

He headed through the gates. It wasn't a game day, and the team was on the road anyway. So he wouldn't be running into packs of fans who would recognize him. What would the typical fan say if they saw him, he wondered? Would they berate him for being a loser who'd abandoned them? Or would they welcome him back like the prodigal son, amped up by the prospect of getting a pitching ace back?

Probably some of both, he decided. His return was sure to set off a firestorm of media and fan attention. If the team would let him come back, that is. He shouldn't get ahead of himself.

He walked into the hallway that encircled the stadium, also known as the promenade. It was lined with flags and pictures of former Yankee legends. Could he make it up there one day? Would he even get the chance to try?

"Hey, Z, there you are," Scott said, appearing suddenly from behind and giving him a hug and a clap on the back. "Good to see you, man."

"You, too," Zach replied, meaning it.

"Okay, so let's go. It's time."

"Yeah, I guess it is...."

They walked together in the direction of the management offices.

Just before they got there, Zach said, "Scott, seriously man, no matter what happens here today, I just want you to know how much I appreciate you setting this up. All I really want is a chance to make things right. This team was always good to me and I, well, you know how I threw that back in their faces."

"No problem, Z. I'm just glad you called me."

Zach couldn't believe how calm he felt. This meeting was something he couldn't have begun to imagine happening even a month ago. And yet here he was, walking through the halls of the stadium as though his entire fate wasn't about to be decided.

But, really, that wasn't true, was it? Emma was the one who held his future in her hands. Hers would be the decision that mattered. If the Yankees told him to drop dead today, he still had options. He could be a pitching coach or try to get a job at ESPN or something along those lines. Yes, baseball was all he knew, but pitching itself wasn't all he had to offer. He was going to be okay, no matter what the Yankees decided.

When the secretary showed Zach and Scott into the conference room, Zach felt emboldened, confident. This meeting wouldn't be easy, but he wasn't going to let it define him either.

He shook the hands of the people around the table. Hal Steinbrenner was there, along with Hank

Wilson, general manager Brian Croft, and a variety of other people he didn't know by name. They each greeted him warmly and said they were glad to see him. He appreciated that he wasn't being met with open hostility. He had figured that might be a real possibility.

Everyone around the table sat down then. It was time.

"So, what brings you here today, Zach?" Brian asked to start things off.

"I'm here today because I owe every single person in this room an apology. You all know the basic facts about what happened—I hit Tommy Layton with a wild pitch, and he got injured so badly he missed the rest of his rookie year. And you all know that I couldn't deal with it. I broke my contract. I quit on my teammates. I quit on Hank. And I quit on the fans." Zach paused for a moment to take a breath. This was starting off well, he felt. It was good to get those words out. "Again, before I say anything else, I want to say that I'm sorry. To all of you and to everyone else I wronged."

"We appreciate you coming here, Z," Brian replied, nodding. "We were sorry to see you go. You left a real hole in the Yankee family."

"I know," Zach told him with a nod of his own. "The entire experience left a real hole in me, too. I've spent the last two years hiding from everything and everyone I ever knew. I couldn't figure out how to get back here or fix what had gone wrong. But I'm finally feeling like myself again. And I know I don't deserve it, but in addition to apologizing to you, I came here today to see if there's any place for me in this organization."

"You look like you kept in shape, but how's the arm?" a woman asked. He didn't remember her.

"I've been religiously working out the whole time," Zach answered immediately. "I think even when I was at my lowest, a part of me always wanted to make sure I could come back when I was ready. I even stayed clean-shaven. I guess some habits die hard."

He paused as a few of them chuckled. Here came the hard part.

"But I haven't actually been *throwing*," he continued. "I feel good. I feel strong. I don't know why I couldn't work the arm back up. But I won't lie to you: There are no guarantees that I've still got it." He was glad he was putting all his cards out on the table.

"Okay, let's say you got a second chance," Hank began. "Let's say you worked your arm back up in time to start next season. How do we know you won't walk back out the door the next time someone gets hit by one of your pitches? That happens, Zach. Players get hit by pitches all the time. Sometimes it's on purpose and sometimes it's by accident. But it happens. You gonna be able to roll with it next time? Because I gotta tell you, everyone in this room is wondering the same thing—does this guy have what it takes? There's a lot of pressure in the Majors, and there's even more when you're in the New York market. The media will go after your story like a dog with a bone. You're sure this is what you want? You're sure you can take it?"

Zach didn't hesitate; he'd been expecting this question and was ready. "I know that I've given all of you no reason at all to believe in me. I did it. I folded and ran. That was me. But before that all happened, I was the cockiest, most confident guy in the room no matter where I was. When Tommy went down, it was like I was seeing that I had human frailties just like everyone else." Zach made a small, self-deprecating laugh. "I know it sounds stupid to say it out loud, but I'd been built up my whole life. After a while, you start believing your press clippings, you know what I mean? But in that moment, all my old confidence disappeared. It took me more than two years to figure all this out, but I've learned a lot. I've grown, and that's because I've suffered. I'm not the same man who walked out of here back then. I've come through the fire. And this time I'm not going to be shocked when I encounter hard times. They are bound to find me again. But this time, when they do, I'll be armed and ready to take them on. To face them."

He stopped then and took a deep breath. He felt drained now, but also triumphant. They might well just tell him to get lost. But he'd still won here today. The words he'd just said hadn't been for show. He really did feel stronger. He was going to make it, no matter what happened next.

Brian whispered something to Hal Steinbrenner then, and they asked if Zach and Scott would mind giving them some time to discuss their options privately.

Once outside the room, Scott sat down in the waiting area. But Zach couldn't do that. As usual, he was too full of energy. He told Scott where to find him, then he headed to the stadium museum, a small room brimming with Yankee history. He'd always loved visiting it, seeing the tokens and mementoes of the great players who'd come before him.

He walked down the length of the long glass wall in the middle. It housed signed balls from myriad Yankees both past and present. DiMaggio, Mantle, Ruth, Rivera, Jeter. He wondered if he'd thrown away his chance to be remembered as a great Yankee. Maybe.

Probably.

He turned then to look at the other displays. Thurman Munson's old locker, kept intact the way the former captain had left it before he died in a tragic plane crash. A display of the different stadium seats that had been gradually upgraded through the years as the stadium had been repeatedly renovated, then torn down and rebuilt. A case of World Series trophies.

The history of the game and the team swirled around him as he wandered. This was *his* world. He was so glad he'd come back and made this attempt to return to the team. It felt good. It felt right. He really was going to be okay now. No matter what.

His phone vibrated with an incoming text.

As usual his first thought was about Emma. Maybe she was missing him, too?

No—it was Scott. He tried not to let the disappointment grab him too tightly.

He read the text. Okay, it was time. The team was ready to talk some more. They were about to deliver their verdict. He would soon find out what the next stage of his life would bring.

He put his phone back into his suit pocket and headed for the door.

He was ready.

Chapter 35

HE STOOD OUTSIDE her door, hand poised over the doorbell in anticipation. This was the next stop on the apology tour. Stop one had been in New York so he could meet with the Yankees. Now, stop two was in Norman, Oklahoma, at the University of Oklahoma, where his little sister Zoe was studying to be a nurse. He hadn't warned her he was coming. Except for getting some nosy-little-sister texts from her that included some not-so-subtle questions about Emma, he really hadn't talked much to his baby sister since she'd left Dublin. She was in for the shock of her life.

Zach rang the bell, smiling as he pictured the happy reception he was about to get.

She opened the door, and then she froze.

"Zach? You just scared me to death. You're the last person I expected to see." She still looked like she wasn't sure if he was a ghost or not.

"It's really me," he said, a little unsure now. He'd thought she would scream and jump up and down in joy, not stare at him like he had an alien growing out of his chest.

"Are you…are you…." Zoe trailed off as tears started to shimmer in her eyes.

"Oh, honey, don't cry. Nothing's wrong. I'm here to tell you that I'm feeling better now. It's good news." And then, in an attempt to make her laugh, "Hey, did you notice? I'm not in Dublin anymore."

But Zoe didn't laugh. Instead, she threw herself into his arms, sobbing.

Okay, of all the reactions she could have possibly had, this one hurt him the most. She'd clearly been covering up how much his exile had hurt her. He had come here wanting to see her laugh and smile and be excited for him. He stupidly hadn't considered that a surprise visit from him would instead serve to pop the cork on two years' worth of pent-up worry and pain.

Sitting in his apartment in Dublin all this time, it had been easy to focus only on how his troubles affected *him*. He hadn't really thought about how they were affecting everyone else in his family. Well, he knew...but he didn't really *want* to know. Not fully.

As Zoe's sobs continued to soak his shirt, he squeezed her tighter.

"I'm sorry, Zozo. I'm so very sorry for what I put you through." He felt the emotion prickling at his own eyes. This was so much worse than facing the Yankees. So much harder. He wished he could just wipe away all the suffering he'd caused her. He had a lot of work ahead of him if he was going to make it up to his family. More than he'd realized until that moment.

"Okay, come on in," Zoe said finally, giving him one last squeeze before pulling back. "Please. Let me get a tissue. Or a whole box of tissues."

He walked into the neat, cheerful apartment and watched Zoe walk down a short hallway, disappear into a room, and reappear a moment later with the promised box of tissues.

She sat down on a recliner, and he took a chair across from her. *May as well face her as I make my apologies*, he thought.

"So what happened, Zach?" Zoe asked. "Last I

knew you were still stuck. Unsure of what to do. But you said Emma was making you feel better. Does your coming back to America have to do with her? I know she's back home in Massachusetts. She mentioned it on Facebook. Did she leave before you could tell her how you felt about her? Is she going to marry her fiancé?"

"You always rattle off about ten questions at once," Zach teased. "I can never remember like the first five of them by the time you get done."

"Sorry," she said, wiping her nose and sniffing. "I just…I can't believe you're actually here."

"Well start getting used to it, because I'm not going back to Dublin. I quit my job and gave up my apartment. My exile is over."

"Oh, thank God! So where are you going to live? New York? Houston?" Then she came to an abrupt halt. "Okay, I'll stop my list of questions there because I really want to know the answers so far."

"Nope and nope," Zach said. "I'm not going to be in New York or Houston."

"Oh, please please please tell me it's going to be Massachusetts! Are you going to go live with Emma?"

"No, not Massachusetts either."

"Okay, you're killing me here. Where are you going?"

"Japan."

"*Japan*?! What? Why?" Now she looked upset again. "What, was Dublin not far enough away from your family for you?"

"No, please Zoe, relax. Hear me out. I promise you're going to think this is a good thing. When I left Dublin, I went to see the Yankees first. I met with them and basically threw myself on the sword. I apologized for walking away and I asked if there was a way for me to come back to the team."

"Okay, that's great. So what happened?"

"Well, because I haven't been throwing in two years, I'm basically an unknown quantity all over again. They aren't sure if they should pump any money into a contract for me that might ultimately net them nothing. So they offered to help me get a one-year contract in Japan. They want to see what I can do there. Watch my progress. See if I still have what it takes."

"Oh, okay. I guess that makes sense. So just one year?" she asked, looking hopeful now.

"Yes, just one year. They already put a call in and talked to a team where they have good contacts from back when Hideki Matsui played for the Yankees. So, long story, but I'm going to be offered a one-year contract to pitch for the Yomiuri Giants in Tokyo. All I have to do is work my tail off and prove to everyone that I can still do it. Then they'll be open to talking with me again."

"Oh, Zach, that's *so* great," Zoe said, still dabbing her eyes. "But I'm going to miss you. I don't want to say goodbye again so soon after getting you back."

"Well, their season doesn't start until April. I'm not sure exactly when pitchers and catchers report, but I'm sure it'll be well after Christmas. So I'll be around a few months."

"Okay...." She still didn't seem very happy at this news. "So why couldn't you just spend the year in the Minors? Why are they shipping you overseas? Did you choose that? So you wouldn't have to be around when Emma marries someone else?"

"First of all, relax about Emma. I've got news to tell you about that situation, too." He laughed as a wave of excitement spread across her face. "But the Yankees picked Japan because it most closely resembles the big-game experience. They're not really going to be able to tell how I do under pressure if I'm pitching for the Tampa Tarpons."

"That's a real team?" she asked with a giggle.

"Yeah. It's a Yankees Single A team."

"K, so tell me the Emma news," she rolled on. "I'm about to die here."

"She broke up with Jim, and we both admitted that we love each other," he said, smiling at her whoop of glee. "Hold on, it's not all doves and roses yet. She also basically kicked me in the head and told me to get my act together, and then she left town without saying goodbye."

"Oh no, Zach. You've got to get her back!"

"That's exactly what I intend to do, little one," he said. "I'm on my apology tour, and she's going to be the last stop. I want to ask her to come to Japan with me."

"Good! Convince her, Zach, because I think she's wonderful. She's exactly what you need in your life."

"I think so, too, and I've actually got a couple favors to ask regarding her. But before I get to that, I want to make sure I don't skip over the part of my apology tour where I *actually* apologi—"

Zoe put a hand up. "Knock it off, Zach. You don't owe me any apologies. Just promise me you're going to keep working at this and moving forward. That's all I need to hear."

"You just sobbed your eyes out when I showed up at the door. That told me more than anything else about how much I've hurt you. I'm sorry. I've been a terrible big brother. I'm sorry I abandoned you."

"But that's the thing, Zach—you didn't. Even in

the middle of your crisis, you were still taking care of us. You've been paying for my tuition and for this apartment from the beginning. I never understood how you found the time. But it made me feel close to you, even when things got really dark. I knew you were still thinking about us and caring for us."

"Well, I'm glad the money went to those things, but that was all Zeke. Before I left, I dumped a bunch into his account and told him to make sure everyone was taken care of. I never thought about it again after that, although it comforted me knowing it would help you guys. I'm sorry it wasn't more personal, though."

"I didn't realize it was Zeke doing it," Zoe said. "But, well, it was still your money. You were still thoughtful enough to leave it with Zeke in the first place. It still shows me a lot, Zach. Stop downplaying it, and please just accept my thanks."

"Okay, well, you're welcome. And thank you for understanding and being there for me. For not giving up on me."

"Never. So what's this favor?"

"I need help shopping," he said. "Can you take me to a jewelry store and a bookstore?"

"A jewelry store? Oh Zach! Are you going to propose to her?" All traces of her former tears were gone now as happiness lit her eyes.

"Yes, I am. I'm hoping she'll marry me this fall and then come with me to Japan," he said. "But I need your help. This is going to be tricky. We're talking about a woman who left Jim's ring at home when she went to Dublin. She said she thought it was too extravagant to travel with. What kind of ring do you get a woman who thinks they're too extravagant? Do I even get a diamond? I'm lost here."

"Why did she break up with Jim?" Zoe asked, looking thoughtful now. "Did she tell you?"

"I don't know exactly. Tracy says they grew apart. Emma never really told me why. But maybe it had to do with me, and her growing feelings for me," Zach mused.

"Well, duh, of course it had to do with that. She didn't take her engagement ring with her?" Zoe asked, her tone incredulous. "He proposed, then she immediately took the ring off and flew away for three months?"

"Yeah, that pretty much sums it up," he replied, nodding.

"Okay, she was never really going to marry him anyway, whether she knew it or not," Zoe said, clearly getting excited again. "There is no way a woman would do that if she was wildly in love with her fiancé. Not a chance. You could give her a plastic ring out of a bubble gum machine, and I promise you, she wouldn't take it off, even if her finger turned green. And speaking of the color green, I *told* you she was into you! You big dummy. It was so obvious by her reaction when she saw me, but you wouldn't believe me."

"I didn't want to hear it, Zoe," he confessed. "I couldn't open myself up to the possibility that an amazing creature like Emma could actually love a guy like me. A guy with so many problems. But I believe it now. I do."

"Good! Then let's go buy that woman the most gorgeous rock in the state."

Zach smiled as Zoe ran down the hall to get her things.

This was good. He was so glad he'd come to see her. Despite her tears, it had gone better than he expected.

Now he just had one more stop to make before he could finally go to Emma.

Chapter 36

I'M SO GLAD I came this far, Zach thought as he got out of the rental car and stood looking at his childhood home. It felt like crossing the finish line, in a way. Being here where his entire journey had begun.

But he was also growing impatient. He couldn't wait to see Emma. The need to see her again, to hold her again, and hopefully to never let her go burned brightly inside him. He was dying to tell her what was happening. So much was changing, and so quickly. He didn't want to go through any of it alone, without her at his side.

The Yankees had reached out to him again through Scott. He'd just gotten the call that morning. They wanted him to spend the rest of the time before Japan in their training facility down in Tampa. They wanted to supervise his throwing and make sure he was building his arm back up the right way, under the supervision of team trainers.

So that rushed things even more. Would Emma would be willing to go to Tampa with him? Was she really just going to abandon her career goals at the drop of a hat? What if she had already secured a teaching position for the fall and signed a contract? Would she want to walk away from that? Would she even want to marry him in the first place? And if they did get married, where would they hold the ceremony? Springfield, Massachusetts, where her parents lived? Or

Houston? Or Tampa? Or even Japan? The only place he'd ruled out was Dublin. He'd had enough of that city to last him a while, even if it was the city that had brought them together.

Emma was going be in heaven with so much planning required. *Planning nirvana*, he thought, an easy smile sneaking its way onto his face as he locked the rental car and headed up the sidewalk to his parents' front door. Okay, well, first things first. It was time to shake off his reverie and focus on making amends with the rest of his family. He'd really put them through the wringer.

He hadn't called ahead, and he'd made Zoe promise not to warn them. So they were in for the shock of their lives.

Zach stopped, his finger poised above the doorbell. The shock of their lives? Holy hell, what was wrong with him? His parents weren't getting any younger. What was he trying to do, give them twin heart attacks?

He clearly hadn't thought this through. As usual. He needed Emma to help him plan his life—that much was clear. He was hopeless when it came to so many things.

He pulled his phone out of his pocket and called the very same house that was in front of him. He smiled as the telephone rang inside, the old-fashioned jangling so loud he could hear it clearly on the front stoop. They had to be the last family in America with a landline, complete with the long, curly cord. When were they going to let him upgrade them to cordless handsets, at least?

"Hello?" his mom's familiar voice asked when she finally answered.

"Hey, Mom," he said, feeling a surge of emotion for her. He was happier than ever that he was here. He'd let far too much time go by without seeing her.

"Zeke, honey? Is that you? What's wrong—did something happen at work?"

"No, Mom, it's Zach," he said.

"Zachary? Oh, I'm sorry. I didn't even recognize you. How are you, honey?" she asked with obvious and tender concern. He was so glad he finally had good news to tell her.

"I'm good, Mom. Really good. So much better than the last time we talked."

"I had a feeling I'd be getting this call soon. Zoe was so hopeful after she came home from seeing you. She said she could tell the tide was turning."

"She was right. Things are better. In fact, I sent you something. A present. It was delivered there today, so open the front door and check, okay? It's a surprise, so don't be too shocked."

"Okay, honey, but do you want me to look for it right now? I'll have to put the phone down."

He chuckled. Good old corded phones.

"Yeah, go ahead and put the phone down."

"Okay, dear. Just a minute...."

He could hear the rustling sound of her setting down the phone and walking away, then her steps as she approached the door. He ended the call and popped the phone back in his pocket as the door swung open.

"Zachary!" she said, with a bright smile and a chuckle. "Well, aren't you the tricky one? Get in here, son!"

"Hi, Mom!" He stepped into the entryway and pulled her into his arms. She looked older, frailer. She had more gray hairs and wrinkles than he remembered. He wondered how many of them he was responsible for. *Probably all of them*, he thought ruefully.

"Come over here," she said, pulling away so she could look up at him and study his face. "Want to sit in the kitchen and have some coffee with me? I could feed that sweet tooth of yours. Wait, have you had breakfast? You're too skinny."

"I'm not skinny at all. And, no, I'm not one for coffee, but I know you like it. Want me to brew you a pot?" He wrapped his arm around her as they walked into the kitchen.

"It's already made. I think I will have a cup. Let's sit down and you can tell me what you being on my doorstep means. I'm afraid to get my hopes too high, Zachary. I want to hear what you've got to say." She pulled a mug from the cabinet. "You sure you don't want any?"

"Nah, I've only had coffee literally once in the last two years," he said, a secret smile stealing across his face as he thought of the coffee he'd shared with Emma when they first met. "You know the caffeine amps me up too much."

"That I do, Zachary." She stirred creamer into her coffee and then came to the table where he was still standing. "So sit down and tell your mother what's going on."

"I've got a ton of news, Mom. It comes in several different categories. Do you want to hear the good news, the better news, or the best news?"

"Let's work our way up," she said. "Start with good."

"Well, the good news is that I'm done hiding from my problems in Dublin. I'm ready to face them head on now. No more sulking around, wondering what happened to my life."

"Is that what you've been doing all this time over there? Trying to figure out what happened?" she asked, looking at him incredulously with the mug frozen midair.

"Yeah, I guess. I couldn't figure out why I was feeling so awful or what I could possibly do about it, you know?"

"Oh, I always knew what had happened," she said, bringing coffee to her lips now and taking a sip. "Always made sense to me."

"What did? That you had a basket case for a son?" He was astonished by her words. How had they not had this conversation before? Had she figured out what his problem was two years before he did?

"Son, the truth of the matter is that you never let yourself feel simple human fears and frailties before. You spent twenty-six years bottling up those feelings and acting like you were invincible." She looked completely unruffled as she laid out these declarations, like absolutely everyone should have been able to reach the same conclusions. "When that pitch hit that poor young man, you also got hit—with the truth that you're a human being. And then all of the things you'd been working so hard to bottle up and ignore came pouring out of you. The rest of us have always felt those same fears and pains, but we felt them slowly, through the gradual course of our lives. You had to deal with twenty-six years' worth in one go. Made sense to me that it would take a while to work its way through your system."

"So if you understood so well, why have Zoe and Zeke been hammering me over the head about how hard this has been on you? They acted like I was killing both you and dad. But it sounds like you understood I just needed time." He felt a little irritated with his siblings now. Had they been shoveling a little too much guilt his way the whole time?

"Zachary, a mother might understand what her child is going through, but don't think for a moment that it's easy to watch." He could see the pain he'd put her through reflected in her eyes. *Okay, yeah, they hadn't oversold it*, he realized. He'd caused everyone in his family a world of suffering. "I just want to say one more thing on this topic, then we can bury it forever if you'd like."

"What's that?"

"Don't let it happen to you again. Be afraid when fear is an appropriate reaction. Get nervous when things get scary. Let yourself have doubts. Don't deny those feelings anymore, honey. Please." She squeezed his arm again and looked at him imploringly.

"I won't, Mom. I've learned a lot through all of this. It won't happen again." He reached over and lay his hand on hers.

"Okay then, good. So what's the better news?"

"The Yankees are willing to give me another shot. I just have to go prove myself in Japan for a year. If I can show them I still have the skills, they'll consider giving me a new contract for the next season. They want me to come to Tampa and start working my arm back up before I head off to Japan this spring."

"Oh, that's wonderful, honey! I can't even imagine what the best news is or how you could possibly top that."

"Well, okay...when Zoe came back from Dublin, did she mention my friend Emma? I had told her that being around Emma was helping me."

"Yes, Zoe was really taken with your Emma," his mom said, nodding.

"That right there is the best news—I'm hoping she'll agree to *be* my Emma. I love her, Mom. I have a flight in two days. I'm going to see her at her parents' house in Massachusetts, and I'm going to ask her to marry me. I'm hoping she'll come with me to Tampa and Japan."

"You don't mess around, son, do you?" she said, looking delighted. "When you decide to get your life moving forward, it really moves!"

"I've got some time to make up for," Zach agreed with a nod.

"I'm sure we're going to love Emma. Zoe talked so much about her. It really tipped me off that maybe there was more going on there than you were admitting to us."

"Yeah, well, we had a lot to work through. She was engaged to someone else, for starters, but then she made the choice to end that. And on my side, well, you know, I had my own boatload of issues to dig through. But I really think we can have a wonderful life together. I just have to get her to agree to marry me."

"She will, honey, I just know it. No one could ever resist you when you turn on the charm." Her pride in him was shining brightly at that moment.

"Thanks, Mom, I'm counting on it. But, well, don't get your hopes up too high. She already turned me down once, sort of. I asked her to stay with me in Dublin and help me get my life together."

"And what did she say?"

"Well, it wasn't good—definitely not my favorite memory, honestly. Basically, she told me to take a hike.

That she wasn't in the business of taking on fix-it projects. Then she left town without another word. Her turning me down, though, was good for me. It's what finally spurred me on to start making changes and to ultimately leave that town behind. I couldn't just let her get away without fighting for her."

"Yes, I'm going to love this girl," his mom said as she drained the last sip of her coffee. "Shoot, I think I love her already. You better do everything you can to make her say yes. She's obviously a keeper."

"Oh, I will, Mom, you can count on it."

Zach smiled at her and sat back in his chair. He absolutely couldn't wait for the chance to talk to Emma again and hear what she was going to say to him. In a couple of days, he'd finally find out whether he'd be bringing his heart along with him to Japan…or leaving the smashed pieces of it behind.

Chapter 37

"SO, EMMA, I guess what I really want to know is whether you're happy or not," Jim said, studying her face from his seat across the table.

He looks older and just…weary, Emma thought, hating that she'd been the one responsible for the lines of sorrow etched on his face.

"Jim, we've been friends a really long time," Emma started cautiously, not sure what she should really be revealing to him. "It feels weird not being able to talk to you, you know?"

"Yeah, it does feel weird," Jim agreed, taking a bite of his quesadilla and chewing slowly. He appeared to be gathering his thoughts before continuing. "But we're here now, together, having lunch and talking again. So tell me, are you happy?"

"Well now, that depends. Do you want the truth, or do you want the 'we just broke up and things are still really raw and painful, and I don't actually want to hear about how your life is moving forward without me' version?" Emma winced as the words came out of her mouth. This was really, really awkward.

"Oh, just unload the whole truth on me, Em. I know we're over," Jim said. "I get it. I'm a big boy, and I can take it. I'm deducing here that you're with the bartender now? Is that it? Is he what's making you happy, Em?"

Emma sighed. How much did Jim really want to

hear? It's one thing to say you are prepared for the truth, and it was another thing altogether to actually hear it.

"No, I'm not with the bartender. And he's not really a bartender anyway, at least not as his full-time occupation. And he's not a tax evader or any of those other things you guessed. He's a professional athlete who had a little bad press, and his name is Zach. But no, I didn't break up with you and immediately jump into another relationship with him or with anyone else. I wasn't lying when I said I needed time."

"Okay, then what do you have to say that would be hard for me to hear?" Jim looked lost now.

"The whole complete and honest truth is that I do have feelings for him. I miss him terribly. I'm sorry I walked away from him and left him in Dublin." Emma mindlessly swirled her spoon through the chicken tortilla soup she'd barely eaten. "I've been pretty lost and miserable since I got here. I just can't get jumpstarted back into the real world. What I should be doing is working on my career, you know? I need to find a job and then find an apartment and really just leap into the next stage of my life. But...I don't know. Something's holding me back from doing any of that. I've basically spent the last month lying in bed, staring at boy-band posters on the walls of my childhood room, and wondering what my problem is."

Jim chuckled and took a drink of his soda. He looked like he was considering his words carefully.

"I absolutely can't believe I'm saying this," Jim said, "but it sounds like you can't move on until you resolve things with this guy. Why'd you leave him in the first place?"

"Well, now, that's the irony of all ironies. He's at a

similar spot in his life—like he hit a fork in the road and can't decide which route to follow. I gave him hell about being stuck, and I rode out of town on my high horse." Emma shook her head in frustration. "And then I seriously got home and slipped into the same sort of rut as him. Who's all high and mighty now, huh? I sure don't have any answers for myself, so why was I such a jerk about *him* not having answers?"

"Again, I'm an idiot for counseling this, but maybe what the two of you aren't realizing is that in order to move forward, you need to do it together?" Jim asked. "Could that be your solution, Em? How serious are you about this guy?"

"Still want the truth?" she asked, a pained look on her face.

"Go ahead. Hit me with it," he replied with a small smile.

"I'm in pretty deep, Jim. I didn't even realize how deep until I left Dublin. It's been…really hard."

It felt good to be able to say these things, but Jim wasn't the person she should be having this talk with. She missed Zach even more than before, and that was saying a lot.

"Then tell him," Jim said, pausing with a quesadilla midair while he added, "Maybe you just need to scratch my name out of your master plan and pencil in his. Maybe that'll make things more clear for you."

"Ouch," she said, annoyed now. "That was a little harsh. And there really isn't a master plan. There isn't. Truly. There never was. I'm just bobbing along in the tide like everyone else, trying to get it right. I don't have any answers here. Obviously."

"Sorry, Emma. I'm just trying to hear what you're saying to me. I'd like to understand what you want and to finally be able to accept what happened to us, I guess."

"No, *I'm* sorry. The truth is exactly what I told you when we were in Dublin. I think we just drifted apart. It just wasn't right for me, not anymore. No master plans. It's just how I feel." Emma looked at him sadly. "And, speaking of which, since this conversation isn't exactly getting any easier, I may as well give you this now while I'm thinking about it."

She reached for her purse and pulled out the ring he'd given her before she headed off to Dublin. *The one I left behind*. She felt bad—she'd barely ever even worn it.

"Here, this is yours. I wanted to make sure I returned it." Emma handed it over.

"Oh, yeah, great. Thanks," Jim said, reaching for it, a small glisten of tears visible now in his eyes. "I appreciate that you gave it back."

"Of course. It wasn't mine to keep."

No doubt desperate for a change of topic, Jim then told her about the classes he'd be teaching that fall, and they ended the lunch on reasonably comfortable terms. *The air between us is definitely less awkward*, Emma thought as Jim drove her back to her parents' house. This lunch had been good for both of them. It felt like a fitting end to their story.

But she couldn't help but mentally pull apart the things Jim had said to her. Was he right? Was Zach the reason she couldn't move on?

When she walked away from Zach and left him in Dublin, she told him she didn't want to set a time limit on his recovery. And she didn't want to pressure him or tie them both to commitments he wouldn't be able to fulfill ultimately.

She still thought that she'd done the right thing for Zach. But it was very clear to her now that it wasn't what was right for *her*. Not at all.

She wasn't moping around because she was in a funk about starting her career. No, she was sad and lost because her heart was breaking. She didn't want to move on without Zach, plain and simple. She wanted to be with him, no matter what.

What did that mean, then? Should she buy an open-ended ticket back to Dublin? Would that ultimately be a good thing? Would having her there help his recovery? Or would that stall him in limbo forever as she had originally suspected?

If this was all about her own happiness, she'd buy a ticket and go back to Ireland today. But it wasn't just about her, it was about Zach, too. And maybe she shouldn't be second-guessing her initial instincts. Those instincts had screamed at her that she couldn't stay there and work through Zach's problems for him. Those solutions and changes absolutely had to come from within him. He had to choose the path that made the best sense for him and his own happiness. She might not be what he thought was best for him. In the way that she'd had to walk away from Jim and their dreams of a future together, maybe Zach needed to do the same thing with her.

She was going to have to face it: He might never be a part of her life. She was going to have to accept that. Going back to Dublin and stealing whatever scraps of happiness she could take just wasn't right. No matter how miserable she was, it absolutely wasn't right. She was going to have to figure out how to live without him. She had to find the strength somehow.

Blinking back the tears that were threatening to

work their way down her face, Emma turned to study Jim's profile as he drove along.

"What?" he said, giving her a quizzical smile.

"I really am happy we were able to meet today. It felt good talking with you, and I appreciate that you want me to be happy. That's all I want for you, too."

Jim pulled up in front of the house then and parked. He looked at Emma for a long moment, then reached out and gently rubbed his thumb on her cheek.

"Are you crying?" he asked.

"No. Yes. I don't know. I told you, I'm just an emotional mess right now. Don't mind me." She laughed as she wiped a tear away.

"Well, come on, let's get this goodbye over with then…."

He opened the car door and stepped out. Then he walked around and opened the passenger door, closing it after as she got out, too.

"I guess this is it," she said. "All these years and I…I just can't…I don't know. I'm just going to miss you."

"Well put," he replied, with a small laugh. "But yeah, Emma. Me too."

Jim opened his arms then, and Emma walked into his embrace. They stood there for long moment, lost in the past and memories, until Emma finally pulled back.

"Goodbye, Jim," she said.

"Can I have a last kiss?" he asked. "For old times' sake?"

"Of course," she said, leaning up and meeting his lips with her own. The kiss felt sad and a little awkward. Emma finally ended it by stepping back and reaching over to squeeze his hand. "Thank you…for everything."

"You too, Emma. Be happy." He walked around the car, got in, and drove off with a final wave.

She stood and watched until his car turned out of her sight.

There, I've done it. She'd completely closed the door to that chapter of her life. College was over. Her relationship with Jim was over. And Zach was gone.

The big question now, of course, was what the next chapter would bring. And whether she'd ever be able to find happiness again.

Chapter 38

HIS HEART WAS LODGED somewhere in his throat. He couldn't breathe or think or…feel. No, this wasn't happening. Emma wasn't back with Jim, please God. It couldn't be true.

And yet, there she was, hugging Jim and kissing him.

I've waited too long....

She'd warned him that she wasn't going to be tied to him. He'd been merrily zigzagging around the country, making stop after stop, slowly working to make amends with the people he'd wronged. He'd saved seeing Emma for last because he'd wanted to get all that other business out of the way first. He wanted to prove to her he was serious about moving forward, and then he wanted to concentrate on making Emma happy for the rest of her life.

What he didn't let himself imagine was that while he was doing all of that, they'd be busy reuniting.

He was frustrated with himself. Was he really already falling into that trap again? Had he been so overly confident that he could just breeze into town and sweep Emma off her feet that, once again, he hadn't considered life might have other plans?

Well...it's too late to sneak off without talking to her, he thought. He'd been standing on her parents' porch, about to knock on the door, when the car pulled up. He'd been so happy to see Emma in the passenger seat…until he saw Jim get out of the driver's side, walk around, and pull her into his arms.

He reached in his jacket pocket and felt the ring box sitting there. He twirled it in his fingers as Jim got back in the car and drove away. Emma stood there watching him leave. She didn't yet realize someone else was standing there, watching *her*.

This was going to be hard, he knew, but he had to at least face her. She'd want to know that he was doing better, even if she wasn't going to be a part of his life.

She started to turn around then and head toward the house. She still hadn't spotted him. *So now I'm going to scare her to death*, he realized. His timing was terrible. He took a deep breath. He had to say something, anything, before he startled her out of her skin.

"Are you and Jim back together, then?" he asked softly.

Emma froze as her eyes flew up to meet his. "Zach!"

"Yeah, it's me."

"You're here!"

"Yeah, I am."

They stared at each other for a long moment, her from across the length of the front sidewalk that led from the house, Zach from his spot on the porch.

"I blew it," he admitted, finally breaking the silence. "I'm sorry. I waited too long to come to you, and now here you've moved on already." He couldn't help feeling a little leap of happiness just to see and talk with her again, despite the pain. He started walking down the stairs.

"You came here for…for me?" she asked.

"Yes, of course," he replied. "I came home to reclaim my whole life, but it's not going to seem whole without you."

"Oh, Z!" Emma said, tears suddenly flowing down her face as though an invisible spigot had been turned on.

"I'm sorry," he said as he approached slowly. "Don't cry. I understand that you decided to go back to Jim. I wouldn't have believed that guy in Dublin would ever get himself together if I were you, either."

"I'm not with Jim. I could never…oh, Zach!" Emma said, as she raced toward him, closing the distance in a few long strides and leaping into his arms. She moved with so much momentum that he had to take a step back to steady himself. Zach held onto her tightly as Emma wrapped her arms around his neck and buried her sobs into his shoulder. Her feet weren't even touching the ground.

Zach was stunned, and his brain churned wildly trying to catch up with everything that had happened and fully process the moment.

"You…you're not with Jim," he asked, his voice muffled in her soft hair.

"No," she said, still pressed firmly against his chest.

"And I'm not stuck in Dublin anymore," he added, shocked as the happy facts lined up and presented themselves to him now. Suddenly his thoughts—and their path to happiness—were beautifully, amazingly clear.

"No, you're not."

"Then it's over," he said, shocked as Emma's tears suddenly sounded like they were ready to level up into sobbing. "Baby, no, please don't cry. It's over now. All our problems and the issues that were standing between us…they're all over. We're together and absolutely nothing will ever get between us again." Zach loved the feel of her in his arms and the wonderful fact that the words he was saying were finally true.

Emma lifted her head and looked into his eyes.

"You did it," she said, a proud smile beaming from her face. "You left Dublin. And...you're in the process of conquering your demons, I can tell. You're really doing it now!"

"Yeah, that's right. Emma, I just couldn't let you walk away from me. No fears, no problems, no issues...nothing could keep me from finding you and...telling...you...." Zach trailed off as the electric feeling of holding her in his arms surged through him. Leaning forward, he touched his lips to hers. The kiss started soft and comforting, but the swell of emotions racing through both of them quickly ignited it into so much more. It burned brightly now, fueled by the pain of their separation and the flooding relief they were both feeling at finally having made their way back to each other. It was passionate and sweet all at once, with the promise of a lifetime of more kisses to come.

"Oh my gosh!" Emma gasped with a laugh, pulling back from him and sliding down until her feet were on the ground again. "We're giving all my parents' neighbors quite a show!"

"Okay, let's sit down on the steps then," he suggested, his chest heaving with the emotional wave they'd both just been hit with. He took her hand and led her to the porch, where they sat next to each other on the top step. "I've got a lot to tell you, Em, starting with the fact that you walking away from me really was the kick I needed. I know it was hard on you, honey. I can't imagine the strength it took you to do that. Trust me when I say it wasn't exactly a fun time for me, either. But it was *right*. I knew that I had to do absolutely everything I could do to win you back, and that's what spurred me to action."

"I'm so glad—you have no idea how happy I am to see you here," she said, looking down at their joined hands and then back up to his eyes. "But before you say anything else, I want to explain what you just saw with Jim. I was simply saying a proper goodbye to him, that's it. We went to lunch and talked. I gave his ring back. And that was the end of it. You just witnessed two people closing the door on their shared past. That's all. I swear I have done absolutely nothing since I got home that didn't involve thinking about you, missing you, wondering if I'd done the right thing, and, from too far away, loving you."

"Thanks for telling me all that, you gave me a bit of a heart attack," he said with a laugh. "I guess I was just so excited to share everything I've been doing, and I just…I'm sorry. My timing was terrible. I shouldn't have witnessed that."

"No, Zach, it's really okay. That part of my life is over. And you're saying that your exile in Dublin is over, too? That we have nothing else standing in the way of our being together?"

"That's exactly what I'm saying," he replied immediately, a wide, easy smile on his face. *This being happy stuff could become a habit*, he thought.

"Okay, so tell me everything," she said.

"Well, first off, the Yankees were willing to meet with me. They're giving me another chance."

"Oh, Zach, that's wonderful! I am so happy for you!"

"Me too. It's good. It feels right. I apologized to every suit they could fit around a conference table. I apologized to my old manager and my agent, too. Then I went home and saw my family. Everything's going to be better now."

"Does that mean you'll be moving back to New York?"

"Well, no, not right away. First they want me to report to Tampa for training this fall," he said.

"Oh," she said, sounding worried. "You know, I haven't thought much about the life of a baseball player. You're going to just head off to Florida and then you'll spend all spring and summer traveling with the team. When will I ever see you?"

"Emma, I don't want any of those things if you're not right by my side to experience them with me. Which is why I've got something to ask you."

He stood up, pulled Emma to her feet, then got down on one knee and took out the ring box, popping it open to reveal the simple platinum solitaire inside.

"Emma Crawford, I love you. I adore you. And it took me a long while to realize this, but it turns out that the curveball that forever changed my life wasn't the one I threw. The most important curveball life had in store for me was you. And I'll forever be grateful for everything that happened that brought you into my life. Emma, will you please marry me and make me the happiest man in the world?"

"Oh, Zach!" she said, the tears falling again. "I have been so miserable without you. I love you so much and, yes! Yes, of course I'll marry you!"

Zach laughed, stood up, and braced himself as she flung herself into his arms again, dropping a flurry of kisses all over his face.

"Here, help me put it on," she said, pulling the ring out of the box and letting him slide it on her finger.

"How's it look?"

"I think it looks gorgeous on you," her new fiancé replied, "but the real question is what do *you* think? Are you going to throw it back in the box and not wear it? You could pick something else out if you'd prefer."

"Oh no you don't! I *love* it. You won't be able to pry this off my finger." She gazed happily as it sparkled and shone on her finger. "There's a big difference this time around."

"And what's that?" he asked.

"You," she said, wrapping her arms around his waist and resting her head on his chest.

He leaned down and hugged her back just as tightly. Yep, he thought, being in her arms still felt like home.

"Oh, I almost forgot," he said then, regretfully pulling away. "I have one more present for you. Hang on...."

He raced down the sidewalk and across the street to his rental car, retrieving what was sitting on the front seat. Then he jogged back and handed her the box that Zoe had elaborately wrapped for him.

"What is it?" she asked, looking confused.

"The traditional way to answer that question is to open it."

"I swear if this is a turtle Pez dispenser, I'm going to give you the ring back," she said, laughing with anticipation as she tore into the paper. "Oh…a book? It's…"

Zach watched expectantly as she turned it right-side up.

"*The Weary Wanderer's Guide to Japan*?" Emma read, then looked at him again. "Huh?"

"The Yankees want me to prove myself for a year,

and they want me to do it on the other side of the world. So I'll be in Tampa this fall and winter, then head to Tokyo for a stint with the Yomiuri Giants. I desperately need someone to plan both those trips...and after that, a wedding. And, on top of all of that, I want to take the story of my return to baseball to the media myself in order to control the information and talk to the reporters I trust. So I'm going to need someone to help me. Maybe we should even plan a trip to ESPN headquarters so I can do the rounds on all their shows. Seriously, it is going to require an absolute ton of planning by someone who knows a lot about travel and sports media. Can you think of anyone who might be up for that job?"

"Oh, you know I am," she said, laughing delightedly. "Zach, I can't believe you got me a travel guide! I absolutely adore it!"

"And I, sweet Emma, absolutely adore you," he replied.

Epilogue

IT WAS AN ORDINARY baseball game in early May. Nothing should have been particularly special about it. There was still plenty of time left in the season before the team's focus would turn to thoughts of getting into the playoffs. They weren't even all that close to the trade deadline. Just another point on the timeline that ultimately formed a Major League Baseball team's long season.

But this matchup between the Yankees, playing at home in their customary blue pinstripe suits, and the Baltimore Orioles wasn't ordinary at all. Actually, it was so out-of-the-ordinary that the media in town had swelled to twice the number that would normally cover something so otherwise routine. The radio hosts were buzzing about it. The newspaper headlines were screaming it. The ESPN television stations were filled with talking heads who were analyzing every moment, the history behind it, and the many theories about what might go down.

And because the story was big, that also meant the pressure was big.

Emma was sitting in the stands, surrounded by the other team wives and families. She knew she shouldn't be letting the tension get to her, but she couldn't help worrying.

Zach had been doing great—fabulous, even—since he re-entered the league. He had worked with a fierce dedication and determination to build his arm back up the winter before they went to Japan. He'd taken a break long enough to marry her in a beautifully intimate ceremony on a Florida beach, with their families gathered around them to help them celebrate. But the next day, he'd headed right back to the training facilities. He had to, if he was going to prove his commitment to the Yankees.

Emma smiled as she watched him walk out of the bullpen and head to the mound so he could start his warm-up throws. He looked good. He looked confident.

All the sweat and hard work he'd put into his time with the Yomiuri Giants had paid off—the Yankees had signed him to a seven-year contract before he even finished his time in Japan. They believed in his recovery, and they trusted that he could be their pitching ace again.

He was going to do it, too; his stats were already backing up that claim. He'd won every game he'd started since his debut back in the Bronx. The Yankees were happy. Zach was happy. And Emma was ecstatic.

Things had been going wonderfully for them. They were together, they were content, and they were talking about starting their own family soon.

But first they had to get through today.

Because this marked the first time Zach would be facing Tommy Layton since the big incident. Since he'd thrown away his life and moved to Dublin.

That's what the media firestorm was about. The sports media couldn't seem to resist talking endlessly about what might happen when Tommy stepped up to that plate again. Would Zach be able to take the pressure? Would he freeze up? Be unable to pitch?

Would he hit Tommy again because he wasn't able to focus?

Emma had complete faith in her husband and his abilities, of course. His talent was amazing to witness. She loved watching him pitch and saw all of his starts, even if she had to watch the daytime games on the DVR in the evening when she got home from the school where she worked in New Jersey.

The faith was there, yes...but she still wasn't sure if Zach was really admitting to her or to himself how much this game might mean to him. He'd laughed it off when she had tried to bring it up. So was it really not a big deal? Was his confidence back to such a high level that he couldn't even see or care about the parallels that everyone else seemed to be drawing today? Or was he just not willing to think back to the dark times? They were in such a wonderful place now; it was easy to block out all the struggles they'd been through to get here.

Zach finished with his warm-up, and the first batter was done taking practice swings in the batter's box. Tommy was hitting cleanup today, which meant that unless one of the first three batters got on base in the first inning, Zach wouldn't even be facing Tommy until the top of the second. Emma didn't know if it would be better to just get it out of the way in the first inning or to let Zach have a bit more time out there before Tommy came to the plate. It was nerve-wracking.

Maybe I should have stayed home and watched the game in privacy.

She'd considered it briefly, but in the end decided she needed to be here in case Zach needed her. She hadn't told him any of that, though. She didn't doubt his abilities, but making it past this first encounter with Tommy was going to be a big hurdle.

Zach got the leadoff batter to hit a slow roller toward the first baseman—an easy out. Still too soon, however, to know if Tommy would come up this inning.

The other wives seemed to sense her worry, and they were politely keeping their distance. Her attention was centered on her husband anyway, who was standing on the mound, all by himself in the middle of the stadium. Emma couldn't wait until they were alone that night. In that moment, she would have given anything to hold him and let him know she was there no matter what transpired here today.

The second batter hit a fly ball then, the crack of the bat startling her a bit. She was so tense and so lost in thought. She knew she should try to relax, but really, that wasn't going to happen. Not until she was certain her husband was really as okay as he claimed to be.

The centerfielder easily caught the fly ball for the second out. At least one more batter to go to either end the inning or bring up Tommy.

What was comforting to Emma was that things were different now for Zach. Even if this game fell apart disastrously, he wasn't really as alone out there as he looked. He had her now. Surely that meant he was stronger now today than he'd been all those years ago, right?

As though he knew what she was thinking, Emma could see Zach glance up in the stands toward the section where she was sitting. She smiled. She could tell he was thinking about her, too.

Zach stared hard at the third batter, went into his wind-up, and delivered a pitch that scorched over the plate. It was a little too high, though. The umpire declared it a ball.

This was so agonizing. Loving someone as deeply as she loved Zach also meant hurting for him sometimes, too. Emma wished this game was over. She wished the media wouldn't swarm his locker afterward, either, although she knew they surely would. She wished he didn't have to go through this trial at all, and definitely not in public.

But it was inevitable—with Tommy Layton fully recovered and back on his old team in the same division as the Yankees, this day was going to come eventually. It wouldn't be a story after this first big match-up was behind them. But for now....

The third batter hit a powerful grounder right up the middle and easily reached first base.

So that's it, she admitted silently. Someone was on base, which meant Tommy was up next. The moment she'd been agonizing about had finally arrived.

A feeling of electricity crackled in the air. Flashes from cameras and phones were suddenly twinkling throughout the stands as people excitedly captured the dramatic sight of Tommy walking to the plate.

Emma realized she was holding her breath. She needed to relax and calm down. Zach had this. He could do it.

A hush fell over the crowd as Zach stared at Tommy, shook off a couple pitch calls from the catcher, and finally went into his wind-up. Emma clapped her hands over her mouth, the anticipation jangling through her body.

Please, honey. Please please please, she thought, chanting it inside.

The first pitch sailed straight across the plate.

Strike one.

Emma released the breath she hadn't previously realized she'd been holding. He was fine. She could tell in that moment Zach really wasn't worried at all.

She watched, frozen in place, as he completed four more pitches and ultimately got Tommy to ground a little dribbler to third. As Tommy jogged back to the visitor's dugout, he very slightly tipped his cap toward Zach. Zach nodded back to him, then looked up in the stands toward Emma again. She smiled back at him, unsure whether he could actually see her or not.

He's done it, she thought as the warmth of pure joy filled her. *He's now faced absolutely every one of his demons and emerged victorious.* She was so proud of him and how far he'd come.

She sat back in her seat then and accepted a few words of congratulations from the other wives seated nearby.

Then she realized her phone was vibrating. She pulled it out and saw that it was Zach. *He's calling me from the dugout?*

"I am so proud of you," she said first.

"There's nothing I can't do with my beautiful wife at my side," he told her.

"Well, you certainly proved there's nothing you can't do just now. You were amazing."

"I didn't make my old mistakes, Em. I didn't go in too confident. I told myself this was a big, nerve-rattling deal. Then I worked through those nerves and let my training and hard work kick in. And in the end, it was no big deal at all."

"Yes it was—it was a *huge* deal, whether you want to call it that or not. This was the last big hurdle for you. It's all really over now, Z. You'll never have to go through that horrible time again or even be reminded of it anymore."

"Oh, I don't know, it wasn't so bad."

"Wasn't so bad? Are you nuts? Did someone hit you with their bat?" she teased.

"I'd go through it a hundred more times as long as I'd be guaranteed to find you at the end."

"I'd never wish your suffering on you, Zach, but I'm so grateful we found each other, too."

"I love you, honey," he told her. "Okay, I gotta go win this game now, Emmy my sweet."

"I love you, too," she replied, disconnecting the call and smiling dreamily now.

She was so happy. Sure, life was going to throw them more curveballs in the future, because that's what life did.

But as long as they had each other, there was nothing to fear.

About the Author

ANNE TROWBRIDGE lives in New Jersey with her husband, kids, and two dogs. When she's not reading or writing, she's working her way through careers like she's marking off a bingo card, with years spent as a newspaper reporter, book editor, middle school language arts teacher, and now writer. She grew up all over the Midwest and somehow still loves to travel and see new places. Anne recently earned her master's degree, exactly 30 years after receiving her bachelor's. It's never too late to chase a dream!

Made in the USA
Monee, IL
06 July 2022

99183919R00187